2

Blackbeard's Secrets by John Kimble

_____

_____

Chapter One

Lucius Dixon sat alone in a wooden straight back chair on the third floor of the law library at the University of Virginia. It was midnight on the eve of his first law school exam, and he was reading through his Contracts notes again.

There was a storm in the area, and the constant pattering of raindrops and rumbling of thunder made it difficult to concentrate. Lightning flashes played tricks on his eyes and cast shadows on the shelves. He was beginning to collect his books to go home, when he heard a noise coming from one of the back shelves. He had been alone on this floor for hours and hadn't seen anyone come up the stairs. Maybe between his studying and the thunderstorm, he hadn't noticed, or maybe the noise had simply been in his head.

Lucius put his books into his backpack and strapped it to his shoulders. He couldn't let his overactive imagination control his life as it had so many times in the past. The library was closing, and he needed to do more studying at home. Lucius started down the stairs. He ignored another noise...the noise of rustling fabric, but he could not ignore what happened next.

Lucius was nearly knocked down the stairs. A young woman went flying past him, banging hard against his shoulder. She vaulted down the stairs, crossed the room, and turned a corner without looking back or uttering an apology. Lucius was already frustrated from his inability to concentrate on his studies, and he briefly considered running after the woman. He changed his mind when he remembered the midterm. He didn't have time to be angry at the woman for her rudeness.

As Lucius headed for the stairs to the first floor, his eyes noticed something lying on the ground. It was a small white card about the size of a typical business card. Lucius picked it up. It wasn't made of paper, but of some sort of plastic. It weighed no more than a credit card. It was blank on one side.

The other side had a small arrow centered on one of its ends pointing toward that end.

Lucius slipped the card into his pocket. He knew that the lost and found would be closed for the night. Maybe he could figure out what it was in the meantime.

As Lucius walked out of the library, the stern librarian furrowed her brow.

"Last one out again?" Her tone was accusatory.

"I think there might be a girl still in there."

"Well, if she's in here, she'll be spending the night here. It's after midnight, and I'm locking up."

Lucius hurried out the door of the library, exited the law school, and stood beneath an awning trying to remember where he had parked his car. Before he could venture out into the rain, he heard a woman's voice behind him. He turned, expecting to have to deal with more wisecracks from the librarian.

"I'm going to need that back." It wasn't the librarian. It was the woman from before. She was tall, nearly six feet. She was in her late twenties and had dark skin and dark eyes. She was wearing blue jeans and a UVA law sweatshirt. She was also uncommonly beautiful.

"What are you talking about?" Lucius' curiosity was getting the better of him. He knew she wanted the card, but he hoped to get some clue as to what it was before giving it back.

"My card."

Apparently, no clues were forthcoming.

Lucius hesitated for a moment, and the woman's expression changed from a smirk to a frown.

"Look, I saw you pick it up. I don't want to have to report you to the honor council for stealing. Just give it back."

Lucius reached into his pocket and pulled out the card. "Yeah, sure, no problem, I was planning to take it to lost and found tomorrow."

The woman quickly grabbed the card from Lucius' hand and spun around, heading back into the law school.

"The library's closed," Lucius yelled at her back.

"I can study on one of the benches outside the library. Nice to have met you." And she was gone again.

6

Lucius pulled his keys out of his pocket and ran out into the rain toward his car. But he couldn't bring himself to get into the car. There was something unusual about that woman. He hesitated for a moment in the cold, rainy night, trying to convince himself that he needed to go home to study. This test was important.

Lucius threw his backpack into his car and walked back into the law school. The library had been locked up, and the librarian was nowhere in sight. There was no one on any of the benches outside the library. Again, Lucius thought about going home. He still hadn't had a chance to review the last section of his notes, and he was beginning to feel drowsy.

He decided to take a quick look around the law school before going home. He should at least find out the woman's name.

So he began wandering the halls, peering through glass windows into the many study rooms. There were a few students still in the law school, but none of them resembled his mystery woman.

Lucius climbed to the second floor and checked the unlocked classrooms. There was still no sign of her. His search seemed futile. Lucius glanced down at his watch. It was nearly two o'clock in the morning. He had wasted two very important hours looking for someone he didn't even know.

Lucius left the law school, got into his car, and drove home. He was too tired to study, so he climbed into bed.

As exhausted as Lucius was, he didn't sleep very well. He awoke nearly every hour. For some reason, the mystery woman was still on his mind. He tried to tell himself that she was just a student, but there was something about her…something alluring.

Lucius climbed out of bed at eight o'clock in the morning. His muscles ached, and he felt sick to his stomach. He showered, brushed his teeth, and left for school. He certainly didn't feel like taking a midterm, but he didn't have a choice.

He arrived at the law school with just enough time to get into the classroom and set up his laptop for the test. His instructor, an older man named Jonas Franklin, entered the room and stood at the lectern silently. His neatly brushed hair was completely white and his face drooped with wrinkles. He was wearing brown tweed pants, a white dress shirt, and a mustard-colored wool jacket. He rarely smiled, but he managed to convey a sense of warmth. Lucius imagined that he taught Contracts the same way it was taught in the nineteenth century.

The class quieted, and Professor Franklin began speaking. He told the students that there was no need to be nervous, that the grade would not be that important in the overall scheme of things, and that the primary purpose of the test was to help the students to improve their test-taking skills.

The papers were passed around, and Lucius let out a sigh before he began reading. The test consisted of one long hypothetical. This particular test was about a liability waiver signed by a drunken teenager before he entered a diving competition in which he was injured. The idea of the test was to notice facts in the hypothetical that tied in with rules learned earlier in the semester. Students at the law school called this type of exam an issue spotter.

On his first reading of the question, Lucius saw only the most obvious issues. He wrote a short essay and began panicking, while everyone else typed furiously. He sat quietly in his seat for a minute or two. He couldn't think of anything else to write. Lucius read through the question again, closed the screen on his laptop, and excused himself from the room. He thought that he might be able to think better if he walked around for a few minutes. He glanced at the clock before he left the room. He had thirty minutes left.

He entered the hallway and walked toward a nearby water fountain. For a moment, he held the hypothetical in his mind and tried to remember all of the contracts rules that he had learned in his few weeks as a law student. But his mind quickly wandered. He couldn't stop thinking about the woman from last night. Why had he never seen her before…and where had she disappeared to when she went back inside?

As he looked up from the water fountain, he saw a tall woman turn the corner about fifty feet away from him. Lucius sprinted down the hallway and turned the corner after her. She heard him approaching and turned around. She looked nothing like the woman from the night before.

"Lucius Dixon, you're losing your mind," he whispered to himself as he skulked away. Lucius always seemed to find mystery in everything, and his paranoid suspicions about people and situations had cost him opportunities in the past. He had to calm down and focus on what was really important.

He nervously walked back to the classroom. He sat down in his seat and stared at the clock. He had lost all ability to concentrate. His leg was shaking uncontrollably.

With about ten minutes left to finish his exam, Lucius decided to try to read through the problem one more time. Amazingly, the issues started popping out. He couldn't believe that he had missed a possible contract of adhesion. They had spent nearly a week on contracts of adhesion. He flipped up the screen on his laptop and began typing feverishly. This grade could be very important, and he only had a few minutes to drastically improve it.

Lucius typed three more pages in the last five minutes of class. He was still typing when the teacher announced that it was time to turn in the exams. Lucius submitted his document electronically, packed up his things, and left the classroom. He wanted nothing more than to go home and sleep. He planned to skip his afternoon classes.

As Lucius stumbled sleepily down the hall, he heard someone calling him. He stopped and turned around.

"Hey, Luke...wait up."

It was Robert Collins, one of his classmates. Robert graduated from Harvard with a degree in journalism. His father was a big shot in Washington, a fact of which Robert was more apprehensive than proud. Robert was small with sunken shoulders, closely-cropped dark hair, and glasses. He liked to talk.

"How'd you do on the test? I noticed you left the room for a while. Are you okay?"

"Yeah, I'm fine. I'm just tired. The test wasn't that bad." Lucius continued walking down the hallway.

"It was a horrible test. I don't mean it was hard, but it didn't really measure how much we knew. It was poorly designed." Robert hovered at Lucius' shoulder, following him down the hallway.

"Well, I suppose it's hard to please everybody." Lucius didn't dislike Robert. In fact, Robert had been very friendly to him since their initial meeting at orientation. Lucius had been nervous about law school, and Robert had calmed him with stories about the friendly atmosphere at UVA. But right now, Lucius just wanted to go home to get some sleep.

"Do you want to go grab some lunch before Torts?"

"I'm not going to Torts. I'm going home to go to sleep."

"What if you get called on? I've heard Sandberg will dock your grade if you're not there on the day when you're supposed to be on call."

"That's probably not true, and anyway, there are one-hundred and twenty people in the class. I'm sure I won't get called on."

"If the odds really worked that way, no one would get called on. You should probably send him an e-mail if you're really planning to skip."

"Maybe I'll do that, Robert. Anyway, my car's right outside, so I'll see you later."

"Yeah, I understand…you're tired. I'll let you know if Sandberg calls on you."

"I appreciate it, Robert. I'll see you tomorrow."

Lucius left the law school and drove back to his apartment. It was kind of a dump, but it was the only reasonably priced one-bedroom apartment that he could find. He didn't want to take on a roommate his first year. He was worried about not being able to study.

As soon as Lucius' head hit the pillow, he was wide awake. His thoughts drifted back to the midterm that he had just taken. He thought of things that he could have written. They all seemed so obvious now. And he silently scolded himself for leaving the room during such an important test. He thought about how he had run down the hallway after a girl simply because she looked like a girl he didn't even know.

His mind drifted to his strange encounter from the previous night. His memory of the event was cloudy. It almost didn't seem real. With a bleary image of his mystery woman's face in his head, he fell asleep. He dreamed about her. In his dream, she walked down the halls of the law school whispering into the ears of his classmates, but never into his ear.

When Lucius awoke, it was dark outside. A quick look at his alarm clock revealed that it was past eight. He had an idea. He would go back to the law school and ask the librarian about the woman. The librarian's name was Gretchen Lewis, and she knew everyone, particularly those who were late leaving and kept her in the library past midnight.

Lucius drove to the law school and went inside. It was pretty empty for a Tuesday night. Ms. Lewis was sitting quietly at her desk reading a celebrity gossip magazine.

"Ms. Lewis, do you remember a woman coming out of the library immediately before or immediately after me last night?"

"I can't say that I do."

"She was tall, and she was wearing a UVA law sweatshirt."

"Oh, I know who you're talking about. Yes, I saw her last night."

"Do you know who she is?"

"She's just a student. I think she's working on some research for one of the professors."

"I wonder why I've never seen her before."

"I don't know. Maybe you have."

"Trust me; I would have remembered this girl."

Ms. Lewis raised her eyebrows. "Well, it's a large law school. What is this about anyway? Did she do something wrong?"

"No, I was just curious about her. That's all. Have you seen her tonight?"

"Not tonight." Ms. Lewis gave him a strange look before returning to her magazine.

Lucius strolled out of the library. She was just a student. He had figured as much last night. He felt dumb for having wasted so much time.

Lucius slept well that night after carefully reading over the material for the classes that he had skipped.

He awoke the next morning with two e-mails waiting for him. The first was from Robert Collins. It was from the previous day.

Hey Luke,

You got called on in Torts today. I hope you sent Sandberg an e-mail. He didn't look happy when you weren't there.

Robert

The other e-mail was from Professor Sandberg.

Mr. Dixon,

I need to speak with you in my office this afternoon. I will be there from 2:00 until class at 3:00.

Daniel Sandberg

Lucius showered and went to school. It was going to be a long day. He had Contracts in the morning, then Civil Procedure, then a meeting with a professor who wasn't happy with him, and then Torts class with the same professor.

He couldn't pay attention in his morning classes. All he could think about was what excuses he could give to Professor Sandberg. He was also worried about Torts class. He expected to be called on again today because he had skipped the previous day. And even though he had read the material, he expected the questions to be difficult.

Finally, it was two o'clock. Lucius took the elevator up to the third floor where Professor Sandberg's office was. He quietly knocked on the door and was called inside.

"How can I help you?" Professor Sandberg was an intimidating man. He was physically very large, and he had an even larger presence. He had dark, wild hair and a thick beard. He had been at a law firm for most of his life. He had only recently come to the University of Virginia.

"I'm Lucius Dixon. You asked me to come."

Sandberg looked up at him above his glasses and frowned. "Yes, Mr. Dixon. I need to talk to you."

"If this is about yesterday, I want to apologize. I didn't get much sleep the night before because I was studying for Contracts. I know it's not appropriate to skip class, but I really needed some sleep."

"I understand. I remember what it was like to be a law student. But that's not why I called you in."

"It isn't?"

"No, Mr. Dixon. I've been hearing complaints that you've been bothering and following one of your fellow students."

Lucius was puzzled. "I'm not sure I know what you're talking about."

"There is a female student here at the law school who has been doing some work for me. She said that you tried to take some of her things and that the librarian told her that you had come in asking about her. We try to investigate these things before they get out of hand. Right now, your behavior has not crossed any lines. However, I would warn you to stay away from this young lady. We don't want to have to take disciplinary action against you."

Lucius was in shock. "I'm so sorry, Mr. Sandberg. I really didn't know I had bothered her. I'll do exactly as you say. I'm not some kind of stalker. I was just curious because I had never seen her before."

"I understand, Mr. Dixon. As I said, we try to investigate these things before they go too far. I'm glad to hear that this will not cause us any further problems."

Lucius gathered his things and left Sandberg's office. He had never felt so foolish. Law school was a great opportunity for him. No one else in his family had ever even graduated from college. The financial support that he would be able to give his family would mean a lot to them. And he was coming close to ruining all of that over a girl he didn't even know.

Torts class was a further embarrassment for Lucius. He was called on at the beginning of class and was not dismissed until the very end. Sandberg was particularly vicious with him.

The questions were very difficult, and he never gave Lucius any clues as to what sort of answer he was looking for. He also made several snide remarks about how Lucius clearly hadn't read the material.

Finally class ended. Lucius was relieved. He hoped that Sandberg would forget all about this in a few days. On his way out, Lucius ran into Robert Collins and their mutual friend Jennifer Morgan.

Jennifer had curly, brown hair, green eyes, and a pug nose. She also had a small but noticeable scar beneath her right eye. Her parents had gone through a very messy divorce when she was six, and she blamed that divorce for her difficulty with relationships. Lucius learned all of this in his first conversation with her. She didn't keep things to herself.

Robert spoke up first. "That was pretty rough. I tried to raise my hand a couple of times to help out, but he ignored me.

Jennifer chimed in, "He was being a jerk." Her ubiquitous smile had been replaced with a scowl. "There was no reason for him to do that. You knew the material better than half the people in the class."

"It's not a big deal. It's a long story, but I think he's mad at me for something else."

The three of them walked out of the law school together, talking about the Contracts' exam and the quirks of their professors. Lucius had had enough adventures for now and planned to put his stalking days behind him.

Chapter Two

A few weeks had passed since the day when Lucius had faced the wrath of Sandberg. He had grown very close to both Robert and Jennifer, at least in part because of the support they had provided on that day. Lucius' relationship with Sandberg had also improved. They even greeted one another with smiles and nods when they saw each other in the hallway.

Lucius was feeling more confident about law school as well. He had gotten back his graded Contracts midterm. He had received an average grade, but Lucius was pleased that his erratic behavior had not ruined his chances for a successful law school career. Everything seemed to be going well. He hadn't even given much thought to his mystery woman...until he saw her again.

Lucius had decided to forego a Halloween party with Robert, Jennifer, and the rest of the first year law students one Friday night. He had fallen a bit behind in several of his classes and needed to study. So he packed up his things and headed to the library. He picked out his usual spot on the third floor of the library and went to work.

He was becoming much more adept at reading case law. At first, it had taken him a couple of hours to read what he could now read in half an hour. And the material had become more enjoyable now that he understood how it fit into the legal corpus. On this night he was studying Criminal Law. It was his favorite subject. He even occasionally considered becoming a public defender. But then he would remember how much money he could make in the private sector working for a big, corporate firm.

Lucius studied hard for a couple of hours and finished up at about half past eleven. He packed his bag and left the law school. He waved to Ms. Lewis, the librarian. He had never figured out if she had suspected him of stalking, or if she had told the mystery woman about his questioning for some other reason. He certainly couldn't read her expressions. She had scowled at him before the incident, and she continued to scowl at him now.

Lucius left the law school and drove home. He planned to watch a couple of hours of television before going to sleep. He particularly enjoyed television shows that didn't make him think. It helped him to relax. This evening he settled in on a marathon of a reality dating show.

He had been watching for only a few minutes when he received a phone call. It was Robert, wondering what the assignment had been for Criminal Law. Lucius opened up his bag to grab his book, and it was nowhere to be found. He must have left it at the library. He apologized to Robert, hung up the phone, and drove back to the law school.

It was getting close to midnight, and Lucius wasn't sure that he would make it to the library before it closed. He turned a corner and headed down the long, carpeted hallway toward the library. When he got about fifty feet from the door, he saw her again.

It was the mystery woman. Without thinking, Lucius ducked into a nearby alcove. He would let her go into the library first, and then get his book. He didn't want to have to face her after the earlier incident. It would be too embarrassing. Lucius waited for a few seconds, and then left his alcove.

The door to the library was still closing behind her, so he walked very slowly down the hallway. As he approached the door, Lucius began to notice something strange. The interior of the library was completely dark. A quick look at his watch revealed that it was past twelve. When he got to the door, his suspicions were confirmed. The door was locked.

Lucius stood at the doorway for a minute trying to figure this out. He had clearly just seen the woman going into the library. He knocked on the door to see if Ms. Lewis had let her inside to get something and would do the same for him. There was no response.

Lucius could get his book tomorrow, but his curiosity was overwhelming. Were his eyes playing tricks on him? Could the woman that he saw have been Ms. Lewis, and not the mystery woman? Perhaps she had left a light or a computer on in the back of the library. But Lucius stopped himself. Ms. Lewis was barely five-feet tall. It couldn't have been her. The woman he saw was much taller.

Lucius decided to go back to his alcove. He could observe the door from there without being visible to anyone coming out of the library. If it was the mystery woman who had gone in, he didn't want her to see him when she came out. She had already caused him enough trouble.

He sat quietly in a red leather chair in the alcove. He could just barely see the door around the corner. After nearly an hour of waiting, Lucius gave up. He wasn't entirely sure what he had seen, and he was annoyed with himself for letting his imagination get the better of him again.

He approached the door one more time to see if he could see anything inside. When he got to the door, he noticed that there was no keyhole in the door. Instead, there was a key card slot right next to the door. Lucius' mind immediately went back to that first night and the card that the woman had dropped.

It had to have been a key card. And that's where she went that night when she disappeared. She went back into the library. Lucius' mind was racing. Why would a student need a key to the library? The library is open for sixteen hours every day. Why go after hours?

For now, Lucius thought it would be best to go home. Something strange was going on, but he didn't think it would be a good idea to confront the woman…at least not yet. Lucius drove home. His mind was so distracted by the mystery woman that he had to slam on his brakes to avoid hitting a young woman crossing the street in front of him. She froze in his headlights, and the look of horror on her face slowly transformed into a look of anger. Lucius waved an apology as the woman slowly finished crossing the street, but she didn't seem receptive. He drove the rest of the way home a little more cautiously.

Could she have stolen the key card from the librarian or some other member of the administration? But what would be the purpose of going into the library? Was she stealing? Lucius also considered the possibility that she was working for one of the professors, as he had been told by Ms. Lewis. Perhaps the professor had given her a key to the library, so that she could work undisturbed. Perhaps she had a job during the day and could only research late at night. But why take the job working for a professor if she already had another job?

None of Lucius' explanations made much sense. And yet he was afraid to go to anyone in the administration to figure out what was going on. He had been told in no uncertain terms to stay away from the woman. Even if she was doing something wrong, he couldn't report her.

Lucius decided that he would call Robert the next day. He was a little afraid to tell anyone about the experience, but he knew he could trust Robert. And perhaps he would have some kind of an explanation for what was going on.

Lucius watched television for another hour, and then went to bed. For the first time in a couple of weeks, he had a fitful night. He continued to try to formulate a believable explanation. Maybe she was planning to steal the computers from the library. But that wouldn't explain why she had used the key a couple of weeks ago. Surely, she would have made her move by now. Maybe she had been evicted from her apartment and had nowhere to sleep.

The last thing that Lucius thought of before falling asleep was Sandberg. It only made sense that the professor that she was working for would be Sandberg. He was not on any sort of disciplinary committee, and yet, the mystery woman had gone to him when she suspected Lucius of stalking her. Lucius even thought that Sandberg might have said something about the woman working for him during their meeting. Finally, Lucius fell asleep.

Lucius awoke the following Saturday morning feeling refreshed. He was nervous about pursuing a solution to the new mystery, but in a way, such a pursuit invigorated him. Law school was sometimes exciting and engaging, but nothing in Torts or Contracts was as interesting as this.

He drove to the law school and picked up his Criminal Law book. It was lying on the table exactly where he had been studying. No one had disturbed it. He called Robert on his cell phone on the way home. Robert agreed to meet him at Lucius' apartment and was there when Lucius arrived.

"The party was terrible. Jennifer and I left early. I had to drag her out of there, though. She's got a crush on some third-year. He said he was dressed as Atticus Finch, but he was just wearing a suit. That's not a costume."

"Yeah, well, I'm sorry I didn't have the assignment for you last night. I left my book at the library. I can tell you the assignment now if you need me to."

"That's okay. I got it from someone else. Did your book get stolen? Is that why you called me over?"

"No, but what I'm about to tell you, you have to keep to yourself. Don't tell anyone." Robert looked at Lucius quizzically, but nodded in agreement. Lucius told him the entire story. He told him about the first encounter in the library and about the frightening meeting with Sandberg. And finally, he told Robert about the woman unlocking and entering the library after it had closed.

Robert paused for a moment as if to take it all in. "I'll bet Sandberg's got something to do with it. I remember that day in class. There was viciousness in his eyes. He attacked you."

"I thought about that, but what sense does it make? First of all, he probably could have gone to the administration and asked for a key to the library if he needed one. If that was the case, then there would have been no need to frighten me away from his research assistant. And secondly, it's hard to believe that this particular research assistant was so good that he had to hire her, even though she couldn't work during the regular library hours. It makes no sense."

Robert looked thoughtful for a moment. "Even so, I still think he might have something to do with her. Otherwise, why would he have been the one to warn you away from her? Do you have an Internet connection here?"

Lucius pointed him toward his bedroom where he kept his computer. "What do you need that for?"

"Sandberg has always intrigued me. I'm going to see what I can find out about him on the web."

Lucius followed Robert into the bedroom and sat down on the bed. Robert slid into the chair next to the computer and turned on the monitor. Lucius zoned out for the next few minutes, until Robert started talking.

"This guy is strange. He finished first in his class at Yale Law. He was editor-in-chief of the Yale Law Journal. And he clerked for Supreme Court Justice Byron White. He had the perfect beginnings of a great legal career. Then he went to some nobody firm called Leeder & Schrum for the next thirty years. He didn't even work on any important cases for them."

Lucius was unimpressed. "That's not so strange. Maybe, he didn't want a high-profile legal career."

"I know the type of person who is editor of the Yale Law Journal, and that's not the type of person who wants to avoid a high-profile legal career. Hell, everyone who attends Yale Law wants a high-profile legal career."

"Well, maybe there was a family connection to the firm."

"I already thought of that, and I couldn't find anything which suggests that. This firm is small. They only have about thirty lawyers."

"Maybe, his family is connected through one of their clients. Maybe his dad was the president of some corporation who always used Leeder & Schrum as their law firm. Maybe he always wanted to work for that firm, ever since he was a kid."

Robert's only initial response was typing. "The odd thing is that I can't find out anything about their clients. Most firms of any size put up a listing of all of their clients. But I suppose it makes sense if you have no big clients."

"What sort of law did Sandberg practice for them? Maybe we can get an idea about what his research interests are."

"Hold on a second, I'll check. And then I'll go to the school's website to see if his bio on there tells what he's researching."

A few minutes later, Robert spoke up again. "He worked on Admiralty and Intellectual Property issues for the Leeder & Schrum. His bio on the UVA website doesn't reveal any interests or what he might be researching now."

"None of this helps. I've got an idea anyway."

"Okay, tell me your idea."

"I'm going to go to the law school tonight at around eleven. I'm going to find the most tucked away spot in the library. I'm going to study until it gets close to midnight, and then I'm going to pretend to fall asleep. If she shows up, I'll follow her from a distance. If she doesn't, I'll sleep there and come home Sunday morning."

Robert didn't hesitate. "That's a horrible idea. You already got into a whole lot of trouble the last time you bothered this girl. The way to approach this situation is through Sandberg...to find out what his connection to her is. If anyone is doing something wrong, it's him."

"I don't think you're right. And I won't get caught anyway. I'll be extra careful. If you want to continue researching Sandberg, feel free, but I've got to know what's going on, and this is the only way for me to find out for certain."

"I can't stop you, so do whatever you want. Just be careful. I'm going to try to find out what sort of research Sandberg is doing now and who he has working for him. Don't worry; I'll keep your name out of it."

The two friends said their goodbyes, and Lucius began preparing for the night. He packed a couple of sandwiches and a soda, and he packed a small camping pillow that he had from his days as a boy scout. At eleven o'clock, he left for the library.

When he arrived, Jennifer was waiting outside the library. She looked nervous.

"Don't be mad at him, but Robert told me the whole story. I don't think this is a good idea. If you'd like, I'm willing to go to the administration to ask them if they know about a girl going into the library after it closes."

"There's too much of a chance that it'll be traced back to me. Professors know that you and I are friends. I could get kicked out for stalking."

"But you could also get kicked out if you get caught hiding in the library after it's closed. We've got a single sanction here. One violation of the honor code, and you're out."

"Only you and Robert know that I will be hiding. To everyone else, I fell asleep in there and got locked in. I can't get kicked out for that."

"Okay, well, Robert told me that you were set on this idea, so I'm going to help. Keep your cell phone with you. I'm going to wait out here for a couple of hours. I'll sit so that I can see the door without being visible myself. If she's coming in, I'll text you. Otherwise, I'll text you before I leave to go home."

"I appreciate it, Jennifer."

"Be careful, Luke."

Lucius explored the library and found the most remote nook that he could find. It was on the second floor. He set his things up and laid his head down on the table.

He awoke to a buzzing in his pocket and complete darkness all around him. Lucius pulled out his phone.

"Shes coming in."

He waited for a moment more until his eyes had adjusted to the darkness. Then he slowly crept to a ledge overlooking the first floor of the library. She had a flashlight and was moving quickly. Lucius was afraid to get too close. When she went up to the third floor, he made his way down to the first floor to see if he could figure out what she had done.

One computer at the very front of the computer lab had been turned on, and the copy machine directly outside the lab had been turned on. Lucius went behind the circulation desk and crouched. From this vantage point, he could see the copy machine and about half of the computer monitor, and only the very top of his head was visible. He waited.

She re-emerged a couple of times over the next few hours carrying law books. Sometimes, she would go to the computer with the books, and sometimes she would copy pages out of the books. So it was some sort of research after all.

At about three o'clock in the morning, the mystery woman re-emerged, turned off the computer and copier, and headed for the door. She used the card to unlock the door and headed out. The door swung open widely and slowly began to close. Lucius crawled quickly over to the closing door, and grabbed hold of the metal doorstop at the bottom of the door. He let the door come as close to closing as he could, and then held it fast.

He waited for a few minutes, until he was certain that she was gone. Then he pulled the door stop out and ran upstairs to get his things. Lucius quickly collected his bag, ran downstairs, pulled up the doorstop, and let the door to the library close behind him as he left.

At least some of his theories from the night before could be put to bed. She wasn't stealing, and she wasn't sleeping there. She appeared to be doing research. Maybe Robert was right, and it had something to do with Sandberg.

Lucius drove slowly home, thinking about what he should do next. He wanted to find out what she was researching. But she returned all of the books, and Internet browsing history can't be seen by other students.

When he arrived at home, he turned on his computer and signed in to his instant messaging service. As he had hoped, Robert was online.

"I'm back."

"What happened?"

"She's researching. I couldn't figure out what she was researching, though."

"I found out some things, too. Have you ever been to the site that lets you see webpages as they were in the past?"

"I've heard of it."

"Well, here's a page from the Leeder & Schrum website from three years ago. It has bios for all of the attorneys that were working there. Sandberg's is interesting."

Lucius clicked on the link that Robert sent him. It took a moment for the detailed page to load. Lucius started scrolling down the list of attorneys; each had their picture and a small bio. He was looking for Sandberg when something else caught his eye.

Under the name Dolores Martinez, a smiling photo of the then second-year associate stared back at him. It was as plain as day. It was his mystery woman.

Chapter Three

For a moment, Lucius simply stared at his screen. An instant message brought him out of his trance.

"Are you still there?"

"She's not a student."

"Who's not a student?"

"The woman with the key to the library. She was an associate at Leeder & Schrum when Sandberg was there."

"Are you sure? Which one is she?"

"Dolores Martinez. Yes, I'm sure."

"Didn't Sandberg claim she was a student?"

"Yes. Something weird is going on."

Lucius' phone started buzzing on the table behind him. He picked it up.

It was Robert. "So before I just thought you were being strange, but now I'm beginning to wonder if you're on to something."

"What's the explanation? Why all the cover-up for something as innocent as research?"

"I don't know. I need to go to bed, but I want to talk about this tomorrow. How about if we meet at that bagel place on 29 at noon tomorrow? I'll bring Jennifer, and we can figure this thing out."

"That sounds like a plan. I'll see you then, Robert."

"Yeah, see you then. You try to get some sleep."

Lucius hung up his phone. His apartment was eerily silent, and he wasn't sleepy at all. He simply couldn't think of an innocent explanation for all of this. Sandberg had lied to him to try to prevent him from figuring out what they were doing. That seemed to imply that Sandberg and Martinez could get into trouble if someone found out.

But how serious was the trouble? If Sandberg could lose his job over this, then he wouldn't hesitate to take out a couple of law students. He was a new professor, but it would be very easy for him to claim he had busted a cheating scandal or caught three students trying to steal someone's laptop. And what could Lucius do? If he reported them, Martinez could simply destroy the key card, and it would be his word against theirs.

And there was always the possibility of an innocent explanation. Maybe Martinez was getting an LLM or some other sort of post-graduate degree. Maybe she was a student.

Lucius decided to try his best to ignore the situation for now. He sat down in his living room and turned on the television. He flipped through the channels, never settling on anything for more than a few seconds. After about an hour of this, Lucius decided to fix himself something to eat.

He pre-heated the oven and put in a frozen pizza. What could they be researching that would require them to be so secretive? Was there a connection to why they had left the firm? Lucius thought again about how Robert had told him that Leeder & Schrum didn't list their clients on their website. Maybe, if they could figure out who Leeder & Schrum represented, and more specifically, who Sandberg and Martinez had represented, they could have a better idea as to what was being researched.

Lucius sat back down in his chair and started flipping through the channels again. A few minutes later, he was asleep.

Lucius awoke to a smoke-filled apartment. For a minute, his mind filled with horror stories. Sandberg was burning down his apartment or trying to smoke him out, so that he could finish him off in a volley of gunshots. Then Lucius remembered his frozen pizza. He ran to the oven and turned it off. A quick look inside revealed a blackened mess and a puff of smoke.

Lucius had unplugged his smoke alarm a few days earlier after a similar cooking mishap. He was too paranoid to open the door, so he cracked a few windows and waved a dish towel around to get rid of all of the smoke. After nearly a half hour of waving the towel at the smoke, it had dissipated enough that he felt he could go back to sleep. He was, however, too afraid to sleep with the windows open, so he closed and locked them. He then turned on his bathroom vent and the fan above the stove. He could worry about cleaning the oven later.

Lucius awoke to his phone buzzing on the table beside his bed. He answered it and apologized to Robert for being late. He looked at the clock. It was half past noon. Robert agreed to wait for him, and Lucius told them to go ahead and order. After a quick shower to try to wash off the smell of smoke, Lucius arrived at the bagel place.

"You smell like smoke," Jennifer said as soon as he arrived at the table.

"I had a little bit of a cooking accident, but it's okay. Everything's fine now."

Robert spoke up. "I told Jennifer about what we found out. We think the best idea is to wait until after finals before we do anything else."

"That sounds reasonable, but we may as well discuss what we'll do after finals. I don't think we can take this to the administration. Not yet, at least."

Jennifer chimed in, "It's the right thing to do, Luke. We're going to put our law school careers in jeopardy if we keep doing all of this spying and sneaking around."

"We put our law school careers in jeopardy if we go the administration. Sandberg may be serious about covering this up. If he wanted to, he wouldn't have a problem getting all three of us kicked out."

"But he wouldn't be able to if we went to the administration first. He couldn't respond to the allegations by accusing the three of us of lying, cheating, or stealing."

"He could say that he had already notified us that we were being investigated for cheating, and that we were simply trying to damage his credibility before he brought the charges against us. The administration will give him the benefit of the doubt, and he could simply have Martinez hide or destroy the key card. Then we have no evidence."

Robert nervously spoke up. "Maybe, we should just stay out of this altogether. It's just legal research. How illegal could it be?"

Lucius was frustrated. "We don't know how illegal it could be. That's why we have to keep investigating. We have to get more evidence before we can go to the administration. And maybe we'll find out that what they're doing is completely innocent. Then we don't have to tell anyone."

Robert and Jennifer both looked at each other for nearly a minute. Then Jennifer spoke up. "Okay, Luke. But we have to all agree about everything we do from now on. You can't keep hiding in the library. That's extreme. And we also have to agree not to do anything until after finals."

Lucius agreed to the demands. He needed the support of his friends, even if he didn't agree with them. They ate their meals in silence, each of them thinking of explanations for the strange goings on at the law school. The three friends finished their food and exchanged goodbyes. Despite what he had told Jennifer, he intended to go back to the library that very night.

Lucius drove home and spent his Sunday afternoon studying. For once, his mind remained focused on the material. He read for nearly ten hours, catching up on all of his reading. He wasn't entirely ready to take a final in any of these subjects, but he wasn't nearly as nervous as he had been when he began law school. If his miserable performance on the midterm had landed him an average grade, he felt comfortable that he could score well above average on the finals...as long as he remained focused.

Once Lucius finished his reading, he began packing his night bag. This time, along with his sandwiches and pillow, Lucius brought along a small flashlight and a notepad. He intended to get a look at what Martinez was researching.

Lucius finished packing and drove to the law school. He kept an eye out for Jennifer or Robert, but there was no sign of them so he went inside the library. He decided to use the same study nook that he had used before. It was hidden away but provided easy access to the landing which looked over the first floor. He set up his things and waited.

After about ten minutes, the lights flipped off and on. Lucius recognized that to be the five-minute warning. He remained in his seat, even as he heard a scuffling just a couple of aisles away. He laid his head down on the desk, in case he was seen. Finally, after a few more minutes, the lights went off for good. Lucius raised his head from the table and looked around.

It took a few minutes for his eyes to adjust to the darkness. Then he walked quietly over to the landing and looked out. It appeared that everyone had gone, so he sneaked down to the lower floor. He planned to find a hiding place near the computer that Martinez had used the night before. He had to see what she was doing.

The computer lab consisted of four rows of five computers. Alongside these four rows were two large machines which operated as printers, copiers, and fax machines. As far as Lucius could tell, neither of those machines was used by Martinez on the previous night. There was a very small corner available between the machine furthest from the entrance to the lab and the back row of computers. Lucius climbed into that corner.

He had a small space between the machine and the wall through which he could see the entrance to the lab. It was, unfortunately, not a comfortable position. He was sitting on wires and more wires prevented him from leaning back against the wall. There was also the fact that the space was far too cramped for him to stretch out his legs. He had to remain in a squatted position. This was not going to be a fun night.

Lucius waited quietly in the dark for what seemed like hours. When his legs began to ache, he finally gave up. She wasn't coming tonight. He crawled out from his corner and checked the front door to the library. It was locked. He wasn't entirely comfortable spending the night in the library, but now he had no choice. He headed upstairs to collect his things and to try to find a comfortable spot. He settled on a spot in the aisle nearest his study nook. He lay down on the floor and tried to make himself comfortable.

He was awakened by blinding light on his face. Lucius couldn't see anything and panicked. He rubbed his eyes and was happy to see, instead of Dolores Martinez with a flashlight in his face, that the lights in the library had been turned on. He collected his things and moved quickly back to his study nook. A glance at his watch revealed that it was a quarter until nine. He had class in fifteen minutes.

He waited for a few minutes and then looked out over the landing. The librarian was nowhere in sight, so he quickly grabbed his things and headed out of the library. He found a nearby bathroom and tried to clean himself up. He still looked rough. His hair was sticking up and would not lie down. He had a five o'clock shadow, and his eyes were bloodshot. Regardless, Lucius couldn't afford to miss any more classes, so he headed for Contracts.

Professor Franklin was a little late to class. Lucius, while looking around the classroom, met eyes with Jennifer. She gave him a disapproving look and mouthed at him to see her after class. Lucius suspected that she had figured out from his appearance what he had done the previous night.

Professor Franklin finally arrived. His lecture on the Statute of frauds was very dry. Lucius stopped paying attention after about fifteen minutes. He started trying to think of ways to explain his appearance, but none of them seemed plausible. Jennifer already knew him too well to accept any excuses. He decided to tell her the truth. He knew she wouldn't turn him in; he only worried that she would stop supporting him in his quest to figure out what Sandberg and Martinez were doing.

After class, he gathered his things and waited outside the classroom. Jennifer arrived momentarily.

"Don't try to give me excuses. I know what you did."

"Please keep your voice down." Lucius pulled her away from the classroom and to a nearby bench where they both sat down. "I'm not going to give you any excuses. I shouldn't have done it, particularly not after I told you and Robert that I wouldn't. But I really couldn't help myself. My curiosity was overwhelming."

"I know, Luke. I'm curious also. But finals are coming up, and you need to be focused on law school, not on solving inane mysteries."

"You're absolutely right. Anyway, in case you were wondering, she didn't show up last night, and I had to sleep on the floor."

"That serves you right. Robert and I are supporting you on this, and you lied to our faces."

"I'm sorry for that, and I won't do it again. I'll tell you the truth from now on. I'm going to go back in tonight."

"No, you're not. This is getting out of hand."

"I'm going back in tonight. It doesn't matter if she does or doesn't show up, this will be the last night. I promise. After tonight, I will focus on finals."

"I don't think it's a good idea, Luke. Ms. Lewis is probably getting suspicious, anyway. You know she sees you going in late and not coming out."

"I've been careful when I go in to make sure she doesn't see me, or at least isn't able to recognize me. And when I left this morning, I didn't see her anywhere."

Jennifer sighed. "Okay. If you go in again after tonight, I'm going to go to the administration and ask them about the girl. I know you don't want me to, but I don't want to let this get out of hand.

"I understand, Jennifer. I know you're looking out for me."

Jennifer left him sitting on the bench. He was finished with class at 4:00. If he could use the breaks between his classes to finish his work, then perhaps he could sleep from 4:00 until 11:00. That way, he wouldn't have to sleep in the library. He could bring some candles and get some work done if Martinez didn't show up again.

The rest of the day dragged on at an even slower pace. When Torts finally rolled around at 3:00, he wanted nothing more than to go directly home to sleep. But he remembered what had happened the last time he had skipped Torts. He didn't want to jeopardize the good relationship that he was trying to build with Sandberg. The law school supposedly had blind grading, but he didn't want to take any chances.

Torts wasn't so bad. The lecture was on *res ipsa loquitur*. The basic rule was that when a specific theory of negligence could not be put forward and the instrumentality of harm was under the exclusive control of a defendant, that defendant could be sued regardless of whether there was a specific theory of harm. Lucius was able to remain awake throughout the class, though there was one scary moment when Sandberg caught him yawning and gave him a disapproving look.

Finally, class ended and Lucius drove home. He climbed into his comfortable bed, a stark contrast from the hard library floor from the night before. He set his alarm for eleven o'clock and slept soundly until it went off.

Lucius packed the same bag from the night before, except he left out the sandwiches and included some small candles. It had seemed like a good idea originally, but he hadn't eaten his sandwiches on either of the previous trips and didn't see himself getting hungry anytime soon.

Lucius headed to the library. This time he was unable to avoid Ms. Lewis. She even waved at him. Nonetheless, he repeated his routine from the night before. He went to the same nook, pretended to be asleep, and then sneaked down to his hiding place in the computer lab when the lights went off. He pushed the machine and the table on which the back row of computer monitors sat in order to create more space. He even rearranged some of the wires to improve his comfort.

Almost as soon as he had settled into his spot, he heard the main door to the library opening. He waited patiently. If her routine from two nights ago was repeated, she would go upstairs at first to retrieve some books. She would then come down to the computer and the copier outside the lab.

A few minutes passed, and then he heard the copier being turned on. He saw her flashlight playing off the walls outside, and then he saw her shadow entering the computer lab. He held his breath. She was less than ten feet away.

She turned on the computer and went back outside. She returned a few minutes later and began typing. She repeated this routine two more times before Lucius had the nerve to move. When she left the computer for the third time and he heard no noise from the copier, Lucius pulled himself out of his hiding place.

He crawled over to the computer. It had been left on. He looked at the screen. She was using an instant messenger service. The user name that she was using was 'AnonWXYZ.' The messages were being sent to 'AnonDCBA.' Lucius pulled out his notepad and wrote down the screen names. Before he could begin writing down the text of the messages, he heard a noise behind him.

He quickly crawled back into his hiding place. Almost as soon as he was in place, he saw her shadow re-enter the room.

She paused for a moment, looking at the computer. He could see her face in the light of the monitor. She looked a little confused, almost as if she suspected that someone had tampered with her work. Lucius worried that he had done something to reveal his presence, but he was pretty sure that he had changed nothing on the computer.

After a few seconds of staring, Martinez sat back down at the computer and began typing. Lucius decided that he would not try to figure out anything more tonight. He would see if Robert could figure out some way to track the second screen name. Perhaps it was Sandberg's.

The next time she left, Lucius crawled back outside to his hiding place near the door behind the circulation desk. He decided to remain there, so that he could leave the library in the same way that he had left two nights ago. She made a few more trips upstairs carrying books back and forth and then finally returned empty handed.

As she was walking toward the door, she glanced near where he was. She then did a double-take, and Lucius ducked. Had she seen him? He tried to stop from breathing heavily but couldn't control himself. He heard no movement from Martinez. Finally, after nearly a minute of waiting, he heard her opening the door.

Lucius let out a sigh of relief and looked up from his hiding place. As the door started to swing shut, he crawled quickly over to it and grabbed the doorstop.

Before he could do anything further, the door swung back open knocking him to the ground. His eyes went blind as the flashlight shined into them. This time he knew it wasn't the lights of the library. This time he knew that he had been caught.

Chapter Four

Lucius was shaking.

"What are you doing?" She whispered at him harshly. Lucius hesitated, not knowing what to say. Had she recognized him? His hesitation was met with a swift kick to the midsection.

"Come on; get away from the door before someone sees you." She motioned with the flashlight for him to go into the computer lab. He did as he was told. When they got there, she again asked for an explanation.

This time he provided one. "I must have fallen asleep upstairs, and I got locked inside. I heard some noises down here, so I came down. When I got down here, you were leaving. I grabbed the doorstop, so I could prop it open and leave after collecting my things."

"That's a lie. I saw you hiding behind the counter near the door. That's why I came back in."

"That's true, but I only hid because I didn't want to be in trouble. I didn't know who you were." Lucius tried to change the subject. "Who are you, anyway?"

She didn't hesitate. "I'm just a student. I left my keys inside, so the janitor gave me a library key to come and look for them."

"Okay, well could you prop the door open, so I can go and get my things? Then we can both get out of here and pretend this never happened." Lucius just wanted to end the conversation as quickly as possible. He was worried that if she had not already recognized him, she would soon.

"I'm sorry I kicked you. I've been nervous lately, and with it being so dark and deserted, I didn't know who you might be."

"It's okay. I've already forgotten it," he said over his shoulder as he walked back toward the staircase. He hadn't. It still hurt.

As Lucius was walking up the stairs, he could see Martinez exiting the library. She pulled down the doorstop and left the door open for him. He collected his things and quickly left the library, pulling the door shut behind him.

As he walked out to his car, he realized that he was still shaking. He tried to convince himself not to be so nervous. He seemed to have avoided giving anything away. He hadn't even given her his name. He tried to figure out what had been going through her mind. Maybe she had recognized him but didn't say anything. What would be the explanation for that? Maybe she remembered that he had previously seen her key card and would realize that her janitor story was a lie. Then why would she tell it? Maybe she just wanted to avoid any sort of confrontation or explanation.

Lucius unlocked his car and climbed in. If she had recognized him, then she would tell Sandberg, and this could mean serious trouble for him. If she didn't recognize him, then it had been a successful evening. He had confirmed that she was indeed researching. He had uncovered two instant message screen names that were being used to transmit information. And he had confirmed that both Sandberg and Martinez were willing to lie to cover up whatever it was that they were doing. After all, Sandberg had claimed that Martinez was a student, and she had identified herself as a student who had lost her keys.

Lucius drove home, still nervous even after he had locked and bolted the door to his apartment. His hopes that Robert or Jennifer would be online were dashed, so he went back into the living room to watch television. There was no way that he was going to be able to sleep.

Early the next morning, he called both Robert and Jennifer to tell them about what had happened. They both agreed that she probably hadn't recognized him. They both also agreed to come forward in support of Lucius if Sandberg tried to have him kicked out. And Lucius agreed to their demand that he leave all of this alone until finals were over.

The next few weeks were marked by nothing particularly interesting. Lucius spent a lot of time outlining for his classes and participating in study groups, primarily with Robert and Jennifer, but also with some of his other classmates.

Sandberg didn't say anything to him or call him into his office, but every time they passed each other in the hallway, Lucius got nervous. Maybe Sandberg knew but didn't want to say anything for fear of what Lucius would reveal about his and Martinez's late-night activities. Or maybe Martinez hadn't recognized him. He knew from his days in the Boy Scouts that faces sometimes looked distorted in the light of a flashlight. And their earlier encounter had only lasted a few minutes.

He worried whenever he saw Sandberg, but on most other occasions, he was able to concentrate on his work. He didn't go anywhere near the library, particularly late at night. He had decided, instead, to work from home. He didn't want to risk seeing Martinez again and possibly raising a dormant memory in her mind of who he was.

All four of his finals came and went. He felt the strongest about his Criminal Law final, but it would be weeks before he would find out any of his grades. Robert and Jennifer went to Washington, D.C. and Atlanta, Georgia respectively to visit their families. Lucius remained at school over Christmas break. His family was in Mississippi. He couldn't afford a plane ticket and didn't trust his car to make the trip.

The break went by quickly. Lucius watched a lot of television and dreamed about Dolores Martinez.

Robert showed up at his house on January 10, three days before school began, with a printed e-mail in his hand. "I've always wanted to be an investigative reporter. I've been thinking about nothing other than Sandberg and Martinez the whole time I was on break."

"What's the e-mail?"

"By the way, we probably won't get much help from Jennifer this semester. She's dating a third-year. She had a crush on him last semester, and they've been hanging out in Atlanta. I'm not entirely sure what she sees in him. He reminds me of Gomer Pyle."

"What's the e-mail?"

"Oh, yeah, sorry. This is the e-mail sent out by Sandberg about the informal get together at his house next Saturday. Everyone in his Torts class is invited."

"I'm not going to that." Lucius was still nervous about seeing Sandberg face-to-face.

"Hear me out. I've got this friend in D.C. He worked with my dad at the Justice Department, and he knows a lot about computers. He didn't know any way to track the screen name 'AnonDCBA,' but he did have an idea. He suggested that if we knew who it might be, we could know for sure by running the instant messenger program on their computer. We could then look at the available screen names." Robert was clearly very excited.

"You want to find Sandberg's computer in his house and run his instant messenger service? Doesn't that sound kind of risky? And what if he's running the program in his office instead of at home?"

"That's doubtful. He would be arousing a lot of suspicions if he were staying at his office until three o'clock in the morning. He's almost certainly receiving the messages at home."

"Fair enough, but what's the point? We're already pretty sure that it's Sandberg. It's too risky of a venture to simply confirm something that we already suspect to be true."

Robert smiled. "That's where the second part of the plan comes into play. My friend also gave me this program." Robert produced a USB flash drive from his pocket. "All you have to do is install it on a computer, and it will tell you all of the saved passwords on that computer."

Lucius was incredulous. "That is way too risky. I feel like I'm on the verge of being kicked out of law school already. If I get caught sneaking into his study with a program like that, I'm finished."

"You don't have to do it. I will."

"What's the point of knowing the password anyway?"

"I'm way ahead of you. We get the password. Then we come over here to your house at around midnight one night. When he logs in, we immediately log in to his account ourselves. Since the service only allows one user to be online for each user name, it will kick him off. We then change the password for his screen name, and he won't be able to sign back in to kick us off.

Then we just receive the information that Martinez sends. There's no need for you to sneak back into the library."

"We would be able to figure out what they're researching, and whether they're planning something illegal." Lucius had to smile. It seemed like a good plan.

"I've got more ideas as well, but we'll carry this one out first. I promise we'll have enough evidence to take them down by the end of the semester." Robert excused himself and left the apartment. Lucius sat perfectly still, trying to take it all in. It was going to be, if nothing else, an entertaining semester.

The week prior to Sandberg's party went by quickly. Lucius had four classes again: Property, Constitutional Law, Criminal Investigation, and Professional Responsibility. After the first week, his favorite was Criminal Investigation. The material was just more interesting to him. Professional Responsibility was his least favorite class. He liked thinking about ethical dilemmas, but the course seemed to primarily consist of memorizing rules of behavior.

Jennifer was in both Property and Constitutional Law with him. One day after class, she came running up behind him.

"How goes the investigation?"

"Hey Jennifer. It's going pretty well. Did Robert tell you about our next move?"

"Nah, he's been acting weird around me lately ever since I started dating Howard."

"He said you wouldn't be helping with the investigation this semester because of Howard."

"I never told him that. I still want to help. I'm still as curious as you guys are to figure this all out. Plus, law school just is pretty boring."

Lucius laughed. "Let's go into one of the study rooms, and I'll tell you the plan."

Lucius and Jennifer found an empty study room and went inside. Lucius told her everything that Robert had told him.

"Sounds like a plan. How can I help?"

"This part seems to be Robert's one-man show. You should come to Sandberg's party with us, though. You can help me keep an eye on Sandberg while Robert finds the computer."

Jennifer agreed, and the two parted ways. Lucius was glad to have Jennifer back on board. Robert had seemed pretty dictatorial in presenting his plan, and Lucius was happy to have support in case any of Robert's ideas needed to be vetoed.

On Saturday at about six o'clock in the evening, the three of them met up at Robert's apartment. The plan was for Jennifer to ask Sandberg's wife, if she was in attendance, where a bathroom could be found. She would then explore that part of the house, looking for a study. Once she found it, she would return and discreetly tell Robert where it was. Robert would then implement the rest of the plan, while Lucius and Jennifer kept their eyes on the Sandbergs.

When they first arrived, there were only two people other than the Sandbergs in attendance. The party was supposed to begin at seven o'clock. They had arrived at half past seven, and hardly anyone was there. No words were exchanged, but all three were noticeably worried by the size of the crowd. If more people didn't show up, it would be impossible to disappear and reappear without being noticed by someone.

After about fifteen to twenty minutes, the crowd started to trickle in. Jennifer excused herself. Mrs. Sandberg walked her down the hall to the bathroom and then returned by herself. Jennifer returned a few minutes later and whispered something in Robert's ear. Robert pulled out a notepad and wrote something down. He then looked at Lucius and passed the pad to him.

Written at the top of the page were the words, 'Second Door on the Left.' Written messily underneath was the sentence, 'I'm too nervous to do this; you'll have to go.' Before Lucius could say anything, Robert passed him the flash drive underneath the table.

For a moment, Lucius panicked. He had only agreed to this plan because Robert was going to be doing the difficult part. And now Robert had bailed on him when it mattered most.

But Lucius needed to get the information, so he didn't have to go back into the library. It would provide an easy way to spy from a distance.

After more than a minute of thinking, Lucius stood up and asked Mrs. Sandberg where the bathroom was. As she was telling him, Mr. Sandberg looked up at him and they stared at each other for a few seconds. Lucius saw no suspicion in Sandberg's eyes, but the stare made him nervous nonetheless.

Lucius walked slowly down the hallway. He looked behind him, and when he saw that no one could see him, he ducked into the second door on the left. It was the study. There were hundreds of books on both sides of the room, an old oaken desk, a print of Bruegel's *Landscape with the Fall of Icarus*, and a computer. Lucius walked quickly over to the computer. Thankfully, it was already turned on.

A quick search of the desktop revealed the instant messenger program. He opened it and scanned the screen names. At the very bottom of the list was the screen name that he was looking for, 'AnonDCBA.' He clicked on it and was delighted to see that the password was saved. He popped the flash drive into the USB port, and then froze when he heard a voice at the door.

"What are you doing in here?" An eight or nine year old boy entered the room rubbing his eyes sleepily.

Lucius thought quickly. "I'm just checking my e-mail. Your dad said it would be okay. Shouldn't you be back in bed?"

"What's your name?"

"Frank. What's yours?" Lucius tried to continue working while he talked to the child. It seemed to be taking forever for the program to install from the disk.

"My name's Edward. Why are you checking your e-mail here? Don't you have a computer at home, Frank?"

"I thought I might have an important e-mail. It couldn't wait until I got home. Now you need to go back to bed before we both get in trouble." Finally, the program installed. Lucius quickly double-clicked on the icon, and the program started running.

Edward starting wandering near the computer when a voice rang out in the hallway. It was his mother. He turned and ran out of the room, but he didn't shut the door all the way. Lucius could hear the conversation in the hallway.

"I thought I told you to go to bed. What were you doing in there?" Mrs. Sandberg was angry.

"I was just talking to that boy." The program revealed the saved passwords, and Lucius quickly wrote down the one for the screen name 'AnonDCBA.' It was a six digit number: '112375.'

"What boy? What are you talking about?"

"The boy who is checking his e-mail in dad's study." Lucius ducked under the desk. He heard the door open further and then close completely. He then heard muffled scolding in the hallway.

"What have I told you about making things up? You get in the bed right now." Edward didn't seem to fight his mother very hard; he seemed to be accustomed to her winning these arguments. Lucius got out from under the desk and made sure that he had left no programs open. He then deleted Robert's program from the computer. After a quick double-check, he walked slowly to the door.

He put his ear to the door, and when he heard no noises outside, he opened it and entered the hallway. He made his way quickly back to the main room.

Sandberg looked at him as he entered. "Did you fall in?"

"What?" Lucius felt as if he were being accused of something.

"The toilet. Did you fall in? You were gone for a while."

Lucius tried to laugh but could only manage a smile. "Nope, I'm fine. I just got a little lost."

It was only then that Lucius noticed both Robert and Jennifer staring hard at him. He nodded his head, and they both smiled. He sat down to talk for a few more minutes. He felt that if they left immediately, it would only draw further attention to them.

Finally, at about 9:00, the three of them excused themselves. They thanked the Sandbergs for having them and said goodbye to everyone else that they knew.

When they got in the car, Lucius felt like he was about to explode. "I got it. I got the password. 'AnonDCBA' is Sandberg, and I got his password."

Robert spoke up. "I don't know what happened to me back there. I got these visions in my head of being caught and having to face my dad. He would kill me. It just seemed too risky. You've got a lot more nerve than I do."

"Don't worry about it, Robert. I couldn't have gotten the password without your idea and your program."

They discussed the situation as they drove home, but Lucius didn't tell them everything. He decided not to tell them about the encounter with Sandberg's son. There was no point. It would only make them worry. When the three of them parted ways and Lucius returned home, he began worrying himself.

Edward was almost certain to repeat the story to his father. And what if his father remembered the long bathroom break? He could put the two together, and then he'd know that Lucius had been on his computer. But what could Sandberg do with that information? Lucius could simply say that he was checking his e-mail. He would apologize for doing so without asking, but there would be no reason for him to be in serious trouble.

Lucius wasn't tired, so he decided to attempt to clean the remains of the frozen pizza out of his oven. He had attempted to clean it weeks ago but had aborted the effort after only a few minutes. He pulled out all of the oven cleaner that he had and a large roll of paper towels. The job was not an easy one. He sprayed and scrubbed for nearly a half hour until the oven looked useable. He nearly filled up the entire trash bag with paper towels.

Lucius closed his oven and went into the living room. He turned on the television and tried to relax. There was no need to worry. He had lied to the kid about his name. That would probably throw Sandberg off his trail. And even if Sandberg figured out that it was Lucius who had used his computer, there was no evidence that he had done anything wrong. He was only checking his e-mail, except...

Lucius felt his pocket. It wasn't there. Had he given it to Robert? No, he had no memory of that.

All of the blood drained out of Lucius' face. He had left the flash drive in Sandberg's computer.

Chapter Five

Early the next morning, Lucius called Robert to tell him the bad news.

There was a pause, and then Robert responded calmly. "Don't worry about it. First off, his wife or the kid might find it first. Secondly, even if he does find it, he won't know what to make of it. He'll probably just toss it aside or repurpose it."

"You don't think we need to try to get back in there…to get the it back?"

"No, that's the last thing we need to do. Right now, that flash drive can't be traced back to us. There's no need to tie ourselves to it. And besides, if he does figure it out, we'll know tonight. He'll almost assuredly change his password, and the plan won't work."

"You still want to do this tonight?" Lucius was reminded of how gung-ho Robert had been about the previous idea until it was time for him to actually do something.

"Yeah, we should go ahead and try tonight. We can't give him time to change his password on the off chance that he does figure out what the flash drive is. And besides, there's never any guarantee that Martinez will send him anything. So we need to try every night until she does."

Lucius spent the rest of the day reading for his classes. He expected the next few weeks to be busy and was hoping to get ahead.

That evening at about eleven o'clock, there was a knock at the door. Lucius opened the door for Robert and Jennifer who were waiting outside. They entered the room arguing.

Lucius tried to remain calm. "What's the problem?"

"Jennifer is starting to get on my nerves. That's all. Why did we have to involve her in this anyway?"

"I've got just as much right to be involved in this as you do."

"No, you don't. Luke didn't tell you what was going on at first. I did. And that was a big mistake."

Lucius interrupted. "What is this about?"

Jennifer quickly chimed in. "It's about Howard. Robert doesn't like Howard, and Howard doesn't like Robert."

"My opinions about Howard have nothing to do with this! I just don't understand why you're trying to tag along with me and Luke."

Lucius tried to play peacemaker. "This is ridiculous. If both of you keep arguing, I'm going to go back to spying by myself."

After a few more harsh words and angry glances were exchanged, Robert and Jennifer calmed down and glumly apologized to each other.

Lucius grabbed a couple of folding chairs from his kitchen table and took them into his bedroom. Robert and Jennifer sat down in the chairs, and Lucius sat down in front of his computer.

He loaded up his instant messenger service and added 'AnonDCBA' to his list. After about ten minutes of waiting in silence, Sandberg logged on. Lucius quickly exited the service and typed in 'AnonDCBA' and the password '112375.' He clicked to log in and waited patiently while the service loaded.

An alert popped onto the screen. "Incorrect Password. Try Again."

Lucius was dismayed. "Sandberg changed the password. This whole thing was a waste of time."

Robert spoke up. "Try it again. Maybe you typed it in wrong."

Lucius carefully typed in the user name and password and crossed his fingers. He looked back at Robert and Jennifer. They were both intently staring at the screen.

Robert stood up from his chair in excitement. "It went through! Now click on the 'change password' icon."

Lucius wheeled around in his chair and did as Robert had told him. He changed the password to 'rosebud.' It was the first thing that he could think of, and there was no way it could be traced back to him if Sandberg was able to figure it out.

As soon as the changes went through, Lucius thought about something that had slipped his mind.

"What if he calls her?"

"What?"

"What if he calls her and tells her that he can't log on?"

Robert spoke up immediately. "He probably won't. He won't know that someone else has logged into his account. He just knows that he can't log on. So he'll assume that she'll see that he's not online and leave the library… or maybe he'll figure it out and call her. We'll just have to wait and see."

Lucius added 'AnonWXYZ' and discovered that she was already logged in.

The next few minutes were tense. There was no way to tell what Martinez and Sandberg were doing. They could be on the phone discussing the situation. Sandberg could be on the phone with tech support trying to figure out what had gone wrong with his service. Or Martinez could be busily researching, and Sandberg could have gone to bed.

Finally, the first message came through. It was a long quotation from a case, followed by a citation. Lucius didn't know what to make of it. From the way it was written, it was easy to identify as an old case. And the case seemed to be British, but other than that, Lucius couldn't make heads or tails of it.

"I think it's British." Lucius said aloud.

Robert's eyes got wide. "Lucius, remember that night when you found out that Dolores worked for the same firm that Sandberg had worked for? When I sent you that old web site? Well, do you remember my saying that there was something interesting about Sandberg's bio that wasn't in his UVA bio?"

"No, but go ahead."

"I forgot to tell you because you were so excited about finding Martinez. About ten years ago, according to the Leeder & Schrum website, Sandberg took some time off. He went to England and got an L.L.M. from King's College in London."

"So what? So he's interested in British law."

"Yeah, but Leeder & Schrum is a small firm. Why are they doing any British law, much less enough British law that one of their partners needed to go study for a year in order to deal with it?"

"I don't know, maybe…" Lucius was interrupted by another instant message coming through. It was more of the same.

Jennifer spoke up. "Be sure you're saving all of this. We can figure out more about these cases tomorrow."

"Yeah, I'm going to save it. Anyway, Robert, maybe one of their clients wanted to expand into England. And maybe that client trusted them so much that he didn't want to switch to another, larger firm. I don't think Sandberg's studying in England is that important at this point."

"Fair enough. But maybe we could get some records from King's College. Maybe we could figure out what type of law he studied while he was there, and that will help us to get a better idea as to what he's researching now."

"Yeah, good thinking. But for now, let's focus on the information that we're getting from Martinez."

The three of them sat in silence for another five minutes. Then 'AnonWXYZ' logged off.

Lucius spoke first. "She's never left the library this early before. What should I do?"

"Just stay online for a minute. Maybe she's coming back." Robert seemed to remain calm.

Jennifer, on the other hand, was noticeably nervous. "He called her, just like Luke thought he would. Change the password and log off before they figure out what's going on and track us."

Robert laughed. "Quit going overboard. There's no proof that they have any idea what's going on. And even if they did, they can't track us."

Jennifer's nervousness turned to anger. "Don't laugh at me, Robert! Your ideas have gotten us into this."

"At least I have ideas, Jennifer."

Lucius intervened again. "Please stop it, you two. We've already got two cases. I'm waiting another minute, and then I'm changing the password back and logging off."

Robert again calmed down and apologized. "I don't know why I've been acting this way tonight. I think I'm just jumpy."

The minute passed without event, and Lucius did as he said he would. First he saved the conversation to his hard drive, and then he changed the password back and logged out. He logged back into his own account just to see if either Martinez or Sandberg got back online.

Jennifer spoke up first. She had also calmed down a bit. "Maybe she just finished early tonight."

Robert added, "And even if he did call her and tell her that he couldn't log in, they'll most likely think that it was some sort of computer problem. I don't think they'll suspect that someone has stolen his account in order to get the information."

As quickly as Robert and Jennifer were regaining their cool, Lucius was losing his. "Unless they put this together with the flash drive left in Sandberg's computer. Then they'll know that someone stole Sandberg's password. They can infer from that and what happened tonight that the same person logged in and changed the password in order to get this information. Then all that's left is to figure out who took the flash drive in. And Sandberg will immediately suspect me."

"Why would he suspect you, Luke?"

"He looked at me funny when I left to go to the bathroom. And he made some comment about it taking so long when I came back. He could show his kid a picture of me and ask him if that looked like the boy who was on the computer."

"You're being paranoid, Luke. He tossed the flash drive aside, assumed that there was a computer problem tonight, and his kid never even told him about the weirdo in his study." Robert smiled as he spoke. "And now we're starting to collect information. We'll read these two cases tomorrow, and then we'll initiate stage two."

Lucius laughed. "I hope you're right."

Lucius wasn't as calm as he pretended to be, but he laughed and joked with Robert and Jennifer as they left his apartment. He locked his door and went to bed. He lay awake for a nearly an hour, wondering what Sandberg and Martinez knew and what they would do about it. After a while, he realized how pointless it was to hypothesize and fell soundly asleep.

He awoke the next day and attended his first two classes. He wasn't able to pay attention, and as soon as they ended, he practically ran to the library. He pulled the citations out of his bag and began his search. He began with the computers, but quickly discovered that the cases he was looking for were either too old or too obscure to be included on either of the searchable archives available to him.

He next began a physical search of the library. The cases had to be here. Martinez had been able to find them. After nearly an hour of searching, Lucius finally stumbled upon the section that he was looking for. It was on the third floor in a dusty, back corner.

The section contained both of the books that Lucius was looking for. They were old and fragile, so he had to be particularly careful with them. He gently carried them down to the second floor and photocopied the relevant pages. He was excited to attempt to read them, but there was one more class that he had to attend before he could dive in.

After the class ended he raced home. He didn't want to read in the library for fear of being disturbed. He sat down in his chair and began reading. Over the next few hours, he tried his hardest to understand the cases. The facts of the cases were almost as hard to understand as the rules that they conveyed. The language was so antiquated.

He ignored several calls from both Robert and Jennifer as he read. He could tell them what he had learned later. For now he had to concentrate.

The first case that he read was Rex v. Stone from 1694. As best as he could understand them, the facts went something like this: There was a man named Timothy Stone. He was a farmer in northern England, who caused a fire by negligently stacking his hay. The fire spread both onto his neighbor's land and into the nearby town, causing massive damage. Mr. Stone, being a fairly rich man, spent the next few weeks hiding from the law and the bill that he expected to have to pay.

After hiding for a while, Stone managed to set sail for America. Once he got to America, he re-established himself as a man named Timothy Scott. Nearly a year later, his identity and his crime were discovered and reported. The question before the court was whether or not the courts of England had any jurisdiction over Mr. Stone for the civil suit. The holding of the case seemed to be that they did have jurisdiction, though Lucius was unsure of the court's reasoning.

The second case <u>Rex v. Highsmith</u> from 1702 had equally interesting facts. In that case, a young British soldier named William Highsmith was stationed in continental Europe. He served there for several years. One night, he got into a fight in a bar. The fight ended in the death of his opponent. All of the witnesses confirmed that the fight was not started by William and that he had not been particularly vicious, and he was never charged with murder.

Despite that ruling, William disappeared from his post a few days later. He was discovered only a month later. He had married the wife of the man that he had killed and was living with her in a cottage outside of town. They were raising crops as well as goats and pigs. William was charged with desertion, a crime punishable by death, but there was also a civil suit, and that was what this case was about.

The civil suit was brought by the Crown of England against William and his new wife. They maintained that the property that he had obtained rightly belonged to them because William had gotten that property while in the service of the Crown. Despite hours of pondering over the archaic language, Lucius was unable to figure out the result of the case. The rulings of three different judges were provided in the case, and all three seemed to be saying something different.

Almost as soon as Lucius put down the cases and turned on the television, there was a loud pounding at his door. He froze for a moment, then tiptoed over to the door and looked out. It was only Robert.

He let Robert into the apartment and handed him the cases. "You read these. I'm going to go in the other room and use the computer. We'll talk about them when you're done."

Robert grinned from ear to ear and sat down in Lucius' chair. "Why is it that I'm so much more excited to read these cases than I am to read the cases that I have to read for class?"

Lucius smiled back, even though he suspected that Robert would be disappointed. The cases were fairly interesting once Lucius figured out what was going on, but they didn't reveal any secrets of illegal activity by Sandberg or Martinez. What could cases from the turn of the eighteenth century reveal about a modern day crime? And what about these cases was so important that Sandberg and Martinez had to hide their research?

Lucius spent the next couple of hours browsing the Internet. He had no interest in doing anything serious, so he read about the latest movie releases and the evening's television schedule. At one point, he remembered the password: 112375. It looked like it could be a birth date.

But it couldn't have been Sandberg's birth date nor his wife's. He thought briefly that it might have been Martinez's, but she seemed younger than that. A brief search of the Internet revealed nothing particularly important happening on the 23rd of November 1975, other than the death of one of the survivors of the Titanic. But that would seem an odd reason for having the date as a password.

Jennifer came over in the middle of his browsing, and Lucius had a conversation with her while Robert read in the other room. They talked about Robert and how temperamental he had been lately. Lucius suggested that Robert was jealous of Howard, but Jennifer denied that that was the case. She suggested that he was just nervous about all of their extracurricular activities. His dad was very high in the Justice Department in Washington, and it would be a huge embarrassment if he got kicked out of law school. Lucius wasn't so sure. After all, Robert was coming up with all of these dangerous ideas.

The two of them agreed that Jennifer would read the cases the next day, and she left after a few minutes.

Finally, Robert finished reading the cases and entered the room.

"So what did you think?" Lucius quizzed him.

"Well, both cases had to do with someone who at the time of the law suit was living outside of England. That could be important. There's also the fact that both of them were citizens of England when they committed whatever act they were being held liable for, and both were trying to run away from England when they were caught."

"Yeah, that's true. Anything else?"

"Nope. One's a property case and one's a torts case. Both are from approximately the same period in history, so maybe they're just studying the law of that period in England."

"Yeah, but why would they need to hide that?"

"I don't know. It doesn't make much sense. I'm going to look in to how we can get Sandberg's transcript from King's College...or maybe even something that he wrote while he was there. It was only ten years ago, so it shouldn't be that hard."

"Well, what now? What's the next step in your plan, Robert?"

"I already told you. It's stage two. Are you ready for it?"

"Sure...it can't be any worse than stage one."

Robert smiled briefly, and then looked very serious. "In stage two, we follow Martinez."

Chapter Six

They all agreed to wait a couple of weeks before commencing stage two. There was still the possibility that Sandberg was on to them, and they wanted to give things a chance to cool down. The three of them met once a week for the next three weeks to discuss the details of the plan, as well as what other courses of action would be taken after stage two.

Their final meeting was on the Thursday night before the Friday on which they would begin tailing Martinez. They met at a burger place near the undergraduate campus. Their specialty was a hamburger with a fried egg on top. Lucius loved them.

Robert took charge of the meeting from the beginning. "All right, we need to walk through each step of the process. Luke, tell me what's going to happen."

Lucius and Jennifer exchanged glances. They had both found that it was best to let Robert believe that he was in charge. "Tomorrow night at a quarter 'til midnight, Jennifer positions herself in the alcove next to the library. Robert and I wait at my apartment. If Martinez doesn't show up, then nothing happens. If she does show up, Jennifer will call us."

Robert interrupted. "Jennifer will text us."

"Yeah, that's what I meant."

"Well, it's important. We can't take a risk that Martinez will hear the call. Jennifer's hiding spot could be compromised."

Lucius tried not to laugh. "That's true. After Jennifer texts us that Martinez has arrived, we leave in separate cars. I'll park in the lot behind the library, and you'll park in the lot out front. Then we wait. Jennifer will text us again when she leaves the library to let us know which direction she is heading. If she comes out the back way, it will be my responsibility to follow her to her car and to follow her car home. If she goes out the front, it will be your responsibility. Then we write down her address, and we're done."

"Yeah, we're done for Friday night, but what comes next?"

"Do you want to go over that now?"

"Yes, we have to make sure we're prepared."

"All right, then. Next we all go home. At six o'clock on Saturday morning, you take the first shift. You'll watch her car for the next four hours, and then Jennifer will arrive. She'll watch for the next four hours, and then I'll arrive. We'll continue alternating until Sunday evening at approximately ten o'clock at night. Then we'll stop, so we can all get some sleep. If she leaves the house, we follow her wherever she goes, being sure to keep a safe distance, so we aren't noticed."

Lucius saw that Robert was satisfied and turned his attention to his hamburger.

Jennifer finally spoke up. "I don't know how you can eat that thing. It looks disgusting." Jennifer was a vegetarian.

Lucius just shrugged.

After a few more minutes, Robert got up to leave. "We'd better get some sleep tonight. We probably won't sleep well for the next two nights."

They all three collected their things and headed out into the cool night air. February was halfway over, and the temperatures were still below freezing in Charlottesville. Lucius couldn't wait for spring.

Lucius spent the drive home reconsidering the whole thing. He had been reconsidering it ever since he read the two cases. Sandberg and Martinez had been sneaky, and they had both lied. But it didn't seem like researching British law from the turn of the eighteenth century could be that dangerous. But then he started thinking about how dull law school would be without the mystery. He would hardly have anything to talk about with Robert and Jennifer, and he'd probably spend most of his free time watching television. Every time he thought about forgetting about all of this, he talked himself out of it. It was just too interesting.

Lucius slept well that night. He wasn't as nervous about this plan as he had been about the previous plan. It would be much easier to come up with an excuse for driving around in the middle of the night than it would have been to explain sitting in Sandberg's study with password hacking software in his hand.

At noon Robert arranged for the three of them to meet briefly in the lounge outside the cafeteria. He arrived carrying two boxes.

"These are for you guys. I was able to borrow them from a friend of mine. They are cameras…pretty high tech. They have 20x optical zoom, and the quality is amazing."

"What do you expect us to do with them?"

"I was only able to borrow them for the weekend. We're going to use them to take pictures of Martinez…of where she goes and what she does."

Lucius was hesitant. "It might be hard to take pictures of her. Remember, we have to keep our distance from her."

"I know, and if it becomes a problem, don't worry about getting pictures. But it's good to have them, in case we get a chance to use them. We have to start collecting evidence on these two."

Lucius spent the rest of the day worrying about the plan and wondering how he could get Robert to focus more on law school and less on mystery solving. Ever since Jennifer had started dating Howard, Robert had thrown himself into the mystery. He was barely keeping up with his studies, and he never went out anymore. Lucius would receive phone calls and instant messages from him at all hours about what needed to be done next. He was glad to have Robert's support, but he was worried about his friend.

He was thinking about Robert when he heard his Professional Responsibility professor call his name.

"Mr. Dixon, can you give us the facts of the next case?"

"Yes, sir…sir, what case would that be?" Lucius hadn't done the reading for this class in nearly a week. It was unbearably dull.

"Page 216, Mr. Dixon."

"Yes, sir…" Lucius turned quickly to the page and tried to skim the facts.

"Can someone else help Mr. Dixon out?"

Thankfully, a few hands went up and Lucius was spared further embarrassment. It was just another reminder that he also had to spend more time on his schoolwork."

Finally, the day ended, and Lucius headed home. He started thinking about Robert again. He had talked with Jennifer about the situation. They both now agreed that Robert was jealous of Howard, but Jennifer didn't know what to do about it. She had tried to talk to Robert, but he had denied that any such feelings existed. She said that he had acted embarrassed, and that he immediately changed the subject back to Martinez. It was a tough situation to be in, particularly since Lucius was around the two of them together all the time.

Lucius spent the afternoon trying to catch up in Professional Responsibility. He expected to be called on next week, and he wanted to be ready this time. He still disliked the course, but he forced himself to do the reading. He was still sitting at his desk struggling to plow through the cases when his phone rang. It was Robert.

"Are you ready to put this plan into action? Jennifer is already at the law school."

Lucius glanced at his clock. It was 11:25. "Why is she already there?"

"I asked her to go a little early…in case Martinez came in early like she did that first night when you met her."

"Yeah, okay. Come on over here, and we'll wait for her call."

"Her text, you mean. All right, I'll see you in a bit."

Lucius hung up the phone and started getting ready. He put on his winter coat and gloves and waited by the door. Robert arrived a few minutes later. He was dressed completely in black from the black skull cap on his head to the black Doc Martens on his feet. Lucius had to stop himself from laughing.

They waited in silence for the next thirty minutes. Lucius thought about talking, but Robert seemed too nervous. Robert's leg was shaking, and he kept humming what sounded like an upbeat version of "Auld Lang Syne."

At a quarter after midnight, both of their phones buzzed simultaneously. It was the text.

"Shes in there."

Lucius and Robert looked at each other. Lucius was calm. Robert was still shaking. They both left the apartment together and climbed into their respective cars. It was freezing outside, and Lucius had to wait in his car for a few minutes while the windshield defrosted.

Lucius drove over to the law school and parked in the back parking lot. He parked in a space overlooking the exit. He then tried to concentrate on what had to be done, but his mind kept drifting back to Robert.

He knew it wasn't right to hope for the breakup of Jennifer and a guy he'd never met, but he wanted things to go back to the way they were before that relationship began. Even if Robert never had a chance with her, at least the situation would be better if she didn't have a boyfriend.

The next few hours went by quickly, and Lucius' phone was buzzing in what seemed like minutes: "back."

Lucius had turned his car off when he arrived, and he hadn't noticed how cold it had become. He could see his breath. He sat motionless in his car for the next few seconds, afraid to start his engine for fear of startling Martinez and drawing attention to himself. Then he saw her coming out the exit.

Martinez walked quickly and decisively toward her car. It was parked about a hundred feet away. He could tell by the streetlight that it was a dark blue Honda. She got in her car, and Lucius tried to crank his car at the same time she cranked hers. He had seen it done in the movies, but he was a couple of seconds late. As far as he could tell, she didn't notice.

She drove slowly out of her parking space. Lucius waited patiently. When she was almost out of sight, he drove after her. He decided to go ahead and turn his lights on. He worried that she would catch a glimpse of his car in the streetlights in her rearview mirror. Such a glimpse would raise far more suspicions if his lights were off than if they were on.

They drove away from the law school and onto the highway. They drove a couple of miles, and then took an exit. One turn later they were driving through a secluded neighborhood. Martinez pulled into the driveway of a small green house and parked her car. Lucius drove past.

This was going to be more difficult than he thought. It was good that she didn't live very far away and that her house would be easy to get to, but it was bad that she lived in a house rather than an apartment. It would have been much easier to park a car in an apartment parking lot to keep an eye on her. Parking in the street would raise both her suspicions and the suspicions of the neighbors. Lucius drove further down the street and turned around. Her car was still in the driveway when he drove past. As far as he could tell, she was no longer in it.

Lucius drove home and called Jennifer and Robert. He happily reported that everything had gone according to plan. The two of them arrived a few minutes later. They had all decided to spend the weekend at Lucius' house. He had a couch that folded out into a bed and a comfortable chair in the living room. And the whole plan seemed like it would work better if the two of them not on duty remained together.

"She lives just off the Barracks Road Exit. Take a left off the highway. Her neighborhood is the third left, and she lives in a green house. It's about the tenth house down. Her blue Honda should be parked in the driveway."

Robert hadn't calmed down yet. "Nice work, Luke. Did she do anything strange? Did she seem to notice you?"

"Nope. She drove directly home. I didn't see her go inside, but she wasn't in her car when I drove back by. Try to park in the street a few houses down. There aren't any hills, so you should be able to see her house from a long way off."

Jennifer was beaming. "Good job, Luke. Now we'll find out what Ms. Martinez does when she's not breaking into the library."

"Yeah, we'll see."

Lucius told Robert and Jennifer to go to bed. They had the first two shifts and would need plenty of sleep. He went into his room and tried to get some reading done before falling asleep himself.

When he got up the next morning, Jennifer was frying eggs on his stove top. He also smelled coffee. It was nine o'clock.

"Good morning, Luke. Robert was a little late getting out of the house this morning, but he probably got over there by seven."

"That's fine. Six o'clock seemed a little early to me anyway. Did you bring a coffee maker?"

Jennifer laughed. "Yeah, I knew you wouldn't have one."

"Are you going to leave Robert there until eleven or are we going to keep our schedule the way it was?"

"I figured we'd keep our scheduling the way it was. There's no reason to have everything thrown off."

"That makes sense. How did he seem this morning when he left? He was so nervous last night."

"He was really tense this morning. He was in the bathroom for a while. I think he threw up."

"If he keeps this up, we're going to have to forget about this whole thing, or cut him out of it. But it seems to be all he cares about anymore."

Jennifer was silent for a minute. She turned away from Lucius, and then walked quickly past him and into the bathroom. Lucius could hear her through the door. It sounded like she was crying. He let the eggs fry a little longer before taking them out and putting them on a plate.

After about five minutes, Jennifer emerged from the bathroom. "I'm sorry about that. I'm just worried about Robert."

"It's okay, Jennifer. I took your eggs out. If you need me to take your shift, I can."

"That's not necessary. I'll be able to handle this."

Jennifer ate in silence and left the house at a quarter before ten. About twenty minutes later, Robert knocked and entered.

"Martinez didn't leave the house all morning. I enjoyed it anyway."

"She'll have to leave eventually. Jennifer said you were a little sick this morning. Are you okay now?"

"Yeah, I was just nervous. I told her not to tell you about that. Oh, well. Everything's fine now."

"If Martinez doesn't go anywhere important this weekend, we'll have to try this again on a weekday. I wonder if she has a job."

"It'd be difficult for her to keep a regular job with the hours she keeps in the library, but maybe she has something in the afternoons."

The two talked for the next few hours. Lucius occasionally tried to change the subject from Martinez to law school and the classes that they had together, but Robert refused to take the bait. He only wanted to talk about Martinez and Sandberg.

Lucius left at a quarter before two. He drove past the green house with the blue Honda in the driveway and saw Jennifer parked in her car a couple of houses down. He discreetly waved at her as he went by, and when he came back by, she was gone. He parked his car and began the surveillance.

The next few hours dragged by slowly. Martinez didn't leave her house, and Lucius worried about Robert and Jennifer and what sort of arguments they would be getting into. At almost six o'clock on the dot, Robert drove by and Lucius left.

The next few shifts went by in much the same way. Nothing interesting happened until half past three on Sunday afternoon. Lucius was sitting in his car looking forward to going home and being done with this whole operation. It had been a complete waste of time.

He was looking down at his cell phone, and he almost missed it. When he looked up, the blue Honda was driving away in the distance. He cranked his car and tried to remain calm. She was probably just doing some Sunday afternoon grocery shopping. There was no reason to be nervous.

They drove toward downtown Charlottesville, taking a left immediately before entering the main shopping area. They drove a couple of miles, and Lucius drove past Martinez as she parallel parked next to a secluded park.

This seemed strange, but maybe she was just going for a walk.

He made a block and pulled into the parking lot of the library across the street. He turned his car off and watched as Martinez got out of her car and walked over to a nearby bench.

From this vantage point, Lucius had a pretty good view of her. She sat down on the bench and opened up what appeared to be a manuscript of some sort. She was about one-hundred yards away.

Nothing happened for the next few minutes. A few children ran by Martinez, but she didn't look up at all. She just intently read the manuscript. Lucius pulled out his camera and took a couple of shots. The zoom feature was as good as Robert had described it. He could almost read the words on the page of her book.

Lucius put the camera away and reached down to pick up his cell phone. He wanted to let Robert and Jennifer know what was happening. As he raised his head, he was startled by the shadow of a large figure moving past his window only a couple of feet away. As the figure passed, he recognized him by the thick beard. It was Sandberg.

Lucius ducked his head to avoid being seen. He waited for a few seconds, and the expected happened. Sandberg sat down on the park bench with Martinez. Lucius took two more pictures and waited. A few minutes later, a large black SUV with tinted windows pulled up next to the park. It slid into the parking space behind Martinez's car, and a little old man emerged from the passenger seat.

Lucius zoomed in on the old man with his camera. He must have been in his eighties. He was wearing a black suit and a black fedora with a gray overcoat. He wandered slowly over to the parking bench and sat down between Martinez and Sandberg. Lucius zoomed in and took some pictures. They were talking but not looking at one another.

Lucius was excitedly thinking of telling Robert and Jennifer about all of this when he was startled again…this time by a knock on his window.

Chapter Seven

Lucius slowly turned and looked out his window into the eyes of a police detective with a bushy mustache.

Lucius rolled down his window.

"Library's closed, son."

"I'm sorry, sir. I was just waiting for some friends of mine."

"Well, you can't wait here. Move along."

Lucius cranked his car and drove out of the parking lot. He tried to get the license plate of the black SUV as he drove by, but he couldn't get a good view. He drove back to his apartment where Jennifer and Robert were waiting.

Robert met him at the door. "What happened? Why are you back early?"

Lucius told them the whole story.

"Why didn't you get the license plate? I've got a friend who could have run the plate for us and gotten us a name." Robert was upset.

"I couldn't see it on the way out, and I was afraid to go back. I didn't want to get spotted. I've got some pictures of all three of them, and some pictures of the SUV."

"You took pictures? Fantastic! Let's go look at them."

The three of them went into Lucius' bedroom and plugged the camera into his computer. They transferred the pictures to the hard drive and started looking them over.

"I wonder who the old guy is," Jennifer thought aloud.

Robert sat down at the computer and went to the Leeder & Schrum website. He couldn't find a picture of the man on the current site. Robert used the website that kept caches of old websites. Even after several attempts, there was no sign of the old man. It appeared that he hadn't worked for Leeder & Schrum, at least not in the last five years.

Lucius spoke up. "I think we should all go home for now. We're making some progress, but I think we should take a couple of weeks off again...just to make sure they're not on to us."

Robert got out of the chair. "You said they didn't see you. What's the problem? Let's keep going. I've got several more ideas."

"Listen, Robert, I know you want to figure this out. We all do. But there's really no hurry." Lucius was trying to be reasonable.

"Fine, I'll wait a couple of weeks, but I'm going to see if I can find out about this old man on the Internet in the meantime."

Robert and Jennifer left the apartment. Lucius sat in silence for a few minutes thinking to himself.

Why were they meeting in a public park? Who was the old man? If he didn't work at the law firm with them, how was he involved in this?

Lucius finally decided to give up trying to figure everything out for now and picked up his Criminal Investigation book. He laughed to himself thinking about which of their actions would have been Fourth Amendment violations if they were police officers.

Lucius fell asleep in his chair with the book open on his lap. This was the first time he had ever fallen asleep sitting up. All of these adventures were taking a lot out of him.

The next few weeks were relatively calm. Lucius finally received his grades from the first semester: two A's and two B's. He was happy with the grades. He was called on in three of his classes and handled all three situations very well. He caught up in all of his classes and spent only a little time thinking about Sandberg and Martinez. Robert, unfortunately, was not doing so well. When he was called on in Property, he ignored the call pretending to be absent, and every time he saw Lucius outside of class, he wanted to talk about the Sandberg situation. Lucius worried about him.

One day after Constitutional Law, Jennifer caught up with Lucius as he was leaving class.

"I've got some big news."

"What's that?"

"Come with me to my locker. I haven't told Robert yet, so I don't want him to overhear anything."

Lucius turned and looked back. He locked eyes with Robert and waved. Robert waved back.

Jennifer and Lucius walked to her locker area, and Jennifer looked behind them before she began talking.

"I'm transferring to Columbia."

"What? Why?"

"Howard's going to work for a mergers and acquisitions firm in New York, and I wanted to be with him. I didn't want to say anything until my transfer was approved, but I talked to someone from there today, and they said it looked very positive."

"Well, I'm happy for you, though I'll miss having you around."

"Yeah, I'll miss you and Robert, too."

"How are you going to break this to Robert? He's going to be devastated. I'm already worried about how much time he's spending trying to figure out our mystery."

"I'm going to tell him as soon as my transfer is approved. It might be rough on him for a day or two, but I think it'll be better for him in the long run."

"I hope so. Anyway, I'm happy for you. I'm sure you'll do well. I'll keep you up to date with the goings on around here."

Lucius left the locker area and immediately ran into Robert.

"Luke, I've got some good news. I know you told me not to do anything further, but I did a little work on our case."

"Robert, you need to be focusing on schoolwork right now."

"Yeah, I know. I didn't do too much. I'll come by tonight and tell you about it."

"All right, Robert. Take care, and I'll see you then."

Lucius walked toward the cafeteria to pick up something to eat. He didn't believe Jennifer's assertion that things would be better for Robert in the long run. He needed to think of a way to get Robert's mind back on schoolwork.

The rest of the day passed peacefully, and Robert showed up at Lucius' house at about half past seven. He didn't show up alone.

Accompanying Robert was a large thirty-something year-old man. He had blonde hair and pink skin. He was about 6'4 and probably weighed 250 pounds.

"Luke, I want you to meet Lindsey Coleman. He goes by Cole. He used to work at the Justice Department with my dad."

"Nice to meet you, Cole. What's going on, Robert?"

"Cole's going to help us."

"What?"

"Well, I guess it would be more honest to say that Cole has already helped us."

"Robert, tell me what's going on."

Robert pulled a small tape recorder out of his pocket. "I sent Cole in to see Sandberg with some questions. He recorded it for us. Just have a listen."

"Fine, Robert, play the tape."

Robert started the tape recorder.

Cole's voice was heard first. "So first of all, I wanted to thank you for taking the time to answer some questions for me today."

"I'm always glad to help a potential law student."

"Your career interested me because it is similar to what I want to do. I want to work at a small law firm for a while, and then become a professor. What was the transition like?"

"It wasn't so hard. The only initial struggle was with Torts. I volunteered to teach it, even though I didn't have much real-world experience in that area."

"What did you work on at your firm?"

"I was mostly involved in property issues."

"What sort of property issues?"

"Well, I really can't give you anything much more specific than that. One of our clients was a wealthy family, and we advised them of their property rights and helped them with their wills and other conveyances."

"I noticed on your resume that you got an LLM from King's College in London. Why did you do that?"

"I've always enjoyed education, and the firm was willing to allow me a year off to go get the degree. I think you'll find that the small firms are much more flexible with you. Are you interested in coming here to UVA?"

"Yes, sir. What made you leave the firm when you did?"

"I was just ready for something new. Did you have any questions about law school itself?"

"Yes, sir. I'm interested to know about getting research positions…where you do research for a professor."

"Sure. Well, most of the research assistants are second-year or third-year law students. Most first-year students focus primarily on their studies. Basically, the student e-mails a professor that he is interested in working for, and the professor will call the student in for an informal interview."

"What sort of areas do you research in?"

"Mostly property issues…the same sorts of things that I worked on when I was with the firm, but other professors work in a lot of different areas."

"What is the first year curriculum like?"

Robert pressed the stop button on the tape player. "That's all the good stuff. Cole was smart enough to change the subject to prevent Sandberg from getting suspicious."

Cole finally spoke up. "Look, I've got to run. Keep me informed about what's going on, and I'll see what I can do to help."

As soon as he had left, Lucius turned his attention to Robert. "What the hell, Robert? Who is that and why did you tell him about this?"

"I told you. He worked with my dad at Justice. He's a good guy, and he'll be much more helpful than Jennifer. He already got us the information about one of their clients being a wealthy family."

"Why isn't he still at Justice?"

"He failed a drug test, but that's irrelevant. He's trustworthy, I promise, and he's got a lot of good ideas. Plus, no one can tie him to us, so we can get him to do things like this interview."

"Robert, it's over."

"What?"

"It's over. I'm going to confront Dolores Martinez, tell her what we know, and ask for an explanation."

"You can't do that. You could get us all in trouble."

"I don't really care anymore, Robert. This stuff is taking over your life. You're going to fail out of law school fooling around with some people who have nothing to do with you."

"When people come to our law school to do illegal things, they compromise the integrity of the school. This has everything to do with me."

"Robert, we don't know that they are doing anything illegal. You're taking this all too seriously. I'm going to confront Martinez, and there's nothing you can do to stop me."

Robert stammered a few times, and then walked out of the apartment, slamming the door behind him. Lucius wondered if he had done the right thing. He didn't know if the investigation was causing Robert to behave this way, or if he was just throwing his energies into this because of Jennifer. At least this way, he would have to find something else to focus his life on…something more important…maybe even his studies.

The night went by slowly. Lucius tried to work, but he couldn't muster the energy. He just sat in his living room and stared at the television. He was firm in his conviction. He would confront Martinez the next night. He would bring all of this to an end.

After a few hours of doing nothing, he wandered back to his bedroom and went to sleep.

Lucius awoke the next morning feeling refreshed. He felt good about his plan. He would take all of the evidence that they had collected and confront her. She wouldn't be able to lie this time. Because Sandberg and Martinez were being so secretive about whatever it was that they were doing, they would probably be too afraid to try to go after him. If they did, he could release the photos and the instant messaging conversations.

He drove to school listening to the local classic rock station. When he arrived, he tried to turn his focus to his classes, but he didn't have much success. Tonight would mark the end of the mystery that had made law school so interesting. Though he doubted that it would, it could also mark the end of his law school career itself.

The evening arrived quickly, and Lucius set up in the alcove outside the library. He brought with him one of the cameras that Robert had accidentally left at his house. He could use it to get one final piece of evidence.

Midnight came and went, and Lucius was considering giving up on the whole thing; but before he could gather his things, Martinez arrived and headed directly for the library door.

Lucius grabbed the camera and moved to the edge of the alcove. Martinez looked around to see if anyone was watching, and then inserted the key card. Lucius snapped a picture of that, and then turned the camera's flash on. He waited until she had opened the door and then ran around the corner.

"Hey!" Lucius yelled.

Martinez turned around in a panic, and Lucius took a picture. The flash filled the hallway with light.

"Who are you and what are you doing?" Martinez asked as she let the door to the library close behind her, rubbing her eyes from the flash.

"I'm Lucius Dixon...a student. Who are you?"

"I'm just a student. What are you doing?"

"No, you're not. You're Dolores Martinez. You worked for Leeder & Schrum up until about two years ago. Do you want to tell me the rest?"

"I don't know what you're talking about."

"Now you're working for Professor Sandberg. You sneak into the library after hours and send him messages about the research that you're doing."

Martinez stammered and looked around. She seemed to be considering running away.

"It's pointless to run away. We know where both you and Sandberg live. If you don't explain this, we'll just find you and ask again."

"Who's we?"

"That's beside the point. I want answers."

"Okay, listen...let me think for a second."

The two of them stood there in silence for nearly five minutes. At one point, another law student walked past them staring at them with a puzzled expression on her face.

Martinez finally spoke up. "I don't know how to explain to you what's going on, but I'll call Professor Sandberg when I get home tonight. I'm sure he'll be willing to explain all of this to you tomorrow. There's a perfectly reasonable explanation, but I don't feel comfortable giving it to you. I think Sandberg should be the one to do that."

Lucius realized that he had been coming on too harshly, so he agreed to her proposal. He told her goodbye and headed out to his car. When he got home, he had an e-mail waiting for him:

> Mr. Dixon,
>
> Please come by my office tomorrow afternoon. I will be there from noon until about five.
>
> Daniel Sandberg

Lucius let out a sigh. It was all going to come down to this. He was either going to be given the explanation that he had been seeking for the past five months, or he was going to have to face off against a law school professor.

He thought about his parents and his old life back in Mississippi. He had never expected that when he left that life, he would involve himself in something as crazy as this. Maybe there was a simple explanation like Martinez had said, or maybe she was just trying to get out of the situation until they could craft a better excuse. Lucius probably shouldn't have revealed as much as he did. Then he could have caught them in another lie, if they had attempted to go that route.

He called Robert and Jennifer a few minutes after he got home and asked them to meet him at a nearby 24-hour diner. They were already there when he arrived.

"I just wanted to call you both to let you know that I confronted Martinez. She didn't give me an explanation for what was going on, but she set up a meeting with Sandberg tomorrow. He's going to tell me everything."

"Wow, Luke. I can't believe you did that. Do you want Robert or me to go with you to the meeting?" Jennifer seemed concerned.

"No, that's okay. I've kept your names out of it so far, and I promise not to bring either of you into this. You've both helped me a lot."

"Thanks Luke, but if you need anything, just let us know." As Jennifer spoke, Lucius looked over at Robert. He was just staring out of the window overlooking the highway.

Jennifer and Lucius talked for a little while longer. Finally, the three of them left the diner. Robert hadn't spoken the entire time they were there. Lucius pulled Robert aside and apologized to him in the parking lot after Jennifer left. Robert accepted the apology, and even smiled once...but he still seemed depressed when he drove away.

That night and the next morning flew by. Lucius was incredibly excited. He wanted nothing more than to know what was going on, so he headed for Sandberg's office on the third floor as soon as the clock struck twelve.

He rode the elevator up and walked down the hallway. His mind was filled with potential explanations. As he approached the door, he hesitated for a moment. Maybe he didn't want to know what was going on. Maybe this was a bad idea...but he kept walking.

Finally, he reached the door. He held his fist at the door and then knocked emphatically. The door wasn't latched and flew open with the force of his knock.

Lucius froze in the doorway. Sandberg was leaning back in the chair behind his desk. A thin trickle of blood flowed down the bridge of his nose from a small hole in his forehead.

Chapter Eight

When Lucius awoke, he was soaked in sweat.

For a moment, he thought that it had all been a dream, but when his eyes adjusted to the brightness, he realized that he was in the law school.

He was lying down on a couch in a hallway on the third floor of the law school. When he finally opened his eyes, he was greeted by a warm and friendly voice.

"I'm glad you're awake. Would you like some water?"

Lucius turned his head to see his companion. She was probably about thirty years old. She was petite with sandy blonde hair tied in a pony tail and a small turned-up nose. She was wearing a police officer's uniform.

"Thanks. I guess I must have fainted?"

"Yes, you did. You've been out for at least fifteen minutes."

She left for a moment and returned with a small paper cup filled with water. Lucius sat up and drank it eagerly. He hadn't realized how thirsty he was.

"My name is Rita Snow. I'm a police detective. I don't know how much you know, but a man lost his life today."

"Sandberg...?"

"Yes, Professor Sandberg was attacked. Can you tell me your name?"

"I'm Lucius Dixon. Is he going to be okay?"

"He's dead." The voice that answered was not Snow's. Rounding the corner was an olive-skinned man with a bushy mustache. Lucius recognized him immediately. It was the same man that had knocked on his window when he was in the library parking lot watching Sandberg and Martinez. "Why don't you go ahead and tell us what you know?"

"He just woke up, Sergio. Give him a minute to collect his wits."

Sergio crossed the room and sat down in a chair about ten feet away. He propped his feet up on the coffee table in front of him. "Take your time. I've got all day. I'm Detective Torro, by the way."

Lucius spoke up immediately. He wondered if the detective recognized him. "I'm not going to be able to help you much. I came up here to see Professor Sandberg. When I knocked, the door opened by itself, and I saw him."

Lucius paused. His whole body went cold, as he pictured Sandberg's face. He laid his head back down on the couch. "I'm sorry. I had never seen anything like that before."

Lucius lay there for a few moments. Both Detective Snow and Detective Torro remained silent. After a few minutes, he regained his composure enough to start talking again. "He was leaning back in his chair. His eyes and mouth were open, and it looked like he had been shot. I guess I fainted when I saw him."

"All right, son. We need to ask you a few questions. Are you ready to answer them? Or do you need a few more minutes?"

"I should be okay, sir."

"What is your relationship to Professor Sandberg?"

"He was my Torts professor last semester."

"That's the extent of your relationship?"

Lucius started to worry. What should he reveal about the previous months' activities? He didn't want to get himself into trouble for all of their spying, but he didn't want to get caught in a lie and end up as a suspect in a murder case. "Yes, sir."

"Then why were you coming to see him today?"

"I was just coming to get some academic advice."

"What sort of advice?"

Lucius tried to think quickly. "Well, exams are coming up, and I wanted to get his opinion on whether or not it was a good idea to create outlines as part of my preparation."

"And why did you want his advice in particular?"

"I just thought his opinion would be helpful."

"Had you planned any meetings with any of your other professors?"

"No, sir. I went to Professor Sandberg's house earlier this semester, and he told me that if I ever needed anything to drop by his office."

"So you weren't being entirely truthful earlier when you said that the extent of your relationship was that he was your professor last semester?"

"I was, sir. I just wasn't thinking about that get-together."

"You forgot that he invited you into his home?"

"Yes, sir. His entire Torts class was invited, though. I wasn't given any sort of special invitation."

Someone called Detective Torro from down the hallway, and he excused himself.

"Sorry about that, Lucius. He just won't let things go sometimes." Lucius had seen good-cop bad-cop routines on television, but he had never seen one in person.

"It's okay, ma'am. I'll do my best to answer all of his questions."

After a few minutes, Detective Snow got up to leave as well. "I'll be right back. Just try to make yourself as comfortable as you can."

Lucius went over his reasons for the meeting with Sandberg in his head. He tried to make sure that his story had no holes. He was willing to tell the truth as a last resort, but for now he wanted the meeting with Sandberg to seem as innocent as possible. It was doubtful that Torro remembered their brief meeting in the library parking lot. And even if he did, it was very unlikely that he knew that Sandberg was in the park.

Then he started thinking about Professor Sandberg. Had their actions led to Sandberg's death? Had their surveillance unintentionally exposed his clandestine activities to someone else…someone dangerous? Again Lucius thought of Sandberg's face. His eyes had been open, but they were rolled back in his head so that all Lucius saw were the whites of his eyes. He couldn't get that image out of his head.

Then Lucius began to fear for his own safety. If their activities had led to Sandberg's death, then that would mean that whoever killed Sandberg knew about them. And maybe the killer thought that they knew more than they did. He was safe for now because the third floor was crawling with police officers, but what about Robert and Jennifer?

Before he could reach for his cell phone to call either of them, Detectives Snow and Torro returned.

"Sorry about that. Now, where were we?"

"You were asking me about why I was meeting with Sandberg."

"Yeah, okay, enough of that. Had you heard any of your classmates saying anything particularly nasty about Sandberg?"

"No, sir. He was well liked."

"So you can't think of anyone who might have had a motive to kill him?"

"No, sir, but like I said, I didn't know him that well."

"Did you know of a woman named Dolores Martinez?"

It was all Lucius could do to avoid swearing aloud. "No, sir. I didn't. Was she a student?"

"That's not important right now. The name doesn't ring a bell to you?"

"No, sir."

Another officer entered the room and gave Torro some papers. Torro placed a finger to his lips while he scanned through the papers. Detective Snow smiled at Lucius.

Torro spoke. "Mr. Dixon, how did you get in touch with Professor Sandberg to arrange this meeting?"

"I e-mailed him."

Detective Torro looked up from the papers, stared Lucius right in the eye, and smiled. "Want to try again?"

"What do you mean?"

"Do you want to tell me how you got in touch with Professor Sandberg to arrange your meeting? I have a list of all the people who e-mailed Professor Sandberg for the last month, and you're not in here."

Lucius pretended to think for a second and then spurted out, "That's right. I saw him in the hallway and arranged the meeting."

"So this is the second time you've lied to me?"

"I'm not lying to you, sir. Everything's kind of mixed up in my head right now. I'm sorry."

"About fifteen minutes before Sandberg sent an e-mail to you asking you to come in for the meeting, he received a phone call. Do you know who that phone call was from?"

"No sir, I don't."

"All right, Mr. Dixon, I believe that's enough for now."

"So what should I do?"

"Detective Snow will walk you to the elevator. Just try to get back into your routine. We'll contact you if we need you."

Torro walked quickly out of the room, and Detective Snow crossed the room to help Lucius off the couch. "I'm really sorry you had to get yourself involved in all of this. You seem like a nice kid."

"I think I'll be okay. I just want to get home and get some sleep."

The two of them walked in silence toward the elevators. Lucius wondered if he should confess everything while he still had a chance. If he left here and they figured out that he was lying to them, things could get dicey. But admitting the lies now might not be any better at this point. Detective Torro would tear him apart.

They reached the elevators, and Detective Snow held out her hand. She spoke gently as they shook hands. "If you need anything at all, just let me know. I know this is hard for you, but we'll do everything we can to help you through it."

Lucius entered the elevator when it arrived and waved goodbye. He wasn't sure if it was just part of the trick to make him reveal anything that he was keeping to himself, but Detective Snow seemed genuinely nice...and she smelled amazing.

The elevator arrived at the ground floor, and the doors opened. A small area had been taped off around the elevator. Immediately behind the taped-off area stood at least fifty law students. Lucius walked by all of them and headed for his car. He just wanted to go home, but before he could get very far, he was grabbed by the arm.

It was Robert. "Luke, you have to tell me what is going on."

"Yeah, okay, Robert. Call Jennifer and tell her to meet us at the Chinese restaurant off Ivy Road in thirty minutes. I only want to tell this story once." Lucius wasn't hungry, but he wanted to get away from the law school, and he was scared to go home. He worried that he was going to be followed.

"She's in class for the next fifteen minutes. We can just go wait for her outside her classroom if you want."

"That's fine, Robert, but I want to talk about something else until she's done with class."

"Yeah sure, Robert. Should I call Cole?"

"Who?"

"Lindsey Coleman. The guy who recorded his meeting with Sandberg and played it for us the other night."

Lucius was angry. "No, don't call him. You never should have involved him in the first place."

"Okay, fine. What do you want to talk about?"

"Let's talk about Property."

"I'm a little behind in there, but go ahead. I can talk about adverse possession."

The two of them wandered down the hallway toward Jennifer's classroom. Lucius' suggestion to talk about Property didn't fulfill either of its intended functions. Their conversation only glazed the surface of the topic, and Lucius' mind remained filled with ideas of conspiracies, betrayal, and murder.

Finally Jennifer's class was let out, and she came out into the hallway. She read Lucius' face perfectly. "What's wrong, Luke? You're as white as a sheet."

"Are you free now?"

"Sure."

"Come on, I'll tell you about it on the way to the restaurant."

The three of them piled into Robert's car and drove toward the restaurant. Lucius told the story from the confrontation with Dolores to the interrogation by the police. When he finished, the quiet roar of the engine was the only sound for several minutes.

Finally Jennifer spoke up. "I'm just glad you're okay, Luke."

Robert spoke next. "You did the right thing not telling them about what we were up to. They probably would have suspected us of the murder."

"The way this guy Torro talked, I think he suspects me of the murder anyway. He accused me of lying twice."

They arrived at the restaurant and went inside. Robert ordered orange chicken. Jennifer ordered two vegetable egg rolls, and Lucius just asked for water.

He still felt guilty. "Do you guys think we caused this to happen?"

The idea clearly hadn't crossed Jennifer's mind. She looked surprised and concerned but didn't say anything. Robert spoke up. "The way I see it is that we only accelerated something that was already going to happen."

"What are you talking about?"

"Martinez killed him."

For whatever reason, Lucius didn't think so. "She's definitely a suspect. Why are you so sure it was her, though?"

"When you confronted her, she didn't know what to do. She panicked. She knew she couldn't tell you everything, so she told you she'd put you in touch with Sandberg. She knew that if she didn't put you in touch with Sandberg, you'd just go talk to him yourself."

"I'm with you so far."

"After she set up the meeting, she started worrying. Maybe she took what they were doing more seriously than Sandberg, and she was worried that he would reveal everything to you. So to avoid that, she went into his office and killed him. Maybe someone saw her there, and that's why the police detectives were asking you about her."

Lucius let the story settle for a moment, and then spoke up. "I've got a different explanation for why they were asking about Martinez. Torro's last question for me was whether or not I knew who had called Sandberg fifteen minutes before Sandberg e-mailed me to set up the meeting. That was probably Martinez calling him to tell him to e-mail me, so they were asking to see if there was some connection."

Jennifer spoke next. "I don't buy the story of Martinez killing him to protect the research. What could they possibly have been researching that was so important that she would kill him rather than have it revealed? Why wouldn't they just make up a lie? It doesn't make sense. I think it's more likely that there's no connection between the murder and the research."

That idea calmed Lucius, but it roused Robert. "Of course there's a connection. Sandberg was up to something very strange and very suspicious. He was being secretive about it and even lied at one point to cover up what he was doing. On the day when he's supposed to reveal everything to Luke, he gets murdered. That's quite a coincidence."

Jennifer responded. "People don't get murdered over legal research. Here's another idea. Maybe Martinez and Sandberg were having an affair. Maybe the phone conversation started an argument that resulted in Sandberg wanted to break off the affair. Martinez didn't like that idea, so she killed him."

Lucius finished her thought. "Or maybe Sandberg's wife overheard the phone conversation and subsequently found out about the affair. Maybe she shot him out of jealousy."

Robert wouldn't hear it. "Then why kill Sandberg in his office. If it was Mrs. Sandberg, why not wait until he came home and kill him there? If it was Martinez, she could have arranged a meeting that evening and killed him there. The person who killed him knew about the meeting and wanted to make sure that Luke never got the information."

"Robert, do you know what it means if you're right? If you're right, then they definitely know about me, and they probably know about you and Jennifer. That means we're all three potential targets."

"We don't have to be targets because Martinez killed Sandberg before he could tell us anything. There's no need for her to kill us."

"But she doesn't know for sure everything that we know. If she's willing to kill Sandberg in broad daylight in his office, then she probably won't be afraid to knock off a couple of defenseless law students while she's at it."

"All the more reason to bring Cole back into this. He can help us to find Martinez and turn her in to the police."

"We're not bringing Cole back into this. I don't want to involve that guy."

"He could be very helpful. He's a smart guy."

"He's strange."

"No, he's not."

Jennifer tried to play peacemaker. "None of us has any idea what's going on. We're all just throwing out theories. I think the best idea at this point is to get our stories straight and to try to forget about this. I'm personally unwilling to turn our spying activity into a murder investigation. Let's just do the best we can to forget about this and move on with law school. We're out of our league."

Even Robert agreed. They all ate in silence and then Robert drove them back to the law school. Jennifer leaned over and gave Lucius a hug before she left the car. "Everything's going to be okay, Luke." Robert glared at both of them.

Lucius got in his car and drove toward his apartment. He shouldn't have insulted Cole, but Robert was agitating him as usual. He knew he wouldn't be able to concentrate on law school for a few days. He just hoped his ability to concentrate would return sometime before finals.

He got out of his car and entered his apartment. He wanted nothing more than to go to bed. It had been one of the longest days of his entire life.

He headed straight for the bedroom door, but before he could reach the doorknob, he heard a noise coming from inside his bedroom. He stopped where he was, and the door swung open.

Chapter Nine

As the door opened, Lucius thought of several potential courses of action. He could run for the door. He could put his hands up and surrender to the intruder. He could hide. He could push the door back into whoever was coming out. He could jump on the intruder as soon as he emerged.

But Lucius just stood there. The door opened, and he was face to face with Dolores Martinez.

Lucius blurted out, "I don't know anything. I...I...I swear I...I don't know anything."

Martinez smiled sarcastically at him. She glanced around the main room, and then asked, "Are you alone?"

Lucius thought about lying...pretending that his friends were outside and coming in at any minute. But he told the truth. "Yes."

"We need to talk."

"I'm scared out of my mind right now. I can't talk to anyone about anything." Lucius was visibly shaken.

"I'm not going to hurt you. I just need to ask you some questions."

"First, I need you to explain to me why you're in my apartment right now."

Dolores spoke quickly and decisively. "I had to check you out. I don't know anyone else in the area...since Sandberg was killed. You were the only person I could come to."

"The police are looking for you."

"I'm sure they are, but I had nothing to do with that murder."

Lucius didn't know why, but he believed her. There was something about her eyes. "Then why not go to the police and explain yourself?"

"I don't have a decent alibi, and there are some very powerful people who would love to see the murder pinned on me."

"I don't want to hear this. I'm in way over my head, and now I just want out. I want things to go back to normal."

Dolores looked right through him. "It's too late for you to get out. You're involved, and I need your help."

"Who killed Sandberg?"

"I don't know for sure, but I do know that it has something to do with the Ramsden family."

"Ramsden? Like the Senator?"

"Yes, but I'll explain all of that later. For now, I need you to agree to help me with something."

"Does whoever killed Sandberg know who I am?"

"No, they don't. That's why you can help me. As you know, Professor Sandberg and I had been researching a very important case for the past two years…"

Lucius interrupted. "Why was it necessary for the research to be so secretive?"

"There were a couple of reasons. The first is that the case we were planning to bring was against some very powerful, very dangerous people, and we were worried for our safety. Our worries were proven correct today when Daniel was killed."

"Daniel?"

"Professor Sandberg. The other reason for the secrecy was that we would be unable to bring the case ourselves. Ethics rules would prevent it because we once worked on similar cases for the person who we want to bring this case against. We would have been thrown out of court and probably disbarred if we would have brought the case ourselves. So our plan was to research the matter secretly and then to pass the research discreetly on to another lawyer who would bring the case on behalf of the government."

"I'm only halfway done with my Professional Responsibility course, but I'm pretty sure that wouldn't be allowed either. Your previous involvement with the people who you want to bring the case against would prevent you from doing any work, including research, on a similar case against them."

"That's why the research and the passing off of the research had to be secretive."

"Why not just get another lawyer to research the case?"

"No one other than Professor Sandberg was willing to put in the necessary amount of work to research the case. There's not much of a monetary incentive to work on this case, and most people don't believe the facts that we're dealing with anyway."

"What are the facts?"

"I can't tell you that right now. I've already told you too much."

"If you expect me to help you in any way, I need to know everything."

"I'll tell you everything in time, but for now you know enough. Professor Sandberg and I have been conducting some very important research for the past two years, and now he has been murdered over it."

Lucius was angry that Martinez was still holding back information. "Why should I believe any of this? Why shouldn't I think that it was you who killed Sandberg?"

"Why would I be here? Why would I be telling you this?"

"Because you know that I'm the only one who can make the connection between you and Sandberg."

"First of all, that's not true. And even if that were the case, why wouldn't I just kill you and be done with the whole thing?"

"I don't know. Maybe you've gone soft all of a sudden."

Martinez opened her mouth as if to respond, but no words came out. She remained silent for a few seconds before speaking. "Lucius, I need your help. I promise you that everything I've told you is true."

Lucius was moved by her sincerity. "What do you need me to do?"

"I need you to get the research for me."

"What?"

"It's two years worth of work. I have to have it."

"You mean you want to continue to try to bring this case? It can't be worth dying over."

"No one else is going to die. We just have to be more careful. Anyway, the research is complete, so all we have to do is get it and pass it on to the attorney in England who has agreed to bring the case."

Lucius thought of the British cases that he and Robert had read, and he also thought of Sandberg's L.L.M. from King's College in London. "Where is the research?"

"It's in Sandberg's office."

Lucius was furious. "There's no way I'm going back in there."

"I need your help, Lucius."

"Well, you're not getting it. Why don't you get the research yourself?"

"Because the people who did this to Sandberg are looking for me, and the police are looking for me, too. I have to leave town tonight."

"Yeah, well, if I go back into Sandberg's office, the murderers and the police will be looking for me, too."

"If you don't help me, then I guess I'll have to go to Robert Collins."

Lucius was incredulous. "How the hell do you know about Robert?"

"I read your e-mail."

"You did what?"

"I had to make sure you were safe, so I hacked into your account while I was here."

"How do you expect me to believe you when you're doing things like that?"

"My best friend was just murdered. I can't trust anyone right now unless I check them out first."

Lucius didn't respond. He just looked at her. There was something about her that made him want to help her...even though she had broken into his apartment, hacked into his e-mail account, and refused to explain what was going on.

"Lucius, this case is important. It needs to be brought. We can right a very old wrong. Please, I need your help."

"Okay, tell me what to do...and call me Luke."

"Thank you, Luke."

Martinez produced a key from her pocket and handed it to Lucius. "This is the key to Sandberg's office." Next, she produced a piece of paper with two sets of numbers on it. "The first of these numbers is the key code combination to get into the office area after dark. The second number is the combination to the safe in Sandberg's office. It's a small red safe in the back of his office, and that's where he kept the research."

"What if I'm seen?"

"The police won't be in there late at night, and the janitors are done with that area by midnight. Just go in after midnight, and you'll be fine."

"What about the murderer? What if he's watching the area?"

"Whoever killed Sandberg is probably long gone. If he's still in the area, then he'll be looking for me, not keeping an eye on a crime scene."

"How will I find you when I've got the research?"

"You won't. I'll be out of the country by tomorrow night. I'll get back in touch with you soon, and we'll arrange something."

"What am I supposed to do with it in the mean time? A guy was just murdered over this stuff."

"No one except for me knows that you have anything to do with this. The research will be safe in your possession, and no one will come after you. I promise, Luke."

They walked together to the door. Dolores thanked him for his help, and as she left the apartment, she did something unexpected. She leaned back inside the door and kissed Lucius on the cheek. Then she disappeared into the darkness of the night.

After she left, Lucius felt like he was floating back down from a dream. It had all seemed like a dream. He tried to remember all of the things that Dolores had told him. This whole thing had something to do with the Ramsden family...and England, but he couldn't figure it out. Whatever it was all about, Lucius believed Martinez that it was important, and he wanted to help.

He looked at his watch. It wasn't too late, so he picked up his phone and called Jennifer.

"I need your help again, Jennifer."

"Of course, Luke. What do you need?"

"Are you free tomorrow night at about midnight?"

"You're not going back into the library?"

"No, I have to go get something out of Sandberg's office."

"What? Why can't you just go during the day?"

"Because it doesn't belong to me. They won't give it to me."

"So you want me to help you steal something from a dead man's office? I'm willing to help you in whatever way I can, Luke, but this sounds crazy."

"I know it does, but trust me, it's important. I just need you to keep a lookout while I go get it."

Jennifer unexpectedly agreed. "Okay, Luke, I trust you. I'll see you tomorrow night."

"And don't mention this to Robert. I don't want to drag him back into all of this. As far as he's concerned, this whole thing is over, and he can go back to focusing on law school."

"Sure, Luke, I won't tell him."

They said their goodbyes and hung up the phone. Lucius knew that he wouldn't be able to concentrate on reading, so he turned on the television. He put it on a basketball game and zoned out. What if Martinez had been the murderer? Maybe she was planning to set him up. Maybe she would call the police and tell them that the murderer was returning to the scene of the crime. Lucius turned the possibility over in his mind. It would make sense from her perspective. She could very well be the number one suspect right now, and the police wouldn't stop looking for her until they had someone else to pin the murder on. The questioning by Detective Torro had already made Lucius consider the fact that he might be a suspect. Returning to the scene of the crime would only encourage Torro's suspicions.

And it would explain Martinez's story. She would have had to tell him a fantastic story to get him to go back in there, and that's exactly what she did. But why pick him to set up?

Maybe he was the only one who would be willing to go back in there, but if he was caught, he'd tell the police everything. If they believed it, that would only point the finger more strongly at Dolores. Could she just be relying on the police not believing Lucius?

Lucius wanted to call Robert. He wanted to tell him everything. Robert was always so good at coming up with possible explanations and punching holes in Lucius' explanations. But Lucius knew that it wouldn't be right to involve Robert again. The previous experience had seriously interfered with Robert's life. He had stopped doing his schoolwork. He had stopped socializing. He had just spent all of his time focusing on solving the mystery.

For the next few hours, Lucius just sat in his chair thinking about the situation and staring at the basketball game on television. It ended and a sports highlight show began, but he didn't change the channel. On a couple of occasions, he thought about calling Jennifer and telling her to forget about the whole thing. Martinez was leaving the country in the next day or two. He could just tell her that the safe was gone when she called.

But then Lucius started thinking about Martinez's face. She was beautiful and had seemed so sincere. Even though she talked fast and made threats, he could tell that she had also been scared. There was vulnerability under her hard exterior. And she had seemed so grateful when he agreed to help her. The kiss at the end of the conversation hadn't seemed like a kiss of death, but more like a way of expressing a deep gratitude.

Before Lucius fell asleep that night, he had firmly decided to get the research. Martinez hadn't told him which night to go get the research, so how could she have set him up? And he felt like he could talk himself out of the situation if he was caught. He could claim that Sandberg had given him the key and passwords before he died, and that he had left something in Sandberg's office but had been too afraid to return for it until then.

Lucius arose early the next day and headed out for school. He went to all of his classes and paid attention as best as he could. His mind drifted occasionally to the night's activities. He had already decided that he would skim through as much of

84

the research as he could that evening when he got it home. If Dolores wouldn't tell him what was going on, then he would figure it out himself.

A few of the other students had heard that he was the one who had discovered Sandberg's body, so he got a lot of strange looks from people he had never met and a lot of kind words from people he barely knew. All of the professors began their lectures by briefly mentioning Professor Sandberg. All of them said that they hadn't known him well but had known him well enough to know that he was a good person. Lucius' Criminal Investigation professor asked that everyone pray for Sandberg's family, and his Professional Responsibility professor seemed on the verge of tears. He saw Robert in the hallway, but they just nodded at one another. No words were exchanged.

The night came quickly and by ten o'clock, Lucius was sitting outside the library near the elevator. He planned to keep an eye on the elevator for a while. He wanted to know if anyone was going in or coming out at this hour.

A few professors came out of the elevator during the next hour, but no one went up. No one had gone in nor had anyone come out of the elevator for nearly an hour when Jennifer arrived at midnight. Lucius felt pretty good about the whole thing. It was doubtful that the police had been up there waiting for him for the last two hours.

"Are you sure you want to do this?"

"Yeah, I'm sure, Jennifer. I've kept an eye on the elevator for the last two hours. I think I'll be okay."

He stood up and began to cross the hallway to the elevator door, when it suddenly began opening. He turned around and walked quickly back toward Jennifer.

A janitor wheeled his cart out of the elevator and down the hallway in the other direction. He couldn't believe that he had forgotten about the janitor. He had been lucky.

Lucius regained his nerve and walked back over to the elevator when the janitor was out of sight. He entered it when the doors opened and headed up to the third floor. The elevator doors opened to reveal a small lounge. There was very little light. He turned to the right and headed for the office area.

He located the keypad and typed in the code that Martinez had given him. The keypad flashed green, and he heard the door unlock. He let out a sigh as he gripped the door handle and pulled it open. He peered into the darkness, and not seeing or hearing anything, he headed inside.

The carpet was soft underfoot, so his footsteps were silent. He crept slowly down the hallway, checking all of the rooms to make sure no light was coming from under their doors. Finally, he reached the doorway to Sandberg's office. It was marked off with police tape.

Lucius pulled out the gloves he had brought for this occasion. He didn't want to leave any fingerprints. He put them on and unlocked the door. He slid underneath the police tape and into the room. He decided against turning on the lights. He didn't want to draw any attention to his presence. He crept across the room and located the safe near the back window. There was just enough light coming from the streetlight outside for him to make out the numbers on the safe's dial.

He carefully turned the dial back and forth to the numbers indicated on the piece of paper. His hands were sweating in the gloves, even though it was relatively cold in the room. He got it wrong the first time. The safe wouldn't open. He started over, and this time he heard the safe's lock click open when he finished with the combination.

He held his breath as he opened the safe's door. The emptiness of the safe briefly distracted him from the sound of cracking fingernails coming from behind him.

Chapter Ten

Lucius' brain finally processed the sounds in the hallway. He quickly closed the safe's door and crawled under Sandberg's desk. He shivered with nervousness. What if the murderer had returned?

An equally nervous voice resounded from the doorway. "Hey, is...is there anybody in there?"

Lucius held his breath and remained perfectly still. The nervousness of the voice made him doubt that the person outside the door was the murderer or the police, but he would be in trouble if anyone caught him in Sandberg's office.

The standoff continued for what seemed like hours. The man at the door might have suspected that someone was in the office, but he was too afraid to go in and check. Finally, Lucius heard the door being closed. He waited for a few more minutes, and then carefully walked over to the door. He opened it slowly and looked out to ensure that no one was around.

"Hey, who are you and what are you..." Lucius didn't wait for the man to finish. He bolted out of the door, slammed hard against the man knocking him to the ground, and ran down the hallway.

Lucius ran through the propped-open keypad door and found the stairwell entrance. He didn't have time to wait for an elevator. He ran down the stairway, skipping two or three stairs with each stride. He emerged on the first floor next to the elevator. He burst into the hallway, ran past a frightened Jennifer, and ducked around the corner.

He peered out from around the corner to watch the events unfold. He was still breathing heavily. The man emerged from the stairwell door and approached Jennifer. Lucius was too far away to hear the substance of the conversation, but he guessed that the man was asking if she had seen anything. Jennifer pointed away from Lucius down a different hallway, and the man walked in that direction. The pace of his walk suggested to Lucius that he didn't really want to run into whoever he had seen coming out of that office.

Lucius remained where he was, and after a few minutes, Jennifer got up from her post and walked toward him.

When she arrived, Lucius spoke first. "Let's get out of the law school. I don't think there's any way he recognized me, but I don't want to press my luck."

Jennifer laughed a nervous laugh. "Sure, let's go back to your place."

Lucius questioned Jennifer as they walked toward the car, "Who was that guy?"

"He didn't say, but I recognized him as being one of the law school tech support guys…the one who came in to fix the projector in our Property class last week. Did he see you in the office?"

"I don't think he could have gotten a good look at me. It was really dark up there, and he didn't have a flashlight."

"Did you find whatever it was you were looking for?"

"No, it wasn't there. Whoever killed him must have already taken it."

"What was it you were looking for anyway?"

"If I tell you, you have to promise not to tell Robert."

"I promise."

The two of them climbed into Lucius' car and drove toward his apartment.

"Martinez came to see me last night."

Jennifer was shocked. "What did she want with you? Did you call the police?"

"She needed my help, and no, I didn't call the police. I don't think she had anything to do with the murder."

"Luke, this is serious. This isn't a game anymore. A professor was murdered at the law school. You have to leave this to the police."

"I trust her."

"Why? She's lied to you before. Don't you remember her claim that she was just a student who had left her keys in the library?"

88

"Yeah, but that was a different situation. She's not trying to cover up what they were doing anymore. She told me all about it."

"So what were they doing?"

"They were doing research on a very important case. They had to be secretive because there were people willing to kill them over it and because they weren't ethically allowed to be working on the case." Lucius was beginning to wish that he hadn't told Jennifer any of this.

"That sounds like further reason to distrust her. Luke, we have to go to the police."

"That would be pointless. She's already left the country."

The two of them arrived at Lucius' apartment and went inside. Lucius checked all of the rooms before the two of them sat down in the living room.

"So what were they researching?"

"She wouldn't tell me."

"Luke, have you stopped for a minute to consider why exactly you're protecting this woman? She hasn't told you anything, and she almost got you in serious trouble tonight. What if that had been the murderer instead of some tech support guy?"

"Then I would have been dead, but it wasn't, so it doesn't matter. Anyway, I was supposed to be getting their research from Sandberg's office tonight, but it was already gone."

"You have to promise me that if Martinez calls back, you'll notify the police."

"I can't promise you that, Jennifer. It doesn't matter now, anyway. Like I told you, she left the country."

"Okay, Luke. You do what you have to do, but I'm not going to help you anymore. I think you're making a very stupid mistake, and I hope you'll change your mind. With that being said, I won't tell anyone about this. I don't want to put you in any more danger than you're already in."

Lucius drove Jennifer back to the law school. They rode in silence. He dropped her off at her car and waved goodbye. He knew from the expression on her face that it was a serious goodbye. They might still exchange greetings in the hallway of the law school. They might even go out to get something to eat at some point, but a very real part of their friendship had ended that night. In a couple of months, Jennifer would be leaving for Columbia, and Lucius felt that she would be leaving his life forever.

As he drove home, he wondered if Jennifer had been right. Maybe he was wrong to trust Dolores. She had lied to him in the past, and she had broken into his house only one night earlier. But she hadn't set him up. There had been no police officers in the office, and she had told him the truth about the janitor. If she had been the murderer, she would have already taken the research, and there would have been no point in sending him into Sandberg's office. Despite Jennifer's reservations, he still believed that Dolores Martinez was telling him the truth.

Lucius arrived at his apartment and fell asleep as soon as his head hit the pillow. The evening's activities had taken a lot out of him. When he awoke the next morning, he had two e-mails waiting for him. The first was from Robert:

> Hey Luke,
>
> I need to talk to you tonight. Can you meet me at the pizza place downtown at 7:00? It shouldn't take long.
>
> Robert

The other e-mail was from Professor Franklin, his Contracts professor from last semester.

> Mr. Dixon,
>
> If you have any free time this afternoon, please stop by my office. I'd like to talk to you.
>
> Jonas Franklin.

Lucius didn't know what to think of either e-mail, but he sent a response to both. He told Robert that he would be there, and he told Professor Franklin, who had been his Contracts professor, that he would drop by at about half past two.

Lucius spent most of the day trying to figure out what the e-mails had been about. He wondered if Jennifer had broken her promise and told Robert about what was going on. He wondered if the tech support guy had identified him to Professor Franklin. By the time two o'clock rolled around, Lucius was eager to figure it all out.

Professor Franklin's office was away from the other offices. He and some of the other senior professors had offices at the back of the first floor of the library. Lucius walked quickly to the office and knocked on his door. He was called inside.

"May I help you?"

"Yes sir, I'm Lucius Dixon. You wanted to see me."

Professor Franklin smiled widely and stood up to shake his hand. "Thank you for coming in, Mr. Dixon. I'm glad you were able to make it."

"It's good to see you again, sir."

"I just wanted to have you in to talk about the incident the other day. I can remember how hard law school was, and I can't imagine having to deal with something like that on top of law school."

"Yes sir, it's been difficult."

"I wanted to let you know that if there is anything that I can do to help you, I'd be more than happy. Since I've gotten older, I've taken less of a mentoring role, and sometimes I feel bad about that. I'd like to help you in any way that I can."

"Thank you, sir. That's a very kind offer."

"Yes, well, I mean it. I know you probably think that an old man like me couldn't possibly have anything useful to say, but I'm willing to give you advice on anything. Just come to me, if you need it."

"Thank you, sir." Lucius left the office and wandered out into the hallway. His experience with Martinez and Sandberg had made him paranoid. He had seen nothing in Franklin's demeanor to suggest that he was being anything but genuine, and yet there was a part of Lucius that refused to trust him.

Lucius walked out of the library and headed toward the exit of the law school. He was tired and wanted to skip his afternoon class and go home. It had been a rough couple of days.

As he walked by the elevator doors, he noticed someone familiar standing in front of them. It was Lindsey Coleman, Robert's friend who was fired from the Justice Department. One of the elevator doors opened, and Cole stepped inside.

Lucius was too afraid to follow Cole upstairs, but he wondered what he was doing here. He wasn't a student, and as far as he knew, Cole didn't have any sort of job with the law school. He began to suspect that Robert hadn't given up on the investigation after all.

Lucius drove home and took a nap. When he awoke, he rolled over and looked at the clock. It was nearly seven o'clock. He threw on some clothes and ran out the door. On the drive over, he thought about Cole and what he had been doing at the law school. He planned to confront Robert about it.

When he arrived at the pizza place, he was surprised to see that Robert was not alone. Sitting with him was Lindsey Coleman. Lucius was very suspicious and considered leaving immediately. But Robert was his friend, so he approached.

"Hey, Robert. Hey, Cole."

"Luke, it's good to see you. You obviously remember Cole." Robert seemed a little too friendly.

"Yeah, I remember him. What's this all about anyway, Robert?"

"I wanted you to come out because I wanted to tell you this in person."

"Okay, go ahead."

Robert leaned over and spoke softly. "Cole and I are going to solve this murder."

Lucius was angry. "No, you're not, Robert. Stay out of this."

"Luke, this is important to me. You know as well as I do that this has something to do with what we were investigating. We're just going to finish the job."

"Robert, this is a murder. This is serious."

"You don't have to help. I don't expect you to help. I just wanted to let you know that we are going to do it."

"Why don't you let the police handle this job?"

"Because the police are incompetent. Cole still has friends at the Justice Department who are willing to help us. And we've also got a lead on Martinez."

"What sort of lead?"

Cole spoke up. "She was seen at the Charlottesville airport flying out to New York. We're currently trying to figure out if it was a connecting flight."

"Robert, why can't you leave well enough alone? We are all lucky to be alive. We clearly got too close to something that was not our business, and we might have played a part in getting a professor killed. Let's just let it go."

Robert turned red. "Don't you think I feel bad about Sandberg? Don't you think I wished I could have stopped it? And now Cole and I are going to bring the killer to justice. We're going to expose whatever it is that's been going on, and we're going to end it."

"Why is Cole helping you?"

Cole opened his mouth to speak, but Robert spoke first. "He's being compensated."

"Why was Cole at the law school today?"

"Since you're not involved in this investigation, I suppose that's none of your business, Luke."

Lucius didn't know what to do. He felt like he had already lost one friend the night before, and he didn't want to lose another.

"Robert, I really wish I could help you, but I just can't get involved. I'm sorry."

Robert looked at him harshly. "That's what I expected, Luke. I hope you'll have the decency to stay out of our way."

"I'll stay out of your way, Robert. But please be careful. This is a very serious situation."

"We're ready for anything."

Lucius got up from the table and headed toward his car. He didn't have much of an appetite. When he had awoken from his fainting spell two days ago, he had been in a panic. The interrogation had taken a lot out of him. But when he left that situation, he had found his two friends, Robert and Jennifer. They had cheered him up and helped him to carry on...just like they had in the past.

Now, Lucius no longer had their support. He would have to carry on without relying on Jennifer's overflowing sympathy and Robert's eccentric creativity. Sandberg's murder had done something to their friendship. Perhaps, it was because their friendship had always been partially defined by their attempts to solve the mystery. After all, their friendship had initially grown out of that day in Torts when Sandberg had torn him apart and his friends had helped to build him back up.

Lucius drove home in silence. He didn't feel like listening to the radio. Maybe he should have listened to Jennifer and told her that he would report Dolores the next time she called. But what if Dolores was telling the truth about everything? What if the work she had been doing was important? And what if powerful people did want to frame her for the murder?

Maybe he should have participated in Robert's investigation. After all, they were going to do it with or without his help. But he knew how serious this situation was. He didn't want to be involved any more than he was already. And he couldn't steer them away from Dolores without revealing their meeting. He also had exams to worry about. He was, after all, still a law student.

Lucius couldn't sleep that night. He tossed and turned, questioning his decisions and wondering what he should do next. At one point, he tried to call Jennifer. He wanted to apologize for the way he had behaved the other night, and he wanted to ask that she forgive him. He wanted to keep in touch with her. She had been very important to him. But all he got was her voice mail. He decided not to leave a message. In a span of twenty-four hours, he had lost both of his friends...and all for a woman he hardly knew. Lucius felt like crying.

He tossed and turned a little while longer and nearly jumped out of his bed when his phone rang. He grabbed at the phone, knocking it to the ground. He answered excitedly, hoping that it was Jennifer.

"Hello?"

"Luke, this is Dolores."

"Dolores, where are you?"

"That's not important right now. Did you get the research?"

"No, I went in to get it, but the safe was empty."

"Were you seen?"

"No, there was a tech support guy there, but he didn't get a good look at me."

"Okay, Luke. I still need your help. Are you willing?"

Lucius hesitated. She had already cost him so much. "Yes, I'm willing."

"Thank you, Luke."

"No problem, what do you need?"

"There is an electronic copy of the research…in Daniel's house."

Chapter Eleven

There was only silence on the line for the next few seconds.

"Dolores..."

"I know, Luke."

"How am I supposed to get the research from Sandberg's house?"

"No one other than Sandberg and I knew about this copy, so I need you to promise me that you'll tell no one."

"I promise."

"All right. The other copy is stored on a USB flash drive hidden inside a hollowed out section of a book."

"Which book? How will I find it?"

"The book is the 5th Edition of Parker's The Economics of Tort Actions. Just ask Sandberg's wife if you can borrow the book. Tell her Sandberg recommended it before he died."

Lucius jotted down the title of the book on a piece of paper next to his computer. He then wrote "Sandberg's house" beneath it. "So you want me to just waltz into her house and ask for a book right after her husband was killed?"

"Because no one else knows about the book, I think it would be okay for you to give her some time. Drop in on her in a couple of weeks. That'll give her a chance to recover, and it'll also give things a chance to calm down."

"If it's okay, I'll wait until after exams in early May."

"Sure, that's fine."

"I also wanted to tell you about Robert. He and another guy are trying to solve the murder. They think you did it."

"Along with everyone else."

"Yeah, but they tracked your flight to New York and are trying to track you further."

"Thanks. I've been careful, so I should be fine."

"Do you have any leads on who the real murderer is?"

"Do you really want me to answer that question? I thought you didn't want to be involved."

"I'm already involved. I need to know as much as I can to protect myself." In truth, Dolores was right. Lucius wasn't sure if he wanted to know anything more.

"I've managed to get into a couple of e-mail accounts. The information that I've gotten is sparse so far, but I do know that the murderer was either hired by the Ramsden family or someone at Leeder & Schrum at the behest of the Ramsden family. And I also know that the murder was supposed to be blamed on me."

"Wait, so what is the connection between the Ramsden family and Leeder & Schrum? And who has the research that was in Sandberg's safe?"

"The Ramsden family is the only real client that Leeder & Schrum has. They only take other work to give the appearance of independence. I would assume that someone at Leeder & Schrum has the research from Daniel's safe. They are probably reviewing it to anticipate any case that may be brought against the Ramsdens."

"So are you telling me that your old law firm is willing to hire murderers and look through illegally obtained files to protect its only client?"

"Yes, that's exactly what I'm telling you. Listen, Luke. I have to go. Please keep all of this information to yourself. Don't breathe a word of it to anyone, not even Robert."

"I promise."

"Goodbye, Luke...and be careful."

She hung up before Lucius had a chance to say goodbye. Lucius didn't know what to believe this time. The story seemed absurd. Why were these rich and powerful people resorting to the murder of a law professor over some research? And even if Martinez were able to hack into e-mail accounts at the firm, why were they e-mailing about a murder for hire? Shouldn't that sort of thing be taken care of in person? But then again, if it was all a lie, couldn't Martinez have made up a more believable story? Nonetheless, he would get the flash drive for her. It was his only chance to figure out what was really going on.

The next couple of months went by quickly. Lucius focused primarily on his schoolwork. He caught up in all of his classes and prepared himself for his second set of exams. The murder still hung over his head and provided plenty of distractions, but he managed to push on through those distractions.

He saw Jennifer and Robert occasionally in the hallways, but his predictions were correct. Neither of them wanted to talk to him. They would speak to him briefly before walking away. It was difficult to deal with the loss of two close friends, but Lucius did his best. His hope was to be more active in the law school next year. He could find new friends.

He spent more time talking to Professor Franklin than anyone else. Franklin had invited him out for lunch several times. They had discussed how law school had changed over the years and what Lucius should expect in his first years as a lawyer. Lucius began to trust Professor Franklin. He seemed genuinely interested in Lucius' welfare.

After a few of these meetings, Professor Franklin asked Lucius to work for him as his research assistant during the summer. Lucius had planned to go home to Mississippi for the summer, but a job offer was enticing. He decided to accept Professor Franklin's offer and looked forward to a relaxing summer in Charlottesville.

He heard through others about the summer plans of Robert and Jennifer. Robert was going to D.C. to work for the legal office of the State Department. Jennifer was going to New York to summer at a prestigious law firm. She had also gotten engaged to Howard. Lucius was happy for both of them, though he still worried about Robert and his murder investigation.

Finally, exams came and went. Lucius was accustomed to the process this time, and it was a breeze. His exams seemed easier than they had the previous semester. Despite all of the distractions that he had been forced to deal with during the year, he felt like he had managed to improve on his grades from last semester.

On the final day of exams, Lucius drove back to his apartment. He was planning to go to a movie theater that evening to unwind, but he wanted to relax at home for a little while. He popped a bag of microwaveable popcorn. He always craved popcorn when he went to the movies, but it was too expensive. He thought that if he ate a bag at home before going, he could stifle his craving before it started.

Before the popcorn had finished popping, there was a knock at his door. He looked through the peephole, as it was now his habit to do, and saw Robert standing outside looking down at his shoes. Lucius opened the door.

Robert looked up at him and spoke immediately. "I'm sorry for the way I've acted, Luke."

"I'm glad to hear that Robert. I'm sorry, too." Lucius signaled for Robert to come inside, and he did so. Lucius closed the door behind him.

"I've just been so wrapped up in this whole thing, and now with Jennifer getting engaged and moving away, I don't feel like I've got anyone to talk to."

"What about Cole?"

"Cole's fine, but he's older, and we don't really have anything in common other than this investigation."

"How's that going, by the way?"

"We're pretty sure Martinez was the murderer. She's skipped town, and the police are looking for her. We think she's in Eastern Europe, but we don't have any solid leads on her exact location."

"So are you going to continue the investigation?"

"I'm not sure. Cole wants to, but I'm not sure it's worth it. I think I did horribly on my exams, and the main reason was all of the time I spent on the investigation."

"I'm sorry to hear that."

"Luke, do you think I should go after Jennifer?"

"What?"

"Do you think I should go to New York to try to get Jennifer away from this Howard guy?"

"You can't do that, Robert. You have to let that whole thing go. Jennifer's a sweet girl, but she's gone. She's going to be married in a couple of months."

"But I never really told her how I feel about her. I think I'm in love with her."

"Trust me, Robert. She knew you liked her, but she fell in love with someone else."

"You're probably right, Luke. I just wonder sometimes if I've missed out on something important."

"It'll be okay, Robert. There are plenty of other girls here at the law school."

"Yeah, I know…but none like Jennifer."

"You don't know that, Robert. You just have to meet more people."

Robert paused for a moment. He smiled a little. "We'll have to go out more often next year…to the bars I mean."

"Yeah, Robert, we will."

"Do you mind if I check my e-mail on your computer really quickly?"

"Yeah, go ahead. I'll be in here watching television."

Lucius had a smile on his face when he sat down. Robert was back…that is, assuming Lucius could talk him out of following Jennifer to New York. He hoped that after a few weeks of her being gone, he would get over his crush. Then maybe he could talk Robert out of continuing the investigation. Then once he got the flash drive and sent it to Martinez, this whole thing would be behind them. Things could go back to normal.

He flipped through the channels for a few minutes while eating his popcorn. It never tasted as good as the movie theater stuff.

The feeling after exams was always extremely relaxing. It was like a great weight lifted off his shoulders. He was so relaxed that he was half-asleep when Robert emerged from his room.

"Thanks, Luke. I'm going to hit the road."

Lucius opened his eyes. "Oh, yeah, Robert. I'm glad you're not mad at me any more. When are you heading to D.C.?"

"In the next couple of days. We'll keep in touch over the summer, though."

"Yeah, Robert. Be careful this summer. I'm already looking forward to the fall semester."

Robert left, and Lucius fell asleep. He woke up a few hours later. The television was still on, and it was dark outside. He thought for a minute about staying in for the night but decided that he could use some time outside of his apartment. He had been spending most of his time recently either in the law school or in his apartment studying.

He got out of his chair and turned on a light. He checked his apartment to make sure everything was in order before heading out to his car and driving downtown. His favorite theater in Charlottesville sat in the downtown area next to an ice skating rink. Its marquee seemed old-fashioned, and it would occasionally show the relatively obscure movies that Lucius liked.

On this evening, he wasn't interested in obscurity. Lucius bought a ticket to the big budget comic book adaptation that had just opened. He had no interest in a thinking-man's movie tonight. He wanted to relax and enjoy himself. He settled into his seat right as the lights dimmed.

The movie fulfilled its purpose. Lucius was completely satisfied when he got up to leave the theater. He decided to walk around in the downtown area for a while. It was a cool night for early May, but it was a comfortable coolness.

After only a few minutes, Lucius thought better of the idea. It was nearly midnight, and there weren't many people around. It would probably be better if he went home for the evening. As he turned to head toward his car, someone tapped him on his shoulder. Lucius was startled.

"You got any change?" It was a disheveled looking man with a long beard. He was carrying a guitar case.

Lucius dug around in his pocket and produced the two quarters that he had gotten as change from the theater. He gave them to the man and nodded at him.

"Thank you, son. You have a good night."

Lucius was thoughtful as he walked back to his car. Seeing homeless people always helped him to put his problems into perspective. He may have had troubles of his own, but at least he had a comfortable bed to sleep in at night. He made it to his car without incident and drove home. He turned up the radio and enjoyed the drive.

Lucius went to sleep as soon as he got home. He had decided to go to Sandberg's house the next day. He had a week off between school and the beginning of his job as a research assistant. He wanted to get this over with while he had the chance. He also thought that the free week would be a good time to spend poring over the research.

He slept well and didn't wake up until the next afternoon. He took a shower, got dressed, and drove to Sandberg's house. He was nervous. He parked his car on the street next to the house and walked up to the door. He rang the doorbell and waited. After a few seconds, the door opened.

"Yes, can I help you?" It was Mrs. Sandberg. She looked better than he had expected.

"Yes, Mrs. Sandberg. I was one of your husband's students. I thought I would drop by to pay my respects and to ask you a favor."

She smiled at him. "Sure, come on inside. I'll brew us some coffee."

"Thank you. That would be nice." Lucius hated coffee, but he didn't want to rock the boat.

Mrs. Sandberg led him to a seat in the living room, and then left the room for a moment returning with a couple of coffee cups. "It'll be ready in a minute. What did you say your name was?"

"I don't think I said, ma'am. My name is Lucius Dixon. I was in your husband's Torts class last semester."

"You seem familiar. Were you at the little get-together that Daniel and I had here at the house?"

"Yes ma'am, I was. It was very nice."

"Daniel always loved to bring the students over. He had only been teaching for a couple of years, but I think his favorite part of the whole thing was the relationships that he developed with his students. Were you close with Daniel?"

"No ma'am. I just really enjoyed his class. I did go to see him a couple of times outside of class, though. He was very helpful to me."

"I'm glad to hear that, Lucius. He was a wonderful man." She sniffled. "Please excuse me for a moment. The coffee is probably almost ready."

Lucius relaxed, but only for a moment. Before Mrs. Sandberg returned, a watch on the living room table started beeping. Mrs. Sandberg walked quickly back into the room and sat the coffee pot on a potholder. She picked up the watch and said, "Please excuse me a moment. I have to wake up my son from his nap."

Lucius had forgotten about the son and the frightening encounter that night. He had also forgotten about the other flash drive…the one he had left in Sandberg's computer. What if they figured it out? What if they put everything together? Lucius thought about leaving but managed to calm himself down. That was a long time ago. The kid had certainly forgotten him by now.

Mrs. Sandberg returned holding the little boy's hand. "I want you to meet someone, Edward."

Edward rubbed his eyes. "I already know that boy. That's Frank."

"No, Edward, this is Lucius. You say hello to Lucius."

"That's not his name. That's not even a real name. His name is Frank. I already met him before."

Lucius spoke up. "You must have me confused with someone else. It's nice to meet you, Edward."

Mrs. Sandberg looked puzzled but didn't say anything. After Edward said hello and shook Lucius' hand, she led him out of the room and told him to go play.

"He's got quite an imagination. It's only gotten worse since he lost his father."

"It must be hard for him. It must be hard for both of you."

"Yes, it is, but we're making it. Some of our old friends have been very nice during this whole thing. The attorneys at Daniel's old law firm have sent so much stuff that my kitchen is overflowing." Mrs. Sandberg poured coffee into both of the cups and began drinking her own. There was no offer of cream or sugar.

"I'm glad to hear that. He was such a great professor, but I imagine he was equally good as an attorney."

"Yes, he was very successful. I met him while he was at Yale. He could have gone anywhere, but he had his mind set on

103

Leeder & Schrum. He was one of their best attorneys. They gave him all of the most difficult assignments. He was a star."

"Why did he leave the firm?"

"He had disagreements with some of the other partners, but his primary reason was a desire to teach. He said he wanted to take part in the education of tomorrow's lawyers. He felt like it was his calling."

"He did an excellent job. I felt like I learned more in that class than any other class that I took."

"That's good to hear. You said when you came in that you wanted to ask a favor?"

"Yes. Professor Sandberg told us about a book that was particularly good. He said that it would help a great deal in the understanding of Torts. I'm going to be working this summer for another professor at the law school, and I thought reading that book would help me to be a better research assistant."

"I wouldn't be able to help you if you're trying to figure out what the name of the book was."

"No ma'am, I know the name. It's just that Professor Sandberg had said that if we ever needed to borrow a copy to let him know. He said he kept one in his personal library."

An odd expression came over Mrs. Sandberg's face. "What was the name of the book?"

"It was the 5th Edition of Parker's The Economics of Tort Actions."

There was a pause. "I'm sorry young man."

"Why?"

"I just gave that book to another law student earlier today."

Chapter Twelve

Lucius could only stare at Mrs. Sandberg in disbelief.

After a moment, she spoke up. "I'm sorry, son. You can probably get a copy from the library, though."

Lucius tried to compose himself. "Yes ma'am. I'll see if they have it. Thank you for the coffee."

"You're welcome, though you've hardly touched it. I would like to thank you for the kind words about my husband."

"You're welcome, Mrs. Sandberg."

She led him to the door, and they shook hands before he departed. She continued to look at him curiously. Maybe it was the way he had acted after finding out that the book had already been taken, or maybe it was the mere fact that he had tried to borrow the same book that had been borrowed earlier in the day.

Lucius walked to his car and began driving home. Had Dolores grown impatient? Had she returned for the book claiming to be a law student? Had Robert figured out the location of the book? Had Cole figured out the location of the book? Lucius searched his mind for a memory of mentioning the book to anyone. Perhaps he had said something to Professor Franklin, but if he had, he certainly couldn't remember it.

When he arrived at home, he decided to call Robert. If either Cole or he had been the person who took the book, then he would know about it. Unfortunately, Lucius only got Robert's voicemail. He decided not to leave a message.

A brief check of his e-mail revealed a message from Professor Franklin. He wanted Lucius to come in tomorrow for a short chat about the project they would be working on during the summer. Lucius e-mailed him back confirming a meeting, and then wandered back into the living room.

He was still unnerved by the fact that someone had beaten him to the book, and that they had beaten him by only a few hours. He wondered if they had kept an eye on the house after taking the book. Maybe they had seen him going inside later. He worried that the killers now knew who he was. He glanced at his door to make sure it was locked.

Maybe Dolores had just been wrong about the location of the book being unknown to anyone else. Maybe someone had broken into Sandberg's e-mail account or listened in on one of his calls. Of course, there was always the possibility that some student just really wanted to borrow that particular book.

Lucius dreaded the call from Dolores. He didn't know how she would take this news. Dolores and Sandberg had worked long hours to get all of that research. If there was only the copy in the safe and the copy in the book, then both copies could be in the hands of their enemies now. The whole thing would have been a waste.

All of a sudden an idea entered Lucius' mind. He remembered the old man who had met with Robert and Sandberg that day in the park. Robert and he had tried unsuccessfully to connect him to Leeder & Schrum, but perhaps he was somehow tied to the Ramsdens. Lucius walked back into his bedroom and logged onto the Internet.

He didn't really know where to begin, so he started by looking up Wilfred Ramsden, the former United States Senator from Virginia. A quick comparison revealed that this was not the old man who had met with Martinez and Sandberg in the park. He tried unsuccessfully to find pictures of Wilfred Ramsden's family members but gave up after a few minutes. He would have to remember to ask Dolores about the old man the next time they talked.

Lucius spent the rest of the day watching television and wondering about who took the book. He tried calling Robert a couple more times, but to no avail. He went to sleep early and woke up early the next morning.

He decided to go over to the law school a little early. Maybe Robert would be around, and he could see if he knew anything. He instead ran into Jennifer.

"Hi, Jennifer."

"Hello, Luke."

"When are you going to New York?"

"I'm leaving next Wednesday."

"I hope it all works out well for you."

"Thanks, Luke. Same to you."

They nodded at each other and walked away. There was no warmth left in their relationship. Lucius was angry with himself.

He spent a couple of hours walking through the halls. He spoke to a few acquaintances and checked his mailbox. When the time finally arrived, he headed for Franklin's office.

Professor Franklin asked him to come inside, and they began talking about the summer's project.

"I want to write a historical paper about the evolution of the available remedies for breach of contract. There will be a lot of research involved. We'll have to research very old American and English law. Do you think you'll be able to help me?"

"Yes sir. I feel like I picked up some good research skills in my Legal Research & Writing course. Just let me know the specifics of what you need, and I'll do my best to find it."

"I'm glad to hear..." Professor Franklin was interrupted by a knock at the door. "Come in."

The door opened. It was Detective Snow, the woman who had questioned him on the day of the murder. "Professor Franklin, would you mind if my partner and I had a word with Mr. Dixon outside?"

"We were having a meeting, but I suppose if it's only for a minute it would be okay."

Lucius got up and walked outside. Detective Snow shut the door behind them. Detective Torro emerged from a connecting hallway.

Snow spoke first. "Hi, Lucius. We were here investigating the murder and thought we would ask you a few questions while you're here."

"Sure, go ahead."

Torro took over. "When we first talked to you, you said that you didn't have a friendly relationship with Professor Sandberg."

"I didn't say that we weren't friendly. I just said that we weren't close."

"Okay. Well, basically what we're wondering is why you went to his house yesterday to talk to his widow."

"You could just ask her. I went to pay my respects and to borrow a book."

"We already talked to Mrs. Sandberg, and she told us about the book. Why don't you tell me the real reason you went there? What was so special about the book? Why couldn't you just get it from the library?"

Maybe the police had already obtained the book. Maybe they had told Mrs. Sandberg to lie and say that it was picked up by a law student. Maybe they already knew about the flash drive. "I don't know of anything special about the book. Sandberg recommended it and said he had a copy at his house. I thought it would be helpful."

"What was the name of the book?"

"It was The Economics of Tort Law."

"So were you taking an exam on Tort law? Are you doing research this summer on economics?"

"No sir."

"Then why did you need the book?"

"I just thought it would be interesting. I don't know what else to tell you."

"Mrs. Sandberg thought you were acting strange. Why were you acting strange?"

Detective Snow interrupted. "Sergio..."

"Just let me do my job, Rita. Answer the question, Mr. Dixon."

"I was surprised to hear that someone had gotten the book earlier in the day. That's all."

"We also spoke with Mrs. Sandberg's son."

Lucius tried to remain calm. "And?"

Detective Snow interjected. "Sergio, try not to be so hard on him. He's clearly under a lot of stress."

"I'm sure he is, Rita, but that's not important right now. Mr. Dixon, are you telling me that you don't know what little Edward Sandberg told us?"

"That's what I'm telling you, sir. I only met him briefly."

"He told us that you had been at the house before. He told us that you used his father's computer to check your e-mail and that you told him your name was Frank."

"He has me confused with someone else. He kept calling me Frank yesterday when I was talking with Mrs. Sandberg."

"He seemed pretty sure of himself."

"He's just a kid! And Mrs. Sandberg herself said that he had quite an imagination." Lucius was practically yelling.

"There's no need to get upset, Mr. Dixon. I just want to know why you were checking your e-mail on Sandberg's computer. You never mentioned that to us before."

"I never checked my e-mail on his computer!" This response was so loud that it brought Professor Franklin out of his office.

"What is going on out here?" Franklin spoke quietly and evenly.

Detective Torro leaned against a nearby book shelf. "Please, sir, I'm going to ask you to stay out of this. This doesn't concern you."

"It certainly concerns me. This young man is my research assistant. If you people don't leave him alone, he won't be a very effective one." Professor Franklin exuded calmness. His voice never rose.

"Sir, do you realize that this is about a murder investigation? This is very serious."

"Do you realize that you are dealing with a man in his early twenties who just discovered a dead body a few short weeks ago? Do you realize that this young man has been through some very hard times, all the while trying to remain focused on his legal studies? Do you have any idea what this young man has been through?"

Detective Torro looked agitated. "Sir, I understand all of that, but there are a lot of people who want this murder solved, and this young man might have some answers that he's refusing to provide. He may even be endangering your safety. After all, it was one of your fellow professors who was murdered."

Professor Franklin just stared at Detective Torro for a moment. He didn't look angry. He didn't look upset. He just looked right through the detective. After a moment, he opened his mouth and spoke very softly. "If I were twenty years younger, I would have already thrown you out of this law school by your pants. If you don't leave right now, I might try it anyway."

Detective Torro backed down. "Fine, we'll leave. We got the information we needed anyway. Mr. Dixon, we'll be in touch."

And with that the two detectives turned and headed down the hallway. Detective Snow gave Lucius an apologetic smile as they walked away.

Lucius was impressed.

"Mr. Dixon, how would you like to get out of this place and get some lunch?"

"Sounds good to me. Thanks for doing that, by the way."

"Just taking care of a couple of bullies."

The two of them walked out to Professor Franklin's car and drove to a sandwich shop nearby. After they ordered their food, Lucius spoke up. "Why did you help me back there?"

"I just saw that they were annoying you and thought I should help you out."

"Why have you been so nice to me? I mean, I appreciate it. It's just that no one else has reached out to me like you have."

Franklin paused for a moment. "Do you mind if I tell you a personal story?"

"Not at all."

"In 1957 I was a first-year law student here at the University of Virginia. Things were different back then, but not so different. We all worked hard, and we were all nervous. I had done well my first semester, and I decided to go home for spring break, rather than sticking around to study. My family lived in Southwest Virginia in a little town called Norton, so I thought it would be a nice time drive down to see them."

Professor Franklin paused his story when the waiter arrived with their sandwiches. They thanked him, and then the story continued. "I had a 1946 Ford 2-Door Coupe. It was a beautiful car...bright blue. Anyway, I drove home to see my family. There's some amazing countryside between Charlottesville and Southwest Virginia. You should make the trip sometime."

Professor Franklin again paused to bite into his roast beef sandwich. He shifted the food to one side of his mouth and continued the story. "When I arrived at home, my family was on edge. They hadn't said anything to me over the phone because they didn't want me to be worried while I was driving down, but there had been a fight. I only had one sibling...my younger sister Caroline. She was sixteen at the time."

Lucius studied Professor Franklin's face. He was trembling a little as he told the story. He didn't look at Lucius. He looked upward, as if he were searching the ceiling for the details of his story. "She had been dating a young man named Amos Landry. Amos was a troublemaker. My sister thought he was just misunderstood, like James Dean in Rebel without a Cause, but this kid wasn't James Dean. He was mean. If his parents hadn't been the richest people in town, he would have been in jail."

"So this young man had been dating my sister for almost a year, and a few days before I arrived at home in the spring of '57, he had gotten into a fight in a nearby town. One of the boys he had been fighting with had been seriously hurt. He had been sent to the hospital, and no one was sure if he would fully recover. Anyway, my father found out about the fight, and he demanded that Caroline break it off with Amos. Caroline refused."

"So on the day before I arrived Amos had come by the house. He had asked to see Caroline, and my mother had told him to go away. When he insisted, my father went outside and told him that he was not welcome at the house. He told him to never come back. Caroline overheard this upstairs and came running down, but my mother caught her at the bottom of the stairs. She held her while Amos drove away."

"My father told Caroline that she was never allowed to see Amos again. On the day I arrived, all of the yelling had subsided. Everyone just seemed to be ignoring one another. My mother told me the whole story. I remember thinking that my father had made the right move. As I said, Amos was a mean kid."

Franklin paused for another bite of his sandwich. He called the waiter over for a refill of Lucius' soda. "I tried to talk to my sister about the situation. She opened up to me at first, but then she got angry with me as well. She told me that mother and father had become very controlling ever since I left. She blamed me."

"That night I slept fitfully. The next morning when I awoke, there was eeriness in the air. I got out of bed and went to the bathroom. The door was closed but not locked. I opened it to find the body of my sister floating in a bathtub filled with blood. She had slit her wrists in the tub. I fainted on the spot."

Lucius looked down at his sandwich. It suddenly seemed unappetizing. "I'm sorry for telling you all of this, but I wanted to explain why I've been so concerned about you. For the next few months both at home and at the law school, I found little comfort. The story had gotten out, and everyone was more concerned with appearances than with providing me with emotional support. I didn't have anyone to turn to. All of my time was spent thinking about my sister and what I could have done to stop her from killing herself. I nearly drove myself crazy."

"I couldn't concentrate on my work. I almost failed out of law school. The administration seemed to want me to fail. The suicide had been bad publicity for the school, even though it was my sister and not me. No one wanted to help me because no one wanted to think about such a sad situation. It was a very difficult time for me. I only made it through that year on sheer determination."

"When I heard about you, I noticed a lot of similarities. I know that you weren't particularly close to Sandberg, but it still must have been difficult to stumble into that scene. I knew that such a trauma would be hard to bear during your first year of law school. And I knew that I had been through a similar experience and might be able to help you a little to understand it all."

"I hope I didn't upset you with my story; I just wanted to help you to see where I was coming from. When I saw those detectives bullying you, I just thought about all of the people who had bullied and ignored me in the aftermath of my sister's death."

Lucius finally spoke. "You didn't upset me, sir. I'm glad you told me."

"Well, anyway, that was fifty years ago. I'll never forget my sister, but I've learned to put it behind me. You have to learn to do the same with your experience. Take the pain from that experience and channel it into productivity. Don't let anyone tell you how to feel or make you feel guilty. You decide for yourself how to feel about it."

The next few minutes were spent in silence. Lucius thought about Professor Franklin carrying with him the memory of a dead sister for fifty years. He thought about how much more difficult his experience must have been than the experience that Lucius was going through.

After a few minutes, Professor Franklin changed the subject back to the research that they would be doing during the summer. Lucius managed to finish his sandwich, and they drove back to the law school and parted ways.

Lucius drove home. The town was already emptying out. The students were all heading home for the summer. It would be interesting to spend the summer in an empty Charlottesville.

Almost as soon as he stepped inside, his phone began ringing.

"Luke, this is Dolores."

"I've got bad news Dolores."

"What is it?"

"The book...someone else had already gotten it."

"Who did you tell about it? I told you not to mention it to anyone."

"I didn't mention it to anyone."

"You must have. No one else knew anything about it."

"I promise you I didn't mention it to anyone. I have a question for you, if you don't mind."

"I don't have time, Luke. I'll call you later." She hung up.

Lucius walked into his bedroom and sat down at his computer. As he reached down for his mouse, a piece of paper caught his eye. He had forgotten that he had written down the name of the book and where to get it on a piece of paper next to his computer. But who had been in his room? Who could have seen it?

Robert.

Chapter Thirteen

For a moment, Lucius just let the whole situation run through his mind. Martinez had told him that no one else knew about the copy of the research that was hidden in the book at Sandberg's house, but how did she know for sure? Wasn't it possible that the killer had forced that information out of Sandberg before killing him?

Robert and he had fought, but they were still friends. They had been through a lot together, and he had trouble believing that Robert would have stolen the information from him. Why wouldn't he have asked Lucius what it was about? Would he really have stolen the book without saying a word?

Lucius thought about calling Mrs. Sandberg to ask for a description of the student who had borrowed the book, but he knew that it was too risky. Any further involvement with her would only implicate him more in the eyes of Detectives Torro and Snow.

He tried to call Robert, but once again he got no answer. If Robert hadn't been the one who took the book, why wouldn't he answer his phone? Lucius called Jennifer.

"Hello."

"Jennifer, this is Luke."

"Hello, Luke. What can I do for you?"

"It's Robert. Have you seen him lately?"

"No, I haven't, but Robert and I don't talk much these days."

"Well, if you hear anything from him, would you let me know?"

"Why? What's wrong?"

"It's just that I haven't heard from him in a few days, and I'm worried about him."

"Luke." Her tone was disapproving.

"Yeah?"

"Robert is a grown man. He doesn't need you to worry about him. I'm sure he's fine."

"You're probably right, Jennifer. Anyway, I'm sorry I bothered you."

"It's all right. Bye, Luke."

"Goodbye, Jennifer."

He couldn't tell Jennifer what was going on. She didn't want to hear it and wouldn't be able to help anyway. Lucius just sat at his desk and stared at the wall. He felt helpless. He wished Dolores would call back. He could try to explain what was going on. Maybe she would be able to help him to locate Robert or the missing book.

The next few weeks went by in much the same way. Lucius was left out in the cold. He felt like all of the pieces were moving in the background. He wanted to become involved again, but he didn't know how.

He thought about Lindsey Coleman, but he couldn't go to him for help. He didn't fully trust him. He couldn't talk to Jennifer. He couldn't get in touch with Robert or Dolores, and Sandberg was dead. His mind kept going back to the old man that Dolores and Sandberg had met that day in the park. That meeting had been so strange that it had to have something to do with this whole thing.

Because he knew of no other way to reach the old man, Lucius went to the park where the meeting took place. He went there nearly every day after he finished his work for Franklin. He would sit on the bench where they had sat and talked. He didn't know what he expected to happen; he just hoped that something would happen.

After a few weeks of this, Lucius started to calm down. His research for Franklin was interesting. He kind of enjoyed reading through dusty old books and trying to think of clever search terms to use with the online archives. He was able to focus his mind on the project, and he began to relax.

He ate lunch with Professor Franklin once a week. They had grown close. Franklin had become someone on whom Lucius could rely. The only thing he couldn't tell him about was the truth about the Sandberg mystery.

On one occasion a few weeks into the summer, he was walking out of the library when he saw Cole. He decided to put aside his suspicions and approach him.

"Hey, Cole. Wait up."

Cole turned around with a puzzled look on his face. There was no look of recognition after he saw Lucius, but he waited.

Lucius spoke first. "What brings you to the law school?"

"I'm just working on a project for a friend of mine. What about yourself?"

"I'm working for a professor this summer."

Cole seemed impatient. "Well, it's good to see you. I'd better be running along. I've got lots to do."

"Wait, there was something I wanted to ask you."

"Go ahead."

"Have you seen Robert lately?"

"He's gone to New York."

"What?"

"I don't know if I should be telling you this."

"Telling me what?"

"There was this girl. He was obsessed with her. She moved to New York, so he decided to follow her up there."

"Are you sure, Cole?"

"Yes, I'm sure. He told me before he left. He said that it was something he had to do."

"What about his summer job?"

"I don't know. I guess he's not going to do it. Anyway, I've got to go. Try not to worry about Robert. He'll be fine."

Lucius just stood there as Cole walked away. He didn't know what to think. Robert had clearly been considering the idea when he came by his house that night, so it seemed plausible. Maybe he wasn't answering his phone or contacting Lucius because Lucius had told him not to do it.

But the whole thing seemed kind of strange. Robert had been unreasonable in the past, but not this unreasonable. Failing to show up for a summer job at this point would be a really bad idea, not to mention the fact that it was a job at the State Department. How would he explain that to future employers?

And if Robert had gone to New York, who had gone by the Sandberg house to get the book? No one else had been in his apartment since he wrote down the note. And Martinez must have believed that no one else knew about the copy of the research that was hidden in the book. She had been so angry when Lucius told her that it was gone. Lucius was baffled…and he worried about his friend.

He called Jennifer again.

"Hello?"

"Jennifer, it's Luke."

"Hello, Luke. What do you need?"

"I'm calling about Robert again."

"Luke, you're not his mother."

"Jennifer, this is serious. Do you remember that guy Cole that he was hanging around?"

"Yeah, I remember him."

"Well, I saw him in the law school today, and I asked him about Robert because I hadn't seen or heard from him in a few weeks."

"And?"

"He said that Robert had gone to New York. He said that Robert was following you to New York."

There was a pause on Jennifer's end of the line.

Lucius spoke again. "I don't know if it's true or not. I just wanted to call to see if you had seen or heard from him."

"No…I haven't."

"Well, will you promise to call me if you see him?"

"Yeah, I promise, Luke."

"Goodbye, Jennifer."

"Wait, Luke."

"Yeah?"

"I'm sorry I've been so rude to you lately. You're a good friend, and I should try to be nicer."

"Thanks, Jennifer."

"And I'll keep a look out for Robert."

"Thanks."

"Bye, Luke."

"Goodbye, Jennifer."

Lucius was powerless. Robert wouldn't answer his phone, and there was no way to find out who had taken the research. The old man who might have been Lucius' only connection to what Sandberg and Dolores had been doing was nowhere to be found.

In a way, it was just what Lucius had been hoping for. He was done with the mystery; or rather the mystery was done with him. He could focus on law school and his work for Professor Franklin…only he couldn't. Now that the mystery had been finally put behind him, he wanted nothing more than for it to return. He hoped every night when he returned to his apartment that Dolores would be there. He kept his phone with him at all times, hoping that he would get a call from Robert or Dolores, but it never happened. The summer days just slowly passed.

It was early one morning after eating some pancakes at a nearby restaurant and before going in to see Professor Franklin that Lucius had another idea. When it first came to him, he immediately discarded it as being far too dangerous and reckless, but it kept coming back into his head.

Dolores had said that the first copy of the research that had been stolen was probably still in existence. She said that Leeder & Schrum probably had it somewhere studying it to prepare for a possible defense. He couldn't break into the firm to try to find the research. It would be impossible to find the information among their files, and the security would almost certainly be impenetrable for someone like himself.

But he could contact them and ask about interviewing for a summer associate job the next summer. According to Dolores they knew nothing about him. He had not yet been connected to the whole Sandberg affair. So he could go in to the lion's den to try to figure out what was going on. He could snoop around a little while being interviewed.

He tossed the idea around in his head for several days. It seemed remarkably reckless. He could be killed for his curiosity. He would certainly be putting himself in a very dangerous spot. And yet the monotony of waiting around and doing nothing while the gears turned behind him was driving him crazy. There was also the fact that Robert could be in danger. Perhaps he had the research in his hands and had mentioned it to someone who was working for Leeder & Schrum or the Ramsdens.

Finally, late one night in the middle of the summer, Lucius decided to e-mail Leeder & Schrum. He typed up a nice letter asking for an interview and telling them how highly he thought of their firm. He attached a copy of his résumé and sent the e-mail. He sat back reconsidering his decision as the e-mail confirmation screen came up. He couldn't help but think that he had made a big mistake.

The next few weeks passed in much the same way as the weeks before them. Lucius continued to work for Franklin. Their paper was moving quickly forward. His research skills were improving a great deal. He still spent a couple of afternoons every week at the park looking for the old man. It seemed futile at this point, but the possibility still remained that he would show up.

One day after a particularly long day at the law school, his phone rang. He answered it immediately.

"Luke, this is Jennifer."

"Hey, Jennifer. How are you?"

"I'm fine. Are you near a computer?"

"No."

"Okay, I'm going to e-mail you a link, but I want to tell you what it says first."

"All right, go ahead."

"Robert has been reported missing."

"What do you mean?"

"I mean no one knows where Robert is, and the police are looking for him."

"Do you think he's okay? Have you seen him in New York?"

"No, I haven't seen him. I don't know if he's okay. I'm worried, Luke."

"It's okay, Jennifer. I'm sure he's going to be fine. We just have to stay calm. Should I call the police and tell them what I know?"

"Yes, Luke. Call them."

"But how do I explain his going to New York? Do I tell them that he was going after you?"

"Yes, just tell them everything. This is serious, Luke."

"Okay, Jennifer. I will."

"Bye, Luke."

"Goodbye, Jennifer."

Lucius was afraid as he drove home. Was Robert really in New York? Was he just planning to hide out for a while? Why wouldn't he have contacted Jennifer? Why wouldn't he have let someone know that he was okay?

Lucius arrived at home and practically ran to his computer. He opened the e-mail. The article had the headline: Son of Solicitor General Reported Missing. It didn't contain many details. It gave a phone number to call if there was any information. Lucius dialed it.

"Hello."

"Yes, I may have information about the disappearance of Robert Collins."

"Yes, please hold for one second."

Lucius waited.

"Yes, this is Robert Collins, Sr. What can I do for you?"

"Sir, I might have some information about the disappearance of your son."

"Who am I speaking with?"

"I'm a friend of Robert's. My name's Lucius Dixon."

"Yes, Robert has mentioned you. What can you tell me?"

"Are you familiar with a man by the name of Lindsey Coleman?"

"Yes, he is a former employee of mine."

"I was worried about Robert because I hadn't heard from him in a while. He had been hanging around Lindsey Coleman, so when I saw Cole in the law school, I asked him if he had seen Robert. He told me that Robert had gone to New York after a girl."

"After a girl? That's ridiculous."

"Yes, sir. It may be. The only thing is...well, Robert told me himself that he was considering the idea only a few days before he disappeared."

"So do you think it's true?"

"I don't know what to think, sir. Robert is hard to read."

"Thank you. Do you have a phone number where I can reach you?"

Lucius gave Robert's father his information, and then the conversation was over. The whole thing took less than a minute. Lucius hung up the phone. He was a little baffled. Why was Robert's father the one who answered the phone? Shouldn't they have had a police officer handling this? It seemed strange, but Lucius didn't let his mind dwell on it for long. He was concerned about his friend.

He called Jennifer again.

"I called the number that was listed in the article you gave me."

"And?"

"It was Robert's father."

"That's strange. Did you tell him what you heard?"

"Yeah, I told him, but he seemed skeptical. He didn't even ask for your name."

"I'm skeptical, too, Luke. Robert seemed to be getting over the crush he had on me. And why wouldn't he have contacted me by now?"

"I don't know, Jennifer. Part of me wants to believe it because it would mean that he was probably okay. Otherwise…"

"Otherwise what? Luke, do you know something that you're not telling me."

"You told me not to tell you about the Sandberg and Dolores stuff anymore."

"Well, I want to know now. This concerns one of our friends."

"Okay, well, Dolores called me about a copy of the research that had been stolen from the safe. She told me that I could find it at Sandberg's house inside a book. She said no one else knew about it. So I wrote down the information next to my computer and waited a couple of weeks. On the day before I went to get the book, Robert came to my house. He went to check his e-mail while I waited in the living room. He could have seen the information that I wrote down about where to find the book. Then the next day when I went to pick up the book, Sandberg's wife said that another law student had already come to get it."

"So you think Robert got the book first? What would that mean?"

"I don't know, Jennifer. Maybe he disappeared with the book so that he could digest the information without being bothered. Or maybe…"

Jennifer didn't let him finish. "Maybe someone hurt him to get the book."

"Yeah."

"So what do we do?"

"I don't know, Jennifer."

There was silence on the line for nearly a minute. Finally, Jennifer said that she would call him back if anything came up. Lucius hung up the phone and sat silently staring at his computer. His heart was sick for Robert.

A new e-mail popped up onto his screen as he stared. It was from a secretary at Leeder & Schrum.

Mr. Dixon:

We'd love to have you in for an interview. Our hiring process begins in August. We would like to have you in Friday, August 3rd at 9:00 A.M. Please let me know if that time works for you. I will send you a more detailed schedule as the date approaches. Thanks for your interest.

Chapter Fourteen

The next few weeks passed in much the same way. Lucius heard nothing from Dolores or Robert, but he spoke with Jennifer on the phone nearly every day. Their friendship had been rekindled, though nearly all of their conversations concerned Robert. They discussed hundreds of different explanations for his disappearance. None of them made much sense.

Finally, the date of August 3rd arrived. Lucius had agreed to the interview with Leeder & Schrum. He feared for his own safety, but something inside of him made him agree to the interview. If Dolores' stories were true, these were dangerous people. But if there were even a slight chance that he might pick up a lead that would help him to find Robert, then it would be worth it.

Lucius had decided that it must have been Robert who picked up the book from Sandberg's house that day. He had also decided that, despite what Cole had said, Robert's disappearance had something to do with that book. Maybe he had told Cole that he was going to New York, or maybe Cole was lying to cover for Robert, but Lucius didn't believe the story. It didn't make sense.

There were two possibilities. In the first scenario, Robert found the research and began studying it. It was so overwhelming that he had hidden himself from everyone, including his father. He had been so sucked into the mystery that he didn't have time for anyone or anything else. In the other scenario, Robert had mentioned his discovery of the research to the wrong person and had been killed either to obtain the research or to prevent Robert from telling anyone about it.

Lucius shuddered at the prospect of Robert's murder as he climbed into his car at six o'clock in the morning on the 3rd of August. He hoped and prayed that it wasn't true. Either way, he had to do something. He had to figure out what was going on. Before, his motivation had come from mere curiosity. Now he was motivated by the disappearance of his friend…and yet, there was always the possibility that Robert's disappearance had absolutely nothing to do with any of this. Maybe he had just gone to New York to keep an eye on Jennifer.

Lucius let his mind wander as he began the nearly three hour drive to Norfolk, Virginia, the location of the law office of Leeder & Schrum. He thought about all of the research that he had done for the past few weeks. He had researched for Professor Franklin, but he had also spent a great deal of time researching Leeder & Schrum and the Ramsden family.

As for Leeder & Schrum, there simply wasn't much information available. The firm was nearly fifty years old, but Lucius couldn't find evidence of any important cases on which they had worked. They seemed to deal mostly with small cases, but their attorneys had really impressive backgrounds. Of the thirty attorneys currently working at the firm, seven had clerked for Supreme Court Justices. All but one of their attorneys had graduated from law schools ranked in the top fourteen, and eleven of them had served in public offices ranging in importance from city council to the United States Congress.

The lack of information about Leeder & Schrum was countered by an abundance of information about the Ramsden family. They were one of Virginia's oldest and wealthiest families. They had their noses in nearly everything in Virginia, and yet they were still a very small family. Lucius had found a family tree site which had recorded some information about the Ramsden family. It was incomplete, but Lucius had been able to uncover a great deal of information by combining it with his own research.

The family had been in Virginia for hundreds of years. Lucius found several other similar families with which to compare the Ramsdens. All of those other families had spread out into all parts of Virginia and into the rest of the states. The Ramsden family was different. There were less than twenty people alive today who were direct descendants of the Ramsden family that settled in the United States in the early eighteenth century. Among those twenty was Wilfred Ramsden, a former United States Senator, and all twenty lived in Virginia.

Lucius let it all run through his head as he drove down the empty highway toward Norfolk. Leeder & Schrum was a strange law firm. It contained far more than its fair share of powerful, important people, yet Dolores had implied that the Ramsdens were able to control the firm in such a way that people at the firm were willing to murder for the Ramsdens. How could such a small family be so powerful?

Lucius arrived at the law office of Leeder & Schrum at exactly nine o'clock. He checked in with the secretary and waited quietly in the lobby for a few minutes. There was nothing unusual about this place so far. He picked up and browsed a magazine while he waited.

He was greeted after a few minutes by a young associate named Marcus Henry. He told Lucius that he would be Lucius' first interview, and that he would take him to his office. Marcus had the face of a very young man. He appeared to be in his late twenties, but his hair was completely gray, and he walked with a severe limp.

They arrived in Marcus' office, and Marcus directed him to sit down. A quick look around the office revealed that Marcus had graduated from the University of Virginia's School of Law only five years earlier.

Marcus spoke in a friendly tone. "I suppose they chose me to start you off because I graduated from UVA. Well, do you have any questions for me or should I just tell you about the firm?"

"I'd love to hear your take on the firm, and what makes it different from other similarly sized firms."

"Sure. Well, as you probably know, we're a small firm, but we're not a boutique. We do everything. That's why we have to hire only the best attorneys in the United States. There are a lot of lawyers out there who are really good at practicing one area of the law, but there aren't many lawyers out there who are well-rounded enough to work in all areas of the law."

"Does the firm have any specialties?"

"There are some areas that provide us with more work than others, but we pride ourselves on being able to do it all. We were originally founded by Mr. Leeder and Mr. Schrum as a corporate firm. We provided advice for corporations and helped to draft whatever agreements they needed, whether they were merger agreements or simple contracts of sale. Then we began to evolve as the needs of our clients evolved."

"Who are your clients?"

"We count among our clients some of the most powerful people and businesses in all of Virginia. They are all connected through Norfolk."

"And what specific practice areas have you worked in recently?"

"I've done a lot of tax work ever since I was brought in five years ago. Despite promises of a wide variety of practice areas, the first year's worth of work was entirely tax work. After that first year, they started putting me on other projects. My first big case was a real property case. It took nearly two years to complete."

"This may seem like an odd question, but how is this firm able to attract such talented attorneys?"

"We reach out to a very particular type of attorney. There are a lot of lawyers out there who love a specific area of the law and love to learn every facet of that area of the law, but there are also a lot of lawyers out there who would be bored out of their minds if they were forced to work in only one area. Those lawyers come here. Not to mention, the firm compensates its attorneys better than any other firm in the state of Virginia. The benefits are extraordinarily generous, as well."

"I've heard that a lot of the law firms that pay so well work their attorneys really hard."

Marcus laughed. "I'm sure you won't believe me, but that's not the case here. I don't mean to say that we don't work hard, but it has always been the policy of the firm to keep its attorneys happy. We've always believed that if the attorneys are worked too hard, they won't be happy. And if they're not happy, the quality of the work will decline. We get plenty of vacation time, and most of the associates are out of the office by six o'clock every evening."

"That sounds really nice."

"What drew you to the firm initially?"

Lucius had expected this question and had rehearsed his answer several times. "Well, I've always liked this part of the state. It seems like a nice area to settle down. And I like the idea of working in a small firm. As you said before, it gives a young attorney the opportunity to work in many different areas. I worry about the monotony of doing the same thing every day for the rest of my life."

"Do you have any family ties to the area? I saw on your résumé that you were originally from Mississippi."

"That's correct. No, sir, I don't know anyone in Norfolk, but I've visited here before, and I've always enjoyed my stay. I could definitely see myself staying here long term."

"Do you have any more questions for me?"

Lucius wasn't sure if he should bring up the Ramsdens when he came here, but he now decided to go for it. If he wanted to find out anything, he had to ask the questions. "Can you tell me about the Ramsden family? I've heard they are one of your clients."

"Yes, the Ramsdens supply us with a lot of our work. In fact, all of the cases that I've worked on since I've been an associate here have been for the Ramsdens. That real property case that I was telling you about earlier was a dispute between one of their businesses and a town outside of Hampton, Virginia. It was basically a complicated zoning case."

"So they are just a local family that gives you a lot of work?"

"Yes, that's exactly right. They have been very good to this firm. In fact, I've heard partners in the firm say that the firm wouldn't exist without the work given to us by the Ramsdens."

"It seems strange that one family could provide so much work."

"Well, the Ramsdens aren't your typical family. They have a lot going on. Anyway, do you have any more questions, or should I take you to your next interview?"

"If you don't mind before we go, could you describe what a typical work day is like for you?" Lucius wanted to change the subject. He didn't want Marcus to remember this as being the odd interview where the kid kept asking questions about the Ramsdens.

"Certainly...but I should first point out that there really isn't a typical day for an attorney working here at Leeder & Schrum. I come in every morning at nine. Sometimes I have a conference to go to. Sometimes I have a client to meet with. Sometimes I have research that needs to be done. But every day I am dealing with challenging legal issues and coming up with unique solutions to our clients' problems. It is a demanding but very rewarding job."

The rest of the interviews were all pretty much the same. Lucius asked similar questions and received similar answers. No one provided any information about the Ramsdens other than what had already been provided by Marcus. There was never an opportunity for Lucius to snoop around the office looking for the research, and he wouldn't know where to begin anyway. After three of these interviews, one senior partner and one young associate took him to lunch.

Lunch conversation was primarily taken over by talk of the summer program. Lucius was informed that the summer program was an excellent opportunity to experience all that the firm had to offer. They brought in two summer associates every year, and they were given real work...the same sort of work that would have been given to a first or second-year associate had the summer associates not been there. Lucius had done his best to feign interest. He even laughed at a couple of terrible jokes.

After lunch was over, Lucius was taken back to the office. The senior partner walked him to his car.

"I've really enjoyed talking with you, son. You seem like a bright, young man. I've always liked UVA kids."

"Thank you, sir. I've really enjoyed visiting your firm. Everyone has been very nice and helpful."

"Well, I'm glad to hear it. You drive safely back to Charlottesville. I'm not sure if we'll send anyone up there for on-grounds interviews, but if we do, I'll be sure to tell them to get in touch with you."

"Thank you, sir. It's been a pleasure."

The senior partner turned and walked away, and Lucius climbed into his car. He had been too nervous to eat much at lunch, and now that his nerves were subsiding, he had already begun to feel slight pangs of hunger.

As he drove toward the highway that would take him back toward Charlottesville, he couldn't help but to notice all of the different things named after the Ramsdens. There were car dealerships, streets, and grocery stores. Everything in the whole town seemed to be named after that family.

Lucius finally found the highway and started toward home. He didn't feel like stopping to get anything to eat in Norfolk. He wanted to get outside of the city. He hoped to find a small town nearby where he could sit down and have a nice meal. He preferred a small-town atmosphere.

He drove along in silence, thinking about the results of his trip. He wasn't entirely sure why he had come in the first place. There was no way there was going to be a chance to try to snoop around to find the missing research, and it was very doubtful that any of the attorneys were going to reveal anything which would lead him to wherever Robert was. He didn't know exactly what he had expected to gain from the trip.

And yet, he had learned a few things. He had learned that there was a very real connection between the Ramsdens and Leeder & Schrum. Before these interviews, he had only the word of Dolores to rely on. For whatever reason, Lucius still trusted Dolores, but it was nice to have some sort of validation for the things that she was telling him.

His mind wandered back to Robert as he drove. He never should have cut Robert out of the investigation. He should have kept him fully informed. If he had done that, then perhaps Robert would not have resorted to moving behind his back. Maybe they would still be working together. He would be driving home to tell Robert about all that he had learned. They would analyze it and plot their next course of action.

Lucius' thoughts were brought back to the present by his hungry stomach. He saw the signs for a town called Seaford. It seemed like a small town. Lucius took the exit and quickly found a small café. It was just the sort of place that he was looking for.

Lucius parked and went inside. He was one of only two customers. The other was an old man sitting at the bar drinking coffee. Lucius sat in one of the booths by the window.

His waitress arrived a few minutes later. She looked like she was in her seventies. Her smile was one of the friendliest that Lucius had ever seen.

"What can I get you, honey?"

Lucius ordered a hamburger with everything on it, french fries, a house salad, and a milk shake for dessert. He was starving.

When he finished his meal, he had a strange idea. He would ask the waitress about the Ramsdens. It would be interesting to see what some of the regular folk around here thought of the rich and powerful Ramsdens.

He got his waitress' attention and asked her as soon as she arrived, "Do you mind if I ask you a couple of questions?"

"Sure, honey. Go ahead."

"Are you familiar with a family called the Ramsdens?"

A scowl immediately appeared on her face. This was just the sort of reaction that Lucius was hoping for. "Yeah, I know 'em."

"What can you tell me about them?"

"Why do you want to know?"

"I was just passing through Norfolk, and I saw all of the stuff called Ramsden. I asked a guy at a gas station, and he said they were a rich family in Norfolk."

"Yeah, I don't know too much more about them than that. They're old money...real old."

"They've been in Norfolk for a while?"

"Yeah, they've been in Norfolk forever. And I've also heard that you don't want to get on the wrong side of them. They've fought and scrapped with pretty much every big shot in Norfolk. They always seem to win."

"You've never fought with them, have you?"

"No, but one of my cousins has. He worked for a lumber mill right outside of Norfolk. They were competing with one of the Ramsdens' lumber mills. When they started getting ahead, a bunch of city inspectors started sniffing around. They ended up getting shut down for mob influence. There wasn't any mob influence on that mill...not in Norfolk."

It was just the sort of story that Lucius expected to hear. It fit in perfectly with his idea of the Ramsdens. "Thanks very

much. The food was delicious, and I appreciate the information.
I now know not to mess with the Ramsdens."

"That's definitely good advice. Be careful driving,
honey."

Lucius paid his tab and left the restaurant. Almost as
soon as he began driving, it started raining. He thought about
Robert. He thought about Sandberg. He thought about the
Ramsden family and the power that they asserted through both
legal and extralegal means. He was starting to see why Dolores
and Sandberg had been so secretive with their work. This wasn't
a family that messed around. If someone was in their way, they
would take care of the problem.

He drove the rest of the way home in a driving
thunderstorm. He hadn't solved anything. He hadn't found
Robert, or the research, but he was beginning to think that he
was involved again.

Lucius arrived at home and slept peacefully. He was
awakened the next morning by a loud knocking at his door.

Chapter Fifteen

Lucius remained under the covers at first, hoping that the knock was coming from one of the other nearby apartments. He didn't want to get out of bed. The second knock was louder. He climbed out of bed and walked to the door. A quick look through the peep hole revealed Detectives Torro and Snow. Lucius opened the door.

"Good morning, Mr. Dixon." Detective Torro glanced down at Lucius' appearance. He was wearing pajama pants and a white t-shirt. "We didn't wake you, did we?"

"Yes sir, but that's okay. What can I do for you?"

Detective Snow spoke, "Could we come in for a few minutes? We need to ask you a few things."

"Sure, come on in." Lucius motioned toward the couch. "Have a seat." He was nervous but couldn't think of anything incriminating in his apartment.

Detectives Torro and Snow walked into the apartment, crossed the room, and sat down on Lucius' couch.

After a few seconds of silence, Detective Torro spoke up, "Mr. Dixon, what is your connection to the student Robert Collins?"

"Robert was one of my closest friends at the law school."

"So I'm sure you're aware that he's missing?"

"Yes sir, I heard. One of our mutual friends told me. I even called the phone number in the article to tell them the information that I had."

"What information was that?"

"I was unable to get in touch with Robert for a few days. This was before he was reported missing. And one day at the law school, I ran into one of his friends: Lindsey Coleman."

Detective Snow pulled out a small pad and wrote down the name. "I think that's a name we've come across before. Who is he?"

"I didn't really know him, but from what Robert told me, he worked at the Justice Department with Robert's father. He was supposedly dismissed for failing a drug test."

Detective Torro glanced at Detective Snow, then back at Lucius. "Interesting. Go on with your story."

"So I caught up with Cole - that's what Robert called him - and asked him if he had seen Robert. He told me that Robert had gone to New York after a girl. The girl is the same mutual friend who told me about his disappearance."

"What is her name?"

Lucius hesitated. He didn't want to bring Jennifer into this, but he didn't really have a choice. "Her name is Jennifer."

"Last name?"

"Morgan. Jennifer Morgan. Anyway, that's what Cole told me. I didn't believe it then, and I don't believe it now. Robert liked this girl, but he was too sensible to act like that."

"So what do you think happened to Robert?"

Lucius hesitated again. He didn't want to tell them about Sandberg's missing book. "I don't know. I'm just worried about him."

There was another pause.

Detective Snow spoke up sympathetically. "I know how you feel, Lucius. If there's anything you can tell us that might help us to do our job, please do."

Lucius decided not to tell them. It would only serve to make him a more likely suspect, and if the Ramsdens were as powerful as everyone was telling him, then these two police detectives wouldn't be able to do anything about them. "That's all I know."

Detective Torro sighed. "Well, while we're here, we've got a few more things to ask you about. Did Robert Collins have any sort of relationship with Daniel Sandberg?"

"No, sir, not that I'm aware of. We were both in Sandberg's Torts class. That's all."

"So the two of you never discussed Daniel Sandberg outside of class?"

"We would sometimes talk about the class and his lectures, but nothing else."

"And did Robert Collins have any sort of relationship with a woman by the name of Dolores Martinez?"

Lucius felt his lies closing in on him. "I never heard him mention anyone by that name."

"Do you know why his grades were so much lower the second semester?"

Lucius knew but couldn't tell. Robert had spent too much time mystery-solving his second semester. Lucius thought about the fact that despite not having much to do this summer, he hadn't gotten around to checking his own grades. "I don't know."

"Do you know why Robert Collins deleted all of his e-mail accounts in the days before he disappeared?"

This was news to Robert. Perhaps Robert was still alive…unless the person who killed him deleted the accounts. Lucius shuddered. "No, I don't have any idea why he would have done that."

Detective Snow looked at Detective Torro, and they nodded at each other. "Okay, Lucius. Thank you very much for your help. We'll be in touch."

Detectives Torro and Snow left the apartment. Lucius locked the door behind them. He tried to process the new information that he had gotten. Unfortunately, there wasn't much of it. They had been careful to not reveal their hand.

They've connected Robert's disappearance to the Sandberg murder. There were two possibilities for that connection. The first was that they had made the connection solely based on the fact that one of them was a student and one of them was a professor at the same law school. Since both mysteries were unsolved, they thought there might be a connection. The other possibility was that they had made some specific connection.

Perhaps they had gotten an identification of Robert from Mrs. Sandberg. Perhaps she had told them that he was the other student who had picked up the book before Lucius arrived. But if they knew that piece of information, why wouldn't they have brought it up? Maybe they were trying to catch him in a lie, or to get him to reveal something that he didn't want to reveal.

And they still wanted to talk to Dolores Martinez. They weren't alone. Lucius wished that Dolores would call him nearly every day. He had a lot to tell her, and a lot more to find out from her.

Lucius thought about the deleted e-mail accounts. Why would Robert have done that? It could have been to avoid contact if he was going to New York to follow Jennifer, or it could have been to avoid contact while he processed the information that he was learning from Sandberg's book. Or worse, the accounts could have been deleted by someone else...someone who was responsible for Robert's disappearance.

Lucius thought about Robert's falling grades, and then he thought about his own grades. He went into his bedroom and turned on his computer. He logged into his UVA account and waited nervously.

Three A's and a B. Not bad. He had even managed to improve on his grades from the first semester. He leaned back in his chair, briefly feeling pretty good about himself. He was so lost in his own mind that he almost missed hearing the buzzing phone coming from the living room.

Lucius nearly knocked his chair over in getting up. He ran to the living room and answered the phone.

"Hello?"

"Luke?"

"Yeah."

"This is Dolores."

Lucius was elated, though he didn't know exactly why. This was the same woman who had left him hanging the entire summer without telling him what was going on. "Hello, Dolores."

"Are you alone?"

"Yeah, I'm alone."

"I need another favor."

Lucius was a little disappointed. "You only call me when you need favors. I'm going to need information first."

"What do you need to know?"

"My friend Robert is missing. Where is he?"

136

"I have no idea, Luke. I hadn't even heard that he was missing."

"The last time I talked to you, you claimed that you had read the e-mail of people at Leeder & Schrum, and that's how you knew both that they were connected to the Sandberg murder and that you were supposed to be arrested for the murder. That's not true, is it? You didn't read anyone's e-mail."

"No, it's not true. The truth is that I have another contact who has given me some information. I didn't feel comfortable telling you about him at the time."

"The old man?"

"What?"

"I saw you and Sandberg meeting with an old man once in a public park...months ago. He's your contact, isn't he?"

"Yes, he is."

"Well, who is he?"

There was silence on the line. "His name is Garland Ramsden."

"He's a Ramsden? I thought you said the Ramsdens were behind Sandberg's murder."

"Listen, Luke. You have to keep this to yourself. This is very serious. I only mention his name over the phone because I know that you are still unknown to them. If the rest of the Ramsdens knew about what Garland was doing, they wouldn't hesitate to have him killed."

"I promise not to tell anyone. But why is he helping us?"

"If you will do me this one favor, I will let you meet Mr. Ramsden, and you can talk to him yourself. He will tell you everything."

Lucius hated being an errand boy. "All right, fine. What's the favor?"

"I need you to come to the Richmond airport at midnight on August 8th. My flight number is 8036. It's arriving from London. I need you to pick me up."

"Where am I taking you?"

"That's the second part of the favor. Right now, the only people that I can rely on are you and Garland. I have to come to Charlottesville, but I can't let the police or the Ramsdens find me there. I need to stay at your apartment."

"That's crazy, Dolores. Why not just go to the police? Ask them for protection from the Ramsdens."

"It won't work. The police will arrest me immediately. They think I killed Sandberg."

"But you didn't."

"That doesn't matter."

"Why do you need to stay here? Why can't you stay with Garland?"

"He can't be seen with me at this point. He was only able to meet with us before because the other Ramsdens were not aware of what we were doing. They didn't know about the research. He can't be seen with me at all now."

"All right, Dolores. I'll do it."

Lucius' heart was racing as he hung up the phone. He had hoped for many months that all of this would be over. Then it was over, and he had hoped that it would begin again. Now, he didn't know what to think.

He looked up Garland Ramsden on the Internet. Apparently, he was the brother of Wilfred Ramsden, the former United States Senator. Garland had been fairly prominent himself in the academic world. He had a Ph.D. in History from Harvard, and a PhD in Classics from Brown. He was currently retired but had been a professor of colonial history at the University of Virginia for thirty years.

Lucius was relieved that Dolores had known nothing of Robert's disappearance. That seemed to make more likely the possibility that it had nothing to do with all of this. Maybe he had just gone to New York City after Jennifer after all.

The next couple of days went by quickly. He turned in his last memo to Professor Franklin. They had agreed to meet in the fall semester to determine if anything further needed to be done before submitting the paper. Lucius had enjoyed his time working for Professor Franklin. It had been a welcome distraction from Robert's disappearance. Lucius even considered the possibility of becoming a professor himself.

Lucius woke up in the early afternoon on August 8th and sat around watching television for most of the day. He was nervous about seeing Dolores. Despite how close he felt to her, he hardly knew her. He wondered if he was fooling himself by trusting her. After all, she had given him nothing but trouble so far.

Finally the time came to leave for Richmond. Lucius gassed up his car and drove toward the highway. He was excited. He was finally going to hear the whole story. He had been waiting for this for nearly a year. Lucius hit the brakes on his car almost instinctively when he thought about the last time he had had those thoughts.

He had been walking toward Sandberg's office. Sandberg was going to tell him everything. He had been smiling, thinking about how it would all be over, and he could go back to focusing on law school. He had opened the door to Sandberg's office, and he had seen him leaning back in his chair.

Lucius tried to stop thinking about it, but he couldn't get that image out of his head. It would be different this time. He was picking Dolores up at the airport. No one else knew that she was there. She was more careful than Sandberg. She knew that there were people trying to kill her. She would be safe.

Lucius thought of Robert as he drove. School would be starting soon. He hoped Robert would show up. He tried to imagine all of the excuses that Robert could possibly give for his absence this summer. None of them seemed reasonable.

Lucius thought about Jennifer. He should have called her to tell her that the police might be calling to ask her some questions. He worried that she would accidentally tell them something that conflicted with something that he had told them. They might not be able to keep their secrets for much longer.

After about an hour and a half, Lucius arrived at the Richmond airport. He parked his car in the short-term parking and walked into the airport. He found the appropriate departure gate and waited on a bench nearby. His phone started buzzing. He had a text message.

"Just go to your car. I can see you. I will follow."

Lucius got up from the bench and walked toward his car. He looked around but saw no sign of Dolores. Either she was really good at this, or something strange was going on.

He climbed into his car and waited. A few seconds later, the passenger door opened and Dolores climbed in.

She smiled brightly at him. "I had to make sure we weren't followed."

Lucius smiled back. "I'm glad you're okay. You don't have any bags?"

"I travel light."

Lucius cranked up the car and backed out of the parking space. He paid the parking attendant and drove out onto the street.

Lucius confessed, "I did an interview with Leeder & Schrum."

"You did what?"

"I was worried about Robert. I thought his disappearance might have had something to do with this whole thing. I think he's the one that got the research."

"If he got the research, then he's betrayed us. The research is back with the Ramsdens."

Lucius didn't know what to think. He was sure that Robert wouldn't have given the research to the Ramsdens, but they could have taken it from him by force. Lucius still believed in his friend. "Then he wasn't the one who got the research."

"Well, don't worry about it. We'll figure this out, and we'll find your friend. For now, I want you to stay away from Leeder & Schrum. We'll talk to Garland about your friend."

"They didn't seem so dangerous."

"That's only because they didn't know that you were their enemy."

"I talked to some people about the Ramsdens."

"Luke, you have to stop. Your value lies in your anonymity."

Lucius was hurt. "Yeah, well, you weren't helping. I find a dead body. My friend goes missing. I don't know where you are. I don't know if people are trying to kill me. I don't know what's going on."

"I'm sorry, Luke. I had to be sure that I could trust you before I called you again."

They drove in silence for a while. Occasionally, Dolores would peer into the rear view mirror studying the lights behind them. She looked nervous but never said anything.

They finally arrived in Charlottesville. Dolores told Lucius to make a loop before driving to his apartment. She looked relieved when the lights behind them turned in a different direction.

"What was that about?"

"I thought we were being followed. Those same lights were behind us for a long time."

Lucius drove back toward his apartment. He was glad Dolores had come here. He was glad that she had decided to trust him. He felt confident that together they could figure this thing out. They could find Robert and make things right.

They pulled into the parking lot and climbed out of the car. As they were walking toward Lucius' apartment, Dolores suddenly stopped and wheeled around. A door on the parked car opened, and a man emerged.

He was carrying a gun.

As he approached the two of them, Dolores grabbed Lucius' arm. She was shaking. Lucius had never been so scared. This was the first time in his life that he really considered the possibility of his own demise. He tried to speak, "L...l...look, I don't know what you want, but I have money. I can give you money."

The gunman walked underneath a streetlight, and Lucius could see his face. It was Lindsey Coleman.

"Cole, it's me, Luke. What are you doing?"

Cole stopped within a few feet of them and raised the gun toward them. "I'm sorry to do this to you, Luke. You just got involved with the wrong people."

Chapter Sixteen

Lucius couldn't move. He closed his eyes and braced himself for the shot. What he heard next was not a gunshot but screeching tires.

Lucius opened his eyes to see a black SUV moving quickly toward them. Cole turned to face the approaching vehicle and raised his gun, but that was the last thing he ever did. Three bullets hit him in the chest, and he fell to the ground.

The driver of the vehicle emerged with a gun in his hand. He had brown skin and white hair. Lucius tried to process what was happening, but it was all a little overwhelming. The man put the gun in his holster and walked over to Cole's body.

The passenger door opened next, and the old man that Lucius had seen in the park with Sandberg and Martinez emerged. He was wearing a dark gray suit and a black overcoat.

"Garland. You saved us." Martinez let go of Lucius' arm and approached Garland, as if to give him a hug.

"We don't have time for all of that. We have a body to dispose of. Luke, will you help Lavindra put young Mr. Coleman in the back of the car?"

Lucius was still shaking but he complied. Lavindra frisked the body and removed a wallet and some keys which he handed to Garland. He then opened the back of the SUV, and the two of them lifted the body off the ground and placed it in the back. Lavindra slammed the door shut.

Garland spoke again. "All of you get inside. I'll handle the introductions on the way."

Everyone did as they were told, and Garland instructed Lavindra to drive to Greenbrier Marsh.

As they pulled out of the parking lot, Garland was true to his word. "I would first like to introduce my closest friend, and the smartest man I've ever known: Mr. Lavindra Padmini. I think you might have received a poor first impression of him.

142

He is originally from Sri Lanka and is the world's foremost expert on the writings of James Boswell." Lavindra turned briefly and smiled at Lucius and Dolores who were seated in the back.

"Next, we have Ms. Dolores Martinez, a young idealistic attorney. Her companion is Lucius Dixon. He is only a law student but has helped our cause immensely." Lucius wasn't sure that was true.

They drove for about fifteen minutes with Garland giving directions to Lavindra. Finally, they pulled into what appeared to be a park. They drove past a few picnic tables and pulled up beside a piece of swampy terrain.

"Luke, would you mind helping Lavindra once more?" Lucius nodded in agreement. The whole night had been so strange that he really didn't know what else to do.

The two of them emerged from the car. Before he opened the back of the SUV, Lavindra spoke. "I'm sorry that you've been dragged into this, Mr. Dixon. Hopefully it will all be over soon."

Lavindra then opened the back, and the two of them lifted Cole's body out of the back. It seemed heavier. They carried the body about thirty feet, and Lavindra took a couple of steps into the swampy water. They then swung the body back and forth and tossed it into the swamp. They both stood there and watched as the body slowly sank.

It was only as Cole's face disappeared into the murk that Lucius started thinking about the implications of this. Did this mean that Cole was the murderer of Sandberg? How did it all tie in with the other Ramsdens? And what about Robert? He had trusted Cole. Is that why he was missing? Had Cole killed him, too?

After the body had completely disappeared into the marsh, Lavindra motioned for Lucius to get back into the vehicle. He did so, and the odd group began their slow drive back toward Lucius' apartment.

They drove in silence until Garland said, "Luke, could you hand me the duffel bag that is sitting next to you."

Lucius picked up the bag and handed it to Garland. He opened the bag and pulled out a poorly bound manuscript. He

143

handed it to Lucius. "Ms. Martinez said that you were interested in knowing what's going on. Well, it's all in there."

Lucius looked down at the manuscript. As his eyes began to adjust to the darkness, the title slowly came into view: The Secret History of the Ramsden Family.

"You can keep that copy, but you are the only person who is allowed to see it. Keep it hidden whenever you aren't reading it."

"I will, sir, but what is it exactly?"

"It's the history of my family from late in the 17th century until today. I'm quite sure that all of this will make more sense when you've had a chance to digest it all."

When they arrived back at the apartment, Garland turned and spoke to Dolores and Lucius. "Go on inside. Lavindra and I are going to check out Mr. Coleman's car, and then we'll come in for a moment."

Lucius and Dolores got out of the car and walked to the apartment. Lucius unlocked it, and they went inside. He turned on some lights, and the two of them sat down on the couch in the living room. Lucius looked down at the manuscript he was carrying. He wanted to open it immediately, but he thought he should wait.

"Luke, I'm sorry about all of this. You've been wonderful, but I feel like I've asked too much of you."

Lucius tried to add a little levity. "Well, you've certainly made my 1L year much more exciting than I had originally thought it would be."

Dolores smiled. "You're a wonderful person, Luke. Anyone else would have lost patience with me a long time ago."

A knock on the door interrupted the conversation. Lucius got up from the couch and unlocked the door. Garland and Lavindra entered, and he closed and locked the door behind them.

Lavindra began, "A quick search of the car revealed a few things. First, there is a printed e-mail from an anonymous sender. It gives the details of Ms. Martinez's flight. This means that Coleman was tracking you, not Mr. Dixon. He probably only found out about Mr. Dixon's involvement when you got in the car with him."

144

Garland interrupted, "We also found Mr. Coleman's cell phone. He has made no calls in the last six hours. What that probably means is that Mr. Dixon is still an unknown as far as the Ramsdens are concerned. I will put out some feelers in the next few weeks, but I think you can both feel safe here at this apartment."

Lavindra continued, "We also found this piece of paper." He handed it to Lucius.

The paper said, "Sandberg's House, Parker's Economics of Tort Actions." It was in Robert's handwriting.

Lucius struggled to speak, "This is Robert's handwriting. Cole took this from Robert."

Garland saw the pain in Lucius' eyes. "I'm sorry, Mr. Dixon."

"Did Cole kill Sandberg?"

"I don't know."

In the span of an hour, Garland and Lavindra excused themselves, promising to be back in a few weeks, and Martinez went to bed. Lucius had forced her to take the bed, while he slept on the couch.

His mind kept going back to Robert. It was Lucius' fault that this had to happen. He was the one who had gotten Robert mixed up in this whole thing. He had to hope that Robert was still alive. Maybe he had simply given the piece of paper to Cole before he left for New York. Lucius had to hold out hope. He couldn't handle the alternative. As he looked around the room, his eyes fell on the manuscript.

He picked it up and turned it over in his hands. Finally, he opened it to the first page.

Chapter 1: The Brothers

Cecily Leeds was born in a small village in North Yorkshire called Pateley Bridge in the year 1680. Her family was poor, and she was a sickly child. When she was just a teenager, she fell in love with Rowland Ramsden. They spent nearly all of their time together and were married when Cecily turned eighteen.

Only one month later, Rowland died in an apparent mining accident. Five months later, Cecily gave birth to twin sons: Ambrose and Solomon. They were trouble from the very beginning with the birth nearly killing Cecily. She died just a few months later. Her obituary lists her cause of death as grief.

The two boys grew up together in orphanages throughout England. They were kept together but continually moved. When they turned eighteen, they both enlisted in the Royal Navy and were shipped out to America.

They were nearly kicked out of the navy a few times. They were constantly causing problems with Ambrose being the primary instigator. They soon found themselves under the command of Robert Maynard who was famous for dealing harshly with troublemakers. They worked aboard the HMS Pearl for six months until the fateful day of November 19, 1718.

On that day, the two brothers were put on the HMS Ranger in Hampton, Virginia. The boat had been commissioned into the Royal Navy, and the rumor that was swirling among the men was that they were going after Blackbeard, the pirate.

Ambrose writes in his diary that November 19th was the day that his life became meaningful.

Three days later, the ships came upon Blackbeard's ship, The Adventure, anchored on the inner side of Ocracoke Island off the coast of North Carolina. Blackbeard tried to run, but Maynard stayed with him. Maynard told the men on the HMS Ranger to go below into the holds, so that Blackbeard would think that there weren't many men on the boat. Both Ambrose and Solomon went below the deck.

After what seemed like hours, the men heard noises above and ran toward the deck. Blackbeard and his men were boarding the Ranger. Ambrose describes Blackbeard in his diary in much the same way as he has been described in lore. His beard was on fire, and he fought with the strength of several men.

After a few minutes of fighting, Blackbeard and Maynard faced off against each other. Blackbeard wounded Maynard with his sword and closed in for the kill. Solomon Ramsden, who had come to develop a great deal of respect for his captain, tried to intervene. He had a broadsword that he had taken from a dead Highlander, and he charged Blackbeard and managed to cut him in the confusion.

Blackbeard tossed Solomon aside, but the moment's distraction allowed Maynard to reach for his pistol, and he shot Blackbeard in the shoulder. Blackbeard continued to fight. More of Maynard's men charged him, and he flung them aside. He was losing blood at an incredible rate. The deck of the ship was wet with his blood.

Blackbeard knocked Maynard to the ground and pulled out his pistol. Another intervention by Solomon caused Blackbeard's shot to miss. He brought the pistol down hard on Solomon's head and knocked him unconscious. He began to reload his pistol in the midst of the battle. Ambrose could only look on in horror. He was too frightened to make a move to try to save his brother's life.

Before Blackbeard could finish reloading his pistol, the blood loss was finally too much for him. He fell to the deck dead.

"Luke?"

Lucius was startled by the sudden interruption. He turned and saw Dolores entering the room wearing the blanket from his bed. "Dolores. Sorry, you scared me."

"I'm sorry. I didn't mean to. I was just having a little trouble sleeping. How's the book?" She sat down on the couch beside him.

"It's not bad. I'm still completely confused. Have you read this before?"

"I've read parts of it. Garland has told me about most of it, though. It will all start to make sense soon."

Lucius smiled. "I hope so because right now this book is telling me about things that were happening three-hundred years ago."

"The funny thing is that what we're fighting over actually goes back three-hundred years. I just want you to know, Lucius, that we're on the right side. What we're doing does have a purpose. I know you think your friend Robert is dead. If he is dead, he didn't die in vain. We're going to finish this together." She put her hand on Lucius' shoulder.

Lucius didn't say anything. His eyes filled with tears as he thought about Robert.

"It'll be okay, Luke. We're going to get through this."

His mystery woman squeezed his shoulder firmly before getting up from the couch and going back into the bedroom. "Try to get some sleep yourself. You've got to start class again soon."

Lucius sat perfectly still for a few minutes. He would help Dolores to finish this, whatever that entailed.

He picked up the manuscript again, found his place, and continued reading.

> The fight stopped almost immediately
> when Blackbeard hit the ground. The few of his
> men that remained alive dropped their weapons
> and surrendered. Ambrose ran to his brother and
> managed to wake him. The two brothers
> embraced as Maynard approached them.
> He thanked Solomon for saving his life
> and told him that he would be recommended for

a medal for his service. Maynard then took Solomon's broadsword and used it to cut off Blackbeard's head which he hung from the bow.

The men were sent in to Ocracoke Island where they were to spend the night. At about two o'clock in the morning, Ambrose woke his brother up.

"There's treasure on that ship. Blackbeard had more treasure than any pirate ever had."

Solomon just wanted to go back to sleep. He told Ambrose that even if there were treasure aboard, it did not belong to them. Ambrose wouldn't give up. He told Solomon that he had a rowboat that they could use to get out to Blackbeard's ship. Everyone was asleep, so they could look around without having to worry about getting caught.

Solomon finally gave in, and the two of them rowed out to the Adventure. They reached the ship and climbed aboard. They heard noises and Solomon tried to drag Ambrose back to their boat, but his brother wouldn't listen. A guard rounded the corner and asked them what they were doing.

Ambrose lied, "Lieutenant Maynard sent us to relieve you."

The guard didn't believe them and told them to go back to the island before they were disciplined. Solomon again tried to get his brother to go back, but Ambrose refused. He pulled out a knife and charged the guard. Before either Solomon or the guard could react, Ambrose was on top of him and had cut his throat.

Solomon was shocked. He screamed at Ambrose, but Ambrose ignored him, focusing his attention on throwing the guard's body overboard. He then told Solomon that they had the ship to themselves, and he went below deck.

Solomon followed him, trying to talk reason into him. Ambrose quickly found the captain's quarters and began rummaging through the room's contents. Solomon followed him into the room but tripped and fell on a loose board. Ambrose spun around to look at the board. He pulled it up and revealed a large chest.

Ambrose pulled the chest up, expecting it to be full of gold and silver. Instead it was full of papers. Ambrose writes in his diary that he had no idea that those papers were worth far more than any gold or silver that could have fit into that chest.

Ambrose lit a candle to examine the papers and quickly realized that they were journals written by Blackbeard. They also contained detailed directions to the places where he had hidden the money and goods that he had taken over the years. Ambrose packed the journals back into the chest and asked Solomon to help him to carry the chest back to their rowboat.

Solomon, not knowing exactly what to do, decided to help his brother for now. The two of them carried the chest back onto the deck and found a rope, which they used to lower it down into their boat.

They rowed back to the island, but they did not go back to the other men. Ambrose talked his brother into deserting the navy. The two of them rowed to the other end of the island and slept for the night.

They waited a few days before leaving the island. They wanted to make sure that no one was looking for them. Ambrose was sure that no one would miss him. A lot of men had died in the fight, and no one would be entirely sure if he was among the living or the dead, but his brother had received that compliment from the captain. Half the navy knew that he was still alive.

The days went by slowly. They didn't have any food or fresh water, and they were afraid to venture far from the camp for fear of being seen. Ambrose managed to find a spring, and that kept them alive for the few days until their hunger became too overwhelming. They decided to head ashore in their rowboat. They hoped that the Royal Navy was long gone.

They came ashore in the town of Kill Devil Hills. They rented a room under fake names and ate their fill of food with the modest wages that they had from their time with the navy. Ambrose spent hours poring through the journals, while Solomon spent hours lamenting what they had done.

A merchant who came through town a few weeks later brought with him word that Blackbeard's skull had been placed atop a totem near Hampton, Virginia to warn all those who were tempted to break the law.

That night Ambrose began trying to convince Solomon to go with him to Hampton to get the skull. Solomon couldn't understand why Ambrose wanted it. Ambrose tried to explain that they were the keepers of Blackbeard's legacy and that the skull was their rightful property.

Solomon called him crazy and told him that he was going to turn himself in. Ambrose stabbed Solomon in the back and pulled his body back into the room. He covered the body with sheets and put it in one of the beds. He then packed up his things and carried the chest by himself down the stairs.

He departed from the inn and went to Hampton, Virginia, where he set up in another inn with another fake name. He spent a couple of days looking around town for the skull. Finally, he heard a rumor that it was being kept at the spot where the Hampton and James Rivers ran together. The very next night he set out to retrieve it.

The skull was guarded, but Ambrose was not going to let that stop him. He knocked the guard unconscious and took the skull. When he got back to his room at the inn, he wrapped the skull in blankets and put it in the chest with Blackbeard's journals. He then pulled out several pages of the journal and began deciding which of Blackbeard's treasures he should seek out first.

In Ambrose's diary, he says that he was visited by Solomon's ghost that night. The ghost told Ambrose that he would never forget what had happened, and that he would haunt him and his family for the rest of time. Ambrose says that these dreams became more frequent as he got older.

Ambrose moved about on the coast for nearly a year. He became famous in those parts. He was known as the Hunchback of Carolina because he always carried that chest with him wherever he went. Rumors circulated everywhere he went about its contents, but none of the rumors were as outlandish as the truth.

He quickly ran out of money and was forced to take up various jobs. He worked as a blacksmith and as a doctor's assistant. After several months of this, he finally felt confident enough in the location of one of Blackbeard's treasures.

The treasure was hidden right outside the town of Bath, North Carolina. Ambrose hired a local to help him, and the two of them set out to look for the treasure. They followed directions that Ambrose had copied out of one of the journals. They found the peninsula that stuck out between two marshes, and they found the forked tree under which the treasure was supposedly hidden.

Ambrose made his new companion do all of the digging. After several hours of digging, the shovel struck something hard. Ambrose pushed his companion aside and dug around the box. He pulled it out and opened it to reveal that it was filled with bottles. Inside some of the bottles were pills and inside other bottles was some sort of syrup.

Ambrose's companion cursed him for wasting their time. As the companion walked away, Ambrose shot him in the back and threw his body into the marsh. Ambrose took the pills and syrup back to the doctor for whom he had worked. The doctor identified the pills and syrup as being medicines made from mercury.

The doctor was willing to purchase the medicine for a hefty sum, and Ambrose made the deal. The money was enough for him to buy a small house outside of Norfolk, Virginia.

This was the beginning of the Ramsden fortune. The Ramsden's money has always been blood money.

Chapter Seventeen

It was nearly four o'clock in the morning when Lucius put down the book after finishing the first chapter. He was hungry.

As he entered the kitchen, his mind wandered back to the contents of the manuscript. Was the story true? What motivation would Garland Ramsden have for making it all up? Perhaps he was jealous of his brother, the Senator. If it were true, how did it tie in to what was going on now?

Lucius pulled out a loaf of bread and some sliced turkey. He tried to remember the cases that he had read all of those months ago. One of them had been about a soldier, and they both had been really old. Maybe they had something to do with the actions of Ambrose Ramsden three centuries ago. But surely nothing he had done back then could really create legal problems for the family now.

Lucius finished making his sandwiches and walked back into the living room. He opened the manuscript and continued reading as he ate.

Chapter 2: The Succession

Ambrose Ramsden spent the next few years amassing a great fortune. He found no more medicine. He found gold, silver, artifacts, and historical papers. Most of it was sold; some of it he kept.

He occasionally hired assistants to help him to find the treasure. He would pick from the dregs of society, pay them only a small amount, and treat them brutally. None would dare turn on him. He was feared by all.

About a year after the theft of Blackbeard's journals, Ambrose began going by his real name. The authorities quickly tracked him down to ask him some questions about his brother whose body they had identified. According to Ambrose's diary, he paid them to arrest one of his former assistants. That assistant was tried and hung; his comments about Ambrose's wickedness were ignored by the masses that came to watch his execution.

A few months later, Ambrose's eccentricities began to take over. He had Blackbeard's skull hollowed out. He then commissioned a local silversmith to coat the skull in silver and engrave "Deth to Spotswoode" on it. Governor Alexander Spotswood had been the governor who instructed Robert Maynard to hunt down and kill Blackbeard. Ambrose began using the skull as a cup for drinking rum.

It was during this period that Ambrose met his wife. She was a German girl named Millicent Gebauer. She was sixteen years old when they first met. Ambrose was a disgusting character at this point. He was known throughout the town for swearing at children and directing lewd comments toward all of the women, but everyone was too afraid of him to say anything. Rumors abounded that Ambrose was a dangerous pirate or that he had connections to dangerous pirates.

Despite her apparent horror at the proposition, Ambrose began courting Millicent. He would bring her flowers and read to her from poetry books. He also gave money to her father who needed every penny of it to stay afloat. Millicent eventually consented to Ambrose's marriage proposal. She never had any affection for him, but she felt that she had to do it to help her father.

Ambrose did not allow her to leave the house after the marriage. She was told that it was her job to provide a male heir for the family fortune. Once she asked Ambrose about that fortune...about where the money came from. He did not lay a hand on her but lashed her so badly with his tongue that she dared not ask again.

After three years of marriage, Millicent provided Ambrose with a male heir. Ambrose named him Cassius. Ambrose spoiled the child, while his wife suffered from an illness. Millicent died three years after giving birth to Cassius.

A crash of thunder brought Lucius out of the book. The soft patter of rain escalated into a roaring storm. The lights flickered but remained on.

Lucius crumpled the paper towel that had held his sandwiches and went to the kitchen. He threw the paper towel into the trash can and pulled a soda out of the refrigerator. The Ambrose Ramsden described in the manuscript seemed too evil to be real. He seemed like a villain from a bad movie.

Lucius knew that he needed sleep, but he was too enthralled by the manuscript. At least two people had died in the last year, and if Garland was to be believed, both of their deaths had something to do with the contents of this book. Lucius returned to the couch, found his place in the book, and continued.

With Millicent gone, Ambrose took complete control of young Cassius' education. He taught him the math and science that was taught in school, but he taught him history in a very different way.

Ambrose explained to the young boy that he was not allowed to associate with any of the other young people in the town. He told him that the rest of the town hated them because they were friends of the pirates. He told his son that Blackbeard had been a great hero who had tried to bring tax-free goods into America to help those who couldn't afford them. He told his son that the people of this town and others had been jealous of Blackbeard's virtue.

Young Cassius loved the stories. He asked for more every night. Ambrose told him that even he and his brother had been tricked into fighting against Blackbeard. He told his son how his own brother Solomon had helped to kill Blackbeard and how Ambrose had been forced to kill Solomon for his crimes.

When Cassius reached the age of twelve, Ambrose began taking his son with him on treasure hunts. Cassius' first successful treasure hunt happened when he was fifteen. The treasure was located under a tree on the island of New Providence in the Bahamas. It was a chest filled with rum and weapons.

Cassius asked for an explanation. How did his father know where the chest would be buried? Ambrose refused to tell him then. He said that the rest of the secrets would be revealed when Cassius turned eighteen.

The next few years were filled with nightmares for Ambrose. He was haunted by the ghosts of Solomon and Millicent. Millicent blamed him for her death, and Solomon swore that Ambrose's own death would be far worse then either of theirs. These nightmares only increased the vile that Ambrose spilled to his son about the two of them. He told Cassius that Millicent was an evil woman who had constantly wanted to abandon the two of them.

Cassius would later write that his father would wake up screaming in the middle of the night. He would scream the name of his brother. Sometimes he would scream for

157

Blackbeard to save him from their wickedness. Ambrose often brought priests into the house to get rid of the evil spirits. He stopped leaving the house, preferring to send others into town to get food and clothing for him and his son.

When Cassius reached the age of eighteen, Ambrose told him everything. He gave him a copy of his diary...the very diary that was used as a source in creating this manuscript. He told him to read it and to try not to judge his father too harshly.

The diary only gave the son more respect for his father. All of the evil deeds that Ambrose had done were explained away by the stories that Cassius had been taught as a child. These were the people who had killed Blackbeard. His father was only trying to keep the legacy of that great man alive.

Even though he was not yet fifty, Ambrose was a very sick man. He began to spend more and more time in bed. He handed the journals over to Cassius with the promise that he would not reveal the secrets to anyone other than his own son. Cassius gave his word.

Cassius began seeking the remaining treasures on his own. His success rate was even greater than his father's, and their fortune soon grew mountainous.

It was upon returning from an unsuccessful excursion to Oak Island off the coast of Nova Scotia that Cassius found his father lying dead on the floor of his bedroom. His eyes were wide open, and he was clutching the sheets from the bed. A knife lay at his side, but there were no wounds on him.

Cassius Ramsden became the bearer of the secret.

Lucius had reached the end of the second chapter. He put the book down.

It was all a little much for him to handle. He had expected to uncover some sort of secret, but not anything like this. He expected the secret to involve insider trading or corporate corruption, not pirates and murders from three-hundred years ago. He had no reason to trust the author of the book, Garland Ramsden, but he still trusted Dolores. She believed the manuscript to be true, and she didn't seem particularly gullible.

He wanted to wake her up. He wanted to ask her to explain everything to him, but he restrained himself. He had come a long way, and he would figure the rest of it out in time.

Lucius thought about Robert. He held back a laugh, trying to imagine the looks on the faces of Detectives Snow and Torro if he tried to explain that Robert's disappearance and Sandberg's murder had something to do with Blackbeard and the ancestors of Senator Wilfred Ramsden.

But his friend was either dead or missing, and there had to be some sort of explanation. There also had to be an explanation for why Cole had tried to kill them, and for why Cole or someone else had killed Sandberg. The cover-up of an ancient family secret seemed as good of an explanation as anything he could come up with at the moment.

Lucius walked back to the couch and sat down. He grabbed a blanket that was lying on the nearby chair and put it behind his head. His mind was racing, but his physical exhaustion soon caught up with him. He fell asleep with thoughts of pirates in his head.

He woke up to the smell of coffee coming from the kitchen.

"Dolores?"

She emerged from the kitchen. "Yes?"

"Did you leave the house to get coffee?"

"No, you had some in the cabinet above the refrigerator, along with a coffee maker."

Lucius remembered, "Oh, yeah. Jennifer left that here when she and Robert stayed overnight."

Dolores walked back into the kitchen. "Who was Jennifer?"

"She was the other friend who helped when we were investigating you and Sandberg. She transferred to Columbia."

Dolores smiled. "When my coffee's done, I want to hear all about that investigation."

"I'd like to ask you some questions first about that book."

"Yeah, sure. What do you want to know?"

There were too many questions. "Is it true?"

Dolores came out of the kitchen again. "Luke, I know it sounds crazy, but that book is completely true. Garland is an expert on colonial history. He got his information from the local history of that area, as well as from the actual diaries of Ambrose and Cassius Ramsden."

"What does it all have to do with the research that you and Sandberg were doing?"

The coffee maker beeped from the kitchen. "Hold on a second, Luke."

Lucius could hear her pouring the coffee from the other room. She came back into the room and sat down beside him, placing her coffee on the end table.

"All right, Luke, let me explain. The journals of Blackbeard are still around. The Ramsdens have passed them down through the generations. We thought that we could bring a law suit to force them to release the journals because they are stolen. We thought that there was a possibility that we could force them to give up their money because it was also stolen, but even if we couldn't, the release of the journals would expose the truth behind their money."

Winning such a law suit didn't seem possible to Lucius. "In my Property class, we learned about adverse possession. After a while of living on someone else's property without being thrown out, ownership is transferred to the adverse possessor. So wouldn't the Ramsdens own the journals now? Isn't it too late for all of this?"

"What kind of grade did you get in Property?"

"I got a B."

"Well, I'm surprised you did that well. Adverse possession applies only to real property, not to personal property. You can't adversely possess personal property."

160

"So who would the journals belong to?"

"The British government. Spoils of war belong to the government, and Ambrose Ramsden was employed by the Royal Navy when he stole the journals."

"So you think you could have won the case?"

"If we could have found a court that would have believed our facts, we would have had a good chance."

"Well, there's still a chance of recovering the research."

"It's possible. Leeder & Schrum are probably keeping it, in case we finally decide to bring the case."

"So are we still planning to bring the case?"

"Maybe. We'll have to talk to Garland. He's the funding and the planning behind this whole operation."

"Why is he trying to destroy the reputation of his own family?"

"He has a lot of guilt about the whole situation. He feels like all of the advantages that he has had in life are directly due to all of the evil acts performed by his family throughout their history in America."

Lucius had so many things he wanted to ask. "So all of this really begins with Blackbeard, the pirate?"

Dolores smiled. "Yes, the whole thing goes back to Blackbeard. I know it sounds a little crazy. I had to do a lot of research myself before I believed it. Daniel...Daniel Sandberg didn't believe the story when he first heard it either."

"How do you know it's true? How do you know that Garland isn't making the whole thing up?"

"I've seen copies of Ambrose Ramsden's diary, as well as copies of newspapers from that era."

"But the diary could be faked...so could the newspapers."

"The newspapers aren't fake. I went to libraries in North Carolina and Virginia to find copies of them myself. The diary could be fake, but it certainly seemed real. And did you notice how hard the Ramsdens came down on us when they thought we were going to expose them?"

"Maybe Garland set you up."

"What would his motivation be for that, Luke?"

"I don't know. Maybe he wants to use the research for something else...something bad, so he concocted this story to get you to do the research for him. Then he hired people to kill you."

"Couldn't he have come up with something a little more believable? And why would he have saved us last night?"

Lucius hesitated. Maybe it was true after all. Strange things happen all the time. Maybe this was just one of those strange things.

Dolores spoke up again. "So why don't you tell me about the adventures of Luke, Robert, and Jennifer from last year? How did you find out about what Daniel and I were doing?"

"Do you really want to hear all of that?"

"Yeah, I do. I told you about our research and how it tied into Blackbeard, the pirate. It's the least you can do."

"So I was up studying late one night, when I bumped into you. You dropped a white card, which I later found out to be a key to the library. I saw you again later going into the library, so we staked out the library."

Dolores interjected, "At some point, the librarian told me that you were asking questions about me. I told Daniel, and he called you into the office. He said he tried to scare you off, and he thought he had succeeded."

"Yeah, he did scare me for a while, but my curiosity got the best of me. I ended up pretending to sleep in the library and waiting for you to come in. I then followed you to see what you were doing. The second time I did it, you caught me. You even kicked me."

Dolores laughed. "I remember that. That was you?"

"Yeah, you kicked me pretty hard. The whole time I was doing all of this sneaking around, Robert and I were doing research on the Internet."

"What did you find out?"

"We researched Sandberg and you. We found out that you worked at Leeder & Schrum together."

"That's pretty impressive. Go on."

"We even hacked into Sandberg's instant messenger account to get whatever information you were sending out. We got a couple of cases and tried to figure out what we could from them."

"So why did you finally confront me?"

"Robert was becoming obsessed with the whole thing. He wasn't spending any time studying, and I was worried about him."

"Well, now I'm happier than ever that I brought you into this whole thing. You're much more resourceful than you look."

Lucius laughed.

Dolores finished her coffee and took it back into the kitchen.

A sudden knock resounded from the door. Lucius walked slowly and silently over to the door. Dolores leaned out from the kitchen.

Lucius looked out the peephole. It was Detective Torro.

Chapter Eighteen

Lucius turned to Dolores and signaled for her to go into the bedroom. She did so quietly, and he opened the front door.

"Hello, Mr. Dixon. I won't keep you long."

Detective Torro refused Lucius' offer to come inside.

"What can I help you with?"

Detective Torro reached into his pocket and pulled out a stack of photos wrapped with a rubber band. He peeled off the first photo and handed it to Lucius. It was a photo of Dolores Martinez.

"I want you to tell me if you've ever seen this woman."

Lucius hesitated. Had they seen him with her last night? Had they followed her off the plane? She had been sure that no one had followed her, but she had already been wrong about that once. Nonetheless, he had already come too far. "I'm pretty sure I've never seen her."

Detective Torro sighed. "Well, this is pretty serious. We now have concrete evidence that she was the one who killed Daniel Sandberg. They were having an extramarital affair, and she killed him because he wanted to end it. Not only that, we think she may have been involved in other murders."

"What sort of evidence do you have?"

"We have an eyewitness report that puts her near the office at the time of the murder. Her fingerprints were also found on the door to the safe in the office. We believe that something was taken from that safe."

Lucius hesitated again. He could end this all right now. All he had to do was to tell Detective Torro that Dolores was in his bedroom. "Okay, well...I'll let you know if I hear or see anything."

"Thank you, Mr. Dixon. This is very important, so keep your eyes open. She might think that you saw her because you discovered the murder scene. If she does, she will not hesitate to kill you. Be careful."

This all seemed very unprofessional. Why was Detective Torro telling him this? "Thank you, sir. Where is Detective Snow today?"

"She's been taken off the case. It's all on me now."

Detective Torro turned to leave, and Lucius closed the door behind him. He immediately began to question his own judgment. Maybe he shouldn't trust Dolores after all.

Lucius walked back to his bedroom, but Dolores was nowhere in sight. After a moment, she emerged from his closet.

"Who was it?"

"It was the detective in charge of Sandberg's murder case."

"What did he want?"

"He wanted to find you. He said you killed Sandberg, and possibly others."

"That figures. With the real murderer sinking to the bottom of a swamp, we may have to expose corruption in the police force while we're busy exposing a three-hundred year old pirate mystery."

"This is serious, Dolores. They think you did it."

Dolores looked at him hard. "I told you they would blame this on me. The Ramsdens have been doing this kind of thing for centuries. They're good at it."

Lucius remembered the story from the second chapter of Garland's book. Ambrose Ramsden had blamed his brother's murder on someone else by paying off the police. "This is the twenty-first century, Dolores. You can't make the police go after someone by throwing money at them."

"Yes, you can, Luke. This is a powerful family."

"Why wouldn't the attorney general or the police department go after the family?"

"Because they either have no evidence to go after them, or they are on the Ramsden payroll."

"I just find this all a little hard to believe. Putting it on top of a ridiculous pirate story doesn't make it any easier."

Dolores was angry. "What do you think happened, Luke? What do you think is going on?"

"I'm not sure Dolores. Maybe you did it."

"Then who was the guy with the gun pointed in your face last night."

"Lindsey Coleman, who was trying to solve the murder. Maybe he figured out that it was you and planned to punish you himself."

"He was going to kill you also."

"We don't know that."

"He said something about how he was sorry to do this, but that you had gotten mixed up with the wrong people."

"Maybe he was apologizing for killing you in front of me. And maybe you were the wrong people that he was referring to."

"That doesn't make sense, Luke."

"It makes just as much sense as the story you are trying to tell me."

"Maybe Lindsey Coleman killed Sandberg and your friend Robert on orders from the Ramsdens. And maybe he was going to kill us until Garland and Lavindra intervened."

"Maybe. Honestly, I don't know what to think."

"Why would Garland Ramsden, a world-renowned expert on colonial history be saving our lives?"

Lucius walked out of the room, saying over his shoulder, "Maybe he's the one having the affair with you now." He felt bad about it as soon as he said it.

"You don't know who your friends are, Luke." Dolores shut the bedroom door hard behind him.

Lucius walked back into the living room. His eyes again were drawn to the manuscript sitting on the coffee table. He picked it up and started the third chapter.

Chapter 3: The Blind Genius

Cassius Ramsden was a very talented financier. He turned the fortune that his father had given him into the largest fortune in Virginia.

He started exporting businesses in Norfolk and the nearby towns. He purchased a few local stores which eventually became the dominant stores in the area. No rivals could compete.

He put his money into the burgeoning banking industry. This was before the United States of America was an independent country. Businesses were getting off the ground and expanding rapidly. Cassius Ramsden had his money in all of them.

His treasure-hunting methods had changed as well. He began hiring private hunters to seek out the treasure. He paid them well. He would sometimes accompany them on their hunts, but usually he would remain at home, trusting that they would bring him whatever they found. He began to keep some of the items for himself. He kept letters and books, as well as a painting or two.

He also began to earn respect in the town of Norfolk. His father Ambrose had been feared, but not respected. The people of the town left him alone and avoided asking too many questions, but that was only because many believed the stories of his connections to pirates. Cassius developed a much better reputation.

He became more active in community events. He came out of the rapidly expanding estate on the hill to meet the townsfolk. He engaged in conversations on the street with passers by.

Cassius also worked to remove the pirate-loving reputation that the family had developed in his father's time. He denied all of the rumors about the family having ties to pirates. He painted a picture of his father as a devoted researcher, who had made his money in the newspaper business back in England.

In the year 1765, Cassius Ramsden was elected to public office. It was a minor office, but it was an impressive feat considering the reputation that his father had left in the community. He changed all of that in one generation.

Cassius forgave the people of Norfolk for the way they had treated his father. He still believed his father's stories about the goodness of the pirates. He still believed that the townsfolk had been jealous of Blackbeard, and he still believed that his family was mistreated because of their dealings with the pirates.

Despite all of that, Cassius thought that the family would do better if they tried to move on...to forgive and forget. Eventually, remaining apart from the rest of the town would catch up with them. So even though Cassius still held a grudge against the townsfolk, he did not reveal that grudge with his actions.

He became active in the church, and it was there that he met his wife, Louise Huntington. She was widely considered to be the most beautiful woman in Norfolk. Her family was also very wealthy, and she was famous in the social scene. Cassius' marriage to her did even more to improve his family's reputation. Soon the town had almost completely forgiven Cassius for the actions of his father.

Louise gave him four sons: Geoffrey, Gerald, Gerard, and Godfrey. They were each born less than one year after the previous one. There is nothing in any of the journals of Cassius to indicate why he gave them all names that began with the letter G.

The sons were treated well. They weren't spoiled, and they were allowed to go to school with the other children.

Louise was also treated well by all indications. She was Cassius' princess, and he treated her like one. She was not forced to do any housework, and Cassius allowed her to continue to participate in the social functions that she enjoyed so much.

Cassius did not, however, let his wife in on the secret of their wealth. To her he told the same thing that he told to the rest of the people in the town. His father had made his money in the newspaper business while in England. He stayed involved while in the colonies, and Cassius had no idea where the pirate rumors had come from.

The Ramsdens' wealth continued to grow. The investments really began to pay off. Cassius lived through the American Revolution. All four of his sons fought in that war, and all four returned home safely.

Cassius was very proud of his sons. What he did not know was how his sons would react to the truth about their wealth. He did not tell any of them on their eighteenth birthdays. He wondered in his journals if he should tell all of them, or only one. He felt that they were all very close and could maintain the secret as a group, but he worried that he overestimated his sons.

Finally, the day came when he had to make a decision. He was old and sick. He didn't have long to live.

Cassius brought all four of his sons into the office that he had added to the house. It was from there that he had managed the family's wealth.

He told them the truth about the family's fortune. He told them about his father stealing the journals from Blackbeard's ship. He told them about their evil great-uncle Solomon Ramsden who had tried to betray the family. He told them about how Ambrose had been forced to kill Solomon. He told them that the murder had haunted Ambrose for the rest of his life.

The entire story was presented to the sons, who remained attentive throughout. Cassius felt that everything must be told. He then gave his sons the diary of his father, and the journals of Blackbeard. He also gave them the sporadic journals that he had written throughout his own life.

His final direction to his sons was to stop the family's practice of writing things down. He said that they should keep these written documents and pass them on to the next generation, but that they should not write diaries or journals of their own. He told them to not repeat the story to anyone.

The only person who was ever to be told was Geoffrey's eldest son, Geoffrey being the eldest son of Cassius.

The trouble began as soon as Cassius uttered these words. The other brothers immediately wanted to know why they could not pass the information on to their own sons.

The fights that arose were described in the last few journals that Cassius ever wrote. They were continuous and brutal. The other sons were jealous of Geoffrey. Geoffrey tried to quell their jealousy by promising to ask his son to continue to share any money made from the journals of Blackbeard with their sons. The other brothers would not listen.

Cassius tried to explain to his sons that the wealth of the family would be split up evenly among them and their families, but this did nothing to lessen the jealousy.

Cassius died a sad man in the year 1790. He probably knew that he was the only person preventing his sons from literally going for one another's throats. He probably knew that things would only get worse. After his death, the arguments turned violent.

The sons followed their father's advice on the subject of not writing anything down. They did not follow their father's advice on anything else.

Newspaper accounts are useful in recreating the events of the next few years. What is clear is that the youngest brother Godfrey killed the oldest brother Geoffrey in a bar fight. He stabbed Geoffrey multiple times and was arrested on the scene.

The accounts differ as to the motivation. Some suggest that there was a woman involved. Some suggest that the fight was over their inheritance. Anyone who has read the journals of Cassius Ramsden knows the real reason. Godfrey killed Geoffrey out of jealousy.

Godfrey was quickly convicted and hung. There is no record of Godfrey attempting to reveal the secret before his execution. The whole thing was taken care of very quietly. The people of the town remembered Cassius fondly and wanted all of this trouble to go away very quickly.

The trouble did not go away so easily, however. Cassius had not left a solution for a situation in which Geoffrey died childless. Gerald and Gerard were left to handle the situation themselves.

Very public arguments and fights were recorded in the local newspaper. The argument finally ended when Gerald seemingly left town. The reason for his departure was not known, but the suspicion was that he left to avoid another murder.

Other accounts suspect that Gerald was murdered by his brother Gerard, who then created the story about his leaving town to avoid being charged with the murder.

Gerard was more like Ambrose than Cassius. He managed the fortune well, but he lost a lot of the good will obtained by his father.

Even though they had their failings, Cassius Ramsden and Solomon Ramsden were men of conscience. The family would never have another such patriarch.

Lucius put down the manuscript. It was all beginning to make sense. The family had passed down the secret for generations, protecting it through violence. Garland wanted to end all of the evil by exposing the family's secret.

But how had Garland found out about all of this? He was the younger brother of Wilfred. Had their father told both of them, in the same way that Cassius had told all four of his sons? Or had Garland sought out his own answers? Was that why he had become an expert on colonial history?

Lucius walked toward the bedroom and knocked on the door. Dolores opened the door.

"I'm sorry, Dolores."

"It's okay, Luke. I'm sorry I yelled at you."

"I believe you. I believe what Garland wrote."

"Why?"

"I'm not sure. I still think there are other explanations which make more sense, but I believe you."

Dolores smiled briefly. "Thank you, Luke."

"This is all very strange to me. You'll have to be patient."

"I know. I was in the same situation that you're in now. Daniel Sandberg came into my office one day about four years ago. He said to meet him after work at a coffee shop that we both frequented. He said that he had followed my career closely and had played a large part in bringing me to the firm."

"How long had you been at the firm at that point?"

"Not too long. I had worked on a couple of cases for Daniel, but I really hadn't done that much work. We met with Garland Ramsden at the coffee shop. They swore me to secrecy, and then they told me the story of the Ramsdens. They then told me how we could use our own abilities to bring the truth out. Sandberg said that we would be able to work on the project while at the firm, and that Garland would make sure we were compensated."

"What did you think?"

"I didn't know what to think. It was a definitely a fantastic story, but it was being told to me by two seemingly intelligent people. At first, I thought it was a test."

"A test?"

"I thought that maybe the firm was testing me to see how I would react. I considered telling someone else at the firm what had happened, but for whatever reason, I didn't. Instead, I started taking weekends off to drive to the libraries described to me by Garland. He told me where I could find newspapers confirming their story."

"At what point, did you decide that they were telling you the truth?"

"A few months later. I think it was the excitement of it all that finally brought me in. I had wanted to be a lawyer since I was a little girl, and the work that I was getting wasn't living up to the dreams I had about being a lawyer. There was a chance that the story was true, and that chance made it all worthwhile. And they weren't asking that much of me. All I had to do was a little extra research in my off-hours."

"Wasn't that unethical, though? Going behind your firm's back?"

"It was, particularly since the firm represented the very people we were going after. I stopped being a legitimate lawyer when I made the choice to follow Daniel and Garland."

"So when did you end up leaving the firm?"

"The firm found some of our research on Daniel's computer. We convinced them that it was for a pro bono client, but they still asked us to leave the firm. They said that all pro bono projects had to be approved by the firm."

"And Sandberg got a job at UVA?"

"Yeah, Leeder & Schrum didn't tell anyone what happened, so he was able to get another job. Garland said he would take care of us financially, so I just worked full time on

the research. We were almost done when someone at Leeder &
Schrum or one of the Ramsdens found out what we were doing
and Daniel was killed."

Lucius listened quietly and didn't say anything when she
finished. It had to be true. All of it had to be true.

The next few weeks went by quickly. Law school
started, and while Lucius had trouble concentrating in class, he
was enjoying his classes. Robert never showed up, and he only
occasionally talked to Jennifer on the phone. For the most part,
his two best friends were out of his life.

They had been replaced by Dolores. She rarely left the
apartment for fear of being seen, so they spent a lot of time
together. Lucius read several more chapters in the book. Gerard
Ramsden increased the family fortune even more on the backs of
slaves. The family used their money and power in immoral
ways, and they continued to pass the secret down through the
generations.

The calm was broken one day nearly a month after
Dolores' arrival when Lucius received a phone call.

It was a woman's voice. "Mr. Dixon, I am calling on
behalf of Leeder & Schrum. We enjoyed meeting you and
would like to offer you a job as a summer associate."

Chapter Nineteen

There was a long pause.

"Mr. Dixon, are you there?"

"Yes, I'm here. You just caught me a little off guard."

"Well, you have excellent credentials, and we know that you'll be getting many offers. We hope you'll consider us and let us know by the first of November."

"Thank you very much. I'll certainly consider it."

"Feel free to call me if you have any questions. My name is Tammy Hudson, and I am the recruiting coordinator at the firm."

"Thank you very much. I'm sure I'll have questions later."

"Goodbye, Mr. Dixon."

"Goodbye."

This was not a predicament that Lucius had expected to find himself in. Everyone at that firm had such impressive resumes that he felt certain his would not stack up. Maybe it didn't. Maybe they had finally figured out his involvement in all of this and wanted to bring him in just to get rid of him. If Dolores' descriptions of the firm were true, he should probably stay as far away from them as possible.

On the other hand, Lucius had chosen to forego the on-grounds interview process. It was through that process that most of the students found their jobs. Hundreds of firms from around the country would come to the law school and set up fifteen-minute interview segments with interested students.

Lucius had avoided signing up because he knew he would be too nervous to deal with the interview process. He had too much on his mind. He had planned to contact some of the firms later when things had settled down, but maybe now he didn't have to. After all, he had an offer from a really good firm.

Lucius got up off the couch and knocked on the door to his bedroom. It was nearly eleven o'clock in the morning on a Friday, and Dolores was still asleep, but he wanted to tell her about this.

After a few seconds, the door opened and Dolores emerged sleepily.

"What is it, Luke?"

"I'm sorry I woke you up, but I wanted to tell you something."

Dolores rubbed the sleep out of her eyes. "Okay, what is it?"

"Do you remember that I told you I interviewed with Leeder & Schrum this summer before you called me back?"

"Yes, I remember."

"Well, they just called me and made me an offer. They want me to be a summer associate."

Dolores did not hesitate. "You can't do it."

"I was thinking I might."

"No, Luke, this is serious. We need to talk to Garland immediately. We need to find out what they know about you."

"They don't know anything about me. You said so yourself."

"Then why did they make you an offer?"

"That's kind of insulting. I've got a pretty decent résumé."

Dolores huffed. "I wasn't trying to insult you, Luke. This just doesn't sound good."

"Well, let's talk to Garland about it. If I could get a job there, then I could get the research back."

"It's too risky. Have you forgotten your friend Robert so quickly?"

Lucius was annoyed that she had resorted to that tactic. "This doesn't have anything to do with Robert."

"Luke, let's just wait for Garland. We'll see what he says."

"Fine."

Lucius gave his cell phone to Dolores, and she made the call.

"Garland, this is Dolores. We need you to come by soon. I've got some important information for you."

Lucius could hear the voice on the other end, but he couldn't make out what he was saying.

"Okay, that sounds good. I'll tell Luke."

Dolores hung up the phone. Garland is coming over in just a few minutes. He'll call when he gets here."

The two sat on the couch in silence. In a few moments, the phone buzzed. Lucius answered, and Garland said he was coming in.

Lucius got up and answered the door, and Garland strode confidently into the room.

"Why aren't you in class, Luke?"

"I managed to arrange my schedule so that I didn't have to go in on Fridays.

"So what's so important that I had to come by right now?

Dolores looked at Lucius.

Lucius spoke confidently, "I interviewed with Leeder & Schrum this summer. They called this morning to offer me a job as a summer associate for next summer."

Garland looked down at the ground for a second before speaking. "I think you should certainly consider taking the job."

Dolores interrupted. "Garland! This is dangerous. Luke could get himself killed."

Garland's speech was measured. "If we get the research back and get it in the hands of our lawyer in England, can we win the case?"

"Maybe. Daniel thought that we had a chance to win."

"I'm an old man. I don't have much left. That 'maybe' means a lot to me."

"But what about Luke's safety?"

"First of all, Luke knows how to take care of himself. Second of all, I've told you that neither the Ramsdens nor Leeder & Schrum are aware of the part he is playing in all of this."

"How do you know that you're still in the loop, Garland? You didn't know that Daniel and I were targets until it was too late."

Garland seemed injured by the comment. "I told you I was sorry about that. There's nothing I can do to bring Daniel back. We now have to act so as to ensure that his death was not in vain...so as to ensure that all the people killed by my family did not die in vain."

"But Luke is just a kid. This isn't his fight."

Lucius was insulted. "I can take care of myself, Dolores, and this is my fight. These people killed my friend."

"There, you see, Dolores. Luke can help us."

Lucius didn't like having his decisions made for him. "I didn't say I'd do it. I need more information. I need something that will make me believe that all of the stuff in that book is true."

Garland looked thoughtful for a moment before speaking. "I can help you with that, young man. Do you have plans for next Friday?"

"No, sir."

"I want you to be here and awake next Friday at six o'clock in the morning."

"Why? What are you bringing me?"

"I suppose you'll find out next week."

Garland blew out of the room as easily as he had entered. Lucius locked the door behind him.

The next week went by slowly. Lucius tried to concentrate on law school, but he was having difficulty. Dolores was annoyed with him, and his own mind kept wandering to the coming Friday's surprise.

Lucius was taking four classes that semester: Antitrust, Corporations, Conflict of Laws, and Federal Income Tax. The reading was more difficult than it had been in previous semesters, and the material was drier. The good thing was that none of his professors called on students unless they raised their hands. It was a welcome relief for Lucius. He had had enough of cold calling.

He hadn't made any new friends, partly because he didn't hang around the law school very much. But there was also a part of Lucius that didn't want to make friends. He felt that he would only endanger them. He blamed himself for whatever had happened to Robert. If he hadn't seen Dolores that night in the library, Robert would still be alive today.

When Friday arrived, Lucius woke up early and showered. He waited impatiently by the door, his foot tapping out a constant beat.

At exactly six o'clock, there was a knock on the door. Lucius opened the door without looking through the peep hole.

It was Lavindra Padmini.

"Mr. Dixon, it's good to see you again."

"It's good to see you also."

"Are you ready?"

Lucius was confused. "Ready for what?"

"Garland didn't tell you?"

"No, he just told me that I would get some proof today. Did you bring it with you?"

"No. I'm taking you to the proof."

"What?"

"It's not that complicated. You and I are going on a road trip."

"What about Garland and Dolores?"

"Garland doesn't want to draw attention to you by accompanying you, and Dolores can't leave the apartment right now. Have you forgotten that the police are after her? It's okay, though. I'll let you pick the radio stations."

Lucius laughed. "Okay, I suppose I'm ready then. Let's go."

The two of them walked out to the parking lot. Lavindra identified a small blue car as his own, and they climbed inside.

"Where to?"

"We've got quite a drive ahead of us. We're heading for Ocracoke Island."

"What's at Ocracoke Island?"

"That's the island where Blackbeard was anchored when Robert Maynard and the two Ramsden brothers cornered him. That's also where the ship was when the Ramsden brothers broke into the captain's quarters and stole the journals of Blackbeard."

"What is there now?"

"They have some historical newspapers in a small library on that island."

"How long will it take us to get there?"

"I can get us there in six hours."

Lucius tried to make conversation. "So if I remember correctly, Mr. Ramsden said that you were an expert on James Boswell."

"That's correct."

"What's so interesting about James Boswell?"

"Well, he's mostly famous for his Life of Johnson. It's a biography of Samuel Johnson, who was himself a noted 18th Century British author. However, he also kept extensive journals which detailed his own life and his interactions with others. These weren't discovered until the 1920's. The fact of the matter is that Boswell is not particularly interesting, nor was he particularly smart. He even made horrible, uninformed pro-slavery statements."

"So why the attraction?"

"He had a talent for recognizing important things and writing them down. His own personality often disappears into his writings. He was a great biographer. The relationship between biography and identity is very important to me. "

The conversation continued for a while before shifting to the current situation.

"How did you get involved in all of this, Mr. Padmini?"

"All of what?"

"The Ramsdens, Leeder & Schrum, Blackbeard the pirate."

"Garland and I were professors at the University of Virginia together. We always got along well. One night nearly twenty years ago, we were talking in his office, and we started talking about our legacies. Neither of us were particularly productive writers, so we had no great works to leave behind. We then started talking about genealogy. He was working on his and was disturbed by some of the things he had found."

"Like what?"

"There was a lot of violence in his family tree. He told me about the odd way his father had treated his older brother.

Their father was always talking about Wilfred becoming the bearer of the family secret."

"So he didn't share the secret with Garland?"

"No, he was never told the secret. Their father successfully passed down the secret, as well as the journals of Ambrose and Cassius, to Wilfred."

"But Garland had to have gotten the journals of Cassius and Ambrose at some point? His manuscript relies very heavily on them."

"Garland and Wilfred had a younger sister, who was a bit of a socialite. She was also a heavy drinker and a very heavy gambler. She died at a young age, and Garland always suspected that his older brother Wilfred had killed her to avoid a family embarrassment. A few years after Garland and I had our conversation about legacies, Wilfred and his family went on vacation, and Garland went into their house. He was given a key by Wilfred in order to keep an eye on the place, so he didn't do anything illegal. He wanted to find proof that his brother had something to do with their sister's death. Instead, he broke into a locked closet behind the eldest son's bedroom and found the journals of Cassius and Ambrose."

"Did he steal them?"

"He took them home. He made copies of them and returned the originals to the closet. He then began studying the journals. He called me into his office a couple of weeks later and told me what he had learned. We then started talking about different ways to confirm the stories that were in the journals. For the next few years, we worked on the project. We found newspapers and letters which substantiated some of the information. After a lot of research, Garland started writing his book."

"The book I've been reading."

"Yes, that's the one. I always told him that it would be embarrassing for his family if he ever published it. He said that his family deserved the embarrassment. I also told him that no one would believe the stories, even with the newspaper substantiation. People would just think it was a well-crafted lie, and the Ramsdens would go on living the way they've always lived."

"But he kept writing anyway?"

"Yes, he put a lot of work into that book. A few more years went by, and one day his brother came into a huge amount of money. Wilfred had invested in a wildcatting company. They drilled for oil in areas suspected to be oil fields. This particular company stumbled upon a Spanish treasure on the Isle of Shoals off the coast of New Hampshire. Because of the small chance of any oil being on an island off the coast of New Hampshire combined with the small chance of simply stumbling upon a three-hundred year old pirate treasure, Garland became convinced that the journals of Blackbeard - those that were described in the journals of Ambrose and Cassius - still existed."

"Wait, so the whole law suit thing is based on a hunch? Even if you won a law suit saying that Wilfred Ramsden had to release the journals of Blackbeard, he could just deny that they exist."

"Not quite. Another Wilfred Ramsden family vacation occurred, and once again Garland was given a key. This time he asked me to come along. We broke into the locked closet again and found nothing new. We were about to leave when one of my steps made a hollow sound. I got down on my knees and pulled up a loose board. Hidden beneath the floor, we found a small unlocked safe. We opened it, and we were at first disappointed. It seemed to only contain the social security cards and birth certificates of everyone in the immediate family."

Lavindra paused his story for a moment while he took a sip from his water bottle. "But there was a hidden compartment in the safe. In that compartment there was a letter from their father to Wilfred. While it did not mention the journals of Blackbeard, it did hint that something important had been passed down. The envelope had originally held two keys. The letter said that these two keys together opened an anonymously held safety deposit box in a bank in Cape Charles, Virginia. Both of them were needed to open the box. The letter said for Wilfred to keep one key hanging around his neck at all times and to give one key to someone trustworthy without explaining what it opened. The letter also said to burn the letter and the envelope."

"So who has the other key?"

"We never figured that out, but we wrote down the account number, so if we ever brought the law suit, we could demand that the safety deposit box be brought before the judge while the case was being litigated. Then if we won, the journals would be revealed to the world. The Ramsdens would be exposed for what they really were."

"And Garland?"

Lavindra laughed. "Garland would be a hero. He would be the Ramsden who exposed the family secret in the face of family embarrassment. He would have a legacy. He would have done something good with his life."

The two of them drove on in silence for a while. They stopped in a town near Suffolk for lunch at about ten o'clock. They were making excellent time.

They drove on for a couple more hours and then took a ferry across to Ocracoke Island.

They walked down a back road and found the library. It was a small library that sat immediately behind a run-down schoolhouse. As they approached the library, Lucius starting thinking about the past. He started thinking about Ambrose and Solomon Ramsden stealing the journals and hiding on the island. He started thinking about how improbable it was that the journals could have been passed down in secret for all these years.

They entered the library and were greeted by an old man who was almost as dusty as the library. He had thick glasses and a thicker mustache. He was wearing khaki pants and navy blue suspenders over a denim shirt.

"How can I help you folks?"

Lavindra spoke up. "We came to look at some of your historical newspapers...the ones about Blackbeard, the fierce pirate."

The old man laughed. "I can certainly help you with that. Follow me."

He led them into a small room at the back of the library. There were a few pirate-related trinkets under glass in the middle of the room, and a set of large drawers in the corner. The old man pulled out the first drawer. Lavindra looked at it for a moment, and then asked for the next one.

When the old man opened the fourth drawer, Lavindra looked excited. "Read this one, Luke. This one's good."

Lucius looked down at the newspaper. The headline said, "Notorious Pirate Blackbeard Caught and Beheaded."

It certainly looked authentic, but it didn't prove anything. "I didn't have any doubts about that part of the story."

"Read the article underneath."

Lucius' eyes scanned the article looking for something important. The text was old, faded, and hard to read.

After a few minutes, he found what he was looking for.

"A member of the royal navy who had been left to guard Blackbeard's vessel was murdered in the night. Several shipmates suspected pirate sympathizers, while others suspected that it was the ghost of Blackbeard himself."

Chapter Twenty

Lucius read through the rest of the article in silence. When he looked up, Lavindra was smiling.

The librarian spoke up, "What are y'all looking for anyway?"

Lavindra laughed. "We're just a couple of history buffs. This sort of thing has always fascinated me, and I'm trying to teach the next generation a thing or two."

"I've always loved history, too. That's why I moved here and took this job. I was brought up on pirate stories."

"Now that I know that, I wish we had time to stay and chat. Unfortunately, Luke and I have to be on our way. We've got a lot of sightseeing to do."

The old man looked a little hurt. "Yeah, I understand. You folks be safe on the roads. Nobody knows how to drive these days."

They thanked the man, as he walked them to the door.

As soon as they left the library, Lucius spoke up, "Well, you said yourself that without Blackbeard's journals, it just looks like a well-crafted lie."

"That's true. It certainly could be. But what would our motivation be?"

"I'm not sure."

"Well, you try to think about that. In the meantime, we've got places to be."

The two of them got on the ferry and soon found themselves driving up Highway 12 in the outer banks of North Carolina.

"Where to, now?"

"Now, we're going to Kill Devil Hills."

"I remember that place from the book. What's the story with the name?"

"There are lots of different stories. Some say it goes back to the locals scavenging rum from the many shipwrecks that occurred in the area. They hid the rum in the hills, and it was strong enough to kill the devil, or the rum itself was called Kill Devil Rum. Others say that a local trapped the devil in the hills to extort money from him. Everyone will swear that their story is the only true one."

"So this is where Ambrose and Solomon took their boat to after they hid out on Ocracoke Island for a while."

"That's correct. This is also where the story between the two of them turned violent."

In less than three hours, they had arrived in Kill Devil Hills. They drove past a very large memorial to the Wright Brothers and into the parking lot of a small, secluded library.

The two of them went inside. This time, Lavindra didn't engage the services of the librarian. He walked to the back of the library and took Lucius into a secluded room filled with historical newspapers.

"This will take me a minute."

After a few minutes of searching through the files, Lavindra pulled up the relevant article on microfilm. "Take a look at that."

Lucius looked at the microfilm. Underneath the heading "Body Identified", there was the following text: "The body found two weeks ago in the inn has been identified as that of Solomon Ramsden, a war hero."

Lucius tried to remain skeptical. "How come I've never heard of the newspapers these stories are printed in? How do I know that you and Garland didn't create them and plant them in the libraries?"

"There has to be a little trust on your part, Luke. But the fact of the matter is that these stories happened before any of the newspapers you've ever heard of were established. The oldest currently active newspaper is either the New Hampshire Gazette or the Hartford Courant. And neither of those was established until the middle of the eighteenth century."

Lucius' skepticism began to fade. Neither of these news stories proved anything by themselves, but it was all starting to add up. The confirmation of a few of the facts in the manuscript was enough for Lucius to believe that the whole thing was true.

"We've got one more stop, Luke. We've got to hurry if we're going to make it on time."

Once again they were back in the car and driving. It was a little after three o'clock in the afternoon.

"So how did you decide which newspapers to show me?"

"I talked it over with Garland. We wanted to get you to all of them in one day, so we picked three of the best."

"How long did it take you and Garland to find these?"

"Years. We spent a lot of time in this area. That's okay by me, though. It's a beautiful part of the country."

At about half past four, they were in Norfolk. They pulled into the parking lot of another library. They rushed inside, and Garland looked around. He quickly located a room identified as the Sargeant Memorial Room and took Lucius inside.

He began searching through the files and typing on the computer. The process did not go as quickly as it had earlier, and soon the librarian entered the room.

"We're closing in five minutes. Can I help you folks with anything?"

"No, ma'am. We're fine. We should be done before you close."

Almost as soon as the librarian had left the room, Lavindra let out a sigh of relief. "Here it is...finally."

Lavindra walked over to look at another piece of microfilm. This one told of Cassius Ramsden's election to the office of borough council. It briefly mentioned the negative opinion that most of the town had held of his father, and how he had overcome that negative opinion to win the election.

Lucius was smiling as he looked up. "Either all of this is true, or you and Garland have gone to a lot of trouble just to mess with me."

Lavindra laughed. "Let's get out of here before that librarian shows up and throws us out."

They got in the car and began the long drive toward Charlottesville. Lucius again noticed all of the stores named after the Ramsdens. Then in a moment that almost seemed surreal, he looked up and noticed a sign that read, "Ambrose Ramsden for Mayor of Norfolk."

"Who is Ambrose Ramsden? I mean, the Ambrose Ramsden that is alive now."

"The eldest son of Wilfred Ramsden. He's only twenty-five years old, and he's already running for mayor. He'll probably win, too."

"Yeah, I just saw the sign. So he's named after the Ramsden that started this whole thing...the one who stole the journals?"

"Yes. The truth of the matter is that former Senator Wilfred Ramsden has been more obsessed by the history of his family than any other Ramsden. The only reason he likes his brother Garland so much is that Garland is an expert on colonial history and can tell him stories about Blackbeard and life in eighteenth century Virginia."

"So he and Garland are still close?"

"They're still pretty close. Garland does not like his brother, but he continues to tolerate him because he believes that that is the only way to get to the bottom of this whole thing. Wilfred still trusts his brother. He still gives him the key to the house whenever he goes away on vacation."

"So I'm guessing he doesn't know about Garland finding the journals of Ambrose and Cassius, or you and Garland finding the letter?"

"No, he knows nothing about that. We were both careful to return things to where we found them. We're a couple of PhD's, you know."

Lucius laughed.

"Has Wilfred passed the secret down to his son Ambrose?"

"We don't think so, but we're not sure."

They stopped for dinner after another hour of driving, and then drove on home. The conversation never died, and Lucius never had to take Lavindra up on his offer to control the radio. Lavindra had a very strong personality, and more than ever, Lucius wanted to believe that every word he said was true.

188

When they arrived back in Charlottesville, Lavindra told him that they would all meet to discuss their next move on the following Tuesday at nine o'clock in the evening.

The weekend went by quickly. Lucius continued to read the manuscript. While there were apparently more and more newspaper articles being written about the Ramsdens, the actual information about the family decreased. They were being more and more secretive. Apparently, not writing anything down had become a family tradition.

Dolores continued to sleep in his bed, while Lucius continued to sleep on the couch. They argued occasionally, as roommates tend to do, but it never got very serious.

Finally, Tuesday evening arrived. Lucius waited impatiently in the living room, while Dolores, sitting near him on the couch, smiled at his nervousness.

"Where are they? You don't think they got into trouble?"

"They'll be here, Luke. Just calm down."

"I'm perfectly calm. I was just wondering."

Lucius' cell phone started buzzing. He answered it, and Garland told him that they were coming in.

Lucius walked over and unlocked the door. Garland and Lavindra walked quickly into the room.

Garland spoke first. "This will be the last time that I will be able to meet with you like this, so we need to plan far in advance. Mr. Dixon, the first question is for you. Do you feel comfortable going to work for Leeder & Schrum and attempting to retrieve the research that Professor Sandberg and Ms. Martinez spent years collecting?"

Lucius didn't hesitate. "I do."

"Well, then, now we only have to convince Ms. Martinez."

Dolores spoke, "I'm still not sure that it's a good idea. Luke is very smart, but I don't think he realizes how dangerous these people are."

Lucius was frustrated. "Dolores, you know that I lost a good friend to these people. I'm well aware of how dangerous they are. I can be careful, though."

Dolores bit her lip. "I'm willing to give my blessing. I really don't see any other option. There's no way to break into that firm, and starting the whole research process over again without Daniel seems too daunting. Luke, if you promise to be as careful as you can be, I will get on board for this part of the plan."

"I promise, Dolores."

Garland smiled. "Okay, you're next Dolores. The police are after you. You are their primary suspect in the murder of Daniel Sandberg. I'm working as hard as I can without giving myself away to ensure that the police find the real killer. However, in the meantime what would you like to do?"

"What do you mean?"

"Would you like to try to go back to Europe or somewhere else? Or would you rather stay here with Luke?"

"I'd rather stay here. Because they followed us from the airport, we know that they were able to track my movements last time. I think I'm safer staying here with Luke. You've said yourself that he is unknown to them."

"Well then, it's settled. In the meantime, we will just lay low. Luke, in a month, call Leeder & Schrum and tell them that you accept their offer. The rest of us will do nothing until you get to the firm next summer. If you can get the research, then we'll bring our case. If you can't, then we'll figure out the next step from there."

Garland and Lavindra left quickly. The meeting took less than ten minutes from their entrance to their exit.

The next couple of weeks went by slowly. Lucius enjoyed spending time with Dolores, but there wasn't much to do. He went to school, but other than that, he rarely left the house. He didn't feel comfortable leaving her alone at night.

One night when they were sitting in the living room talking, Lucius' phone rang.

It was Jennifer Morgan.

"Hello?"

Jennifer was sobbing. "Luke, this is Jennifer."

Lucius walked into the other room. "What's going on, Jennifer?"

"Everything's crashing down."

190

"Tell me what's wrong."

"I came to New York for Howard. All of my dreams about how my life was going to turn out were built around Howard...and yesterday he broke up with me."

Lucius remembered wishing that this very thing would happen...but that had been months ago. "I'm sorry to hear that, Jennifer. Did he give you a reason?"

"No, he wouldn't say. He just said that we had to stop seeing each other."

"Well, there's nothing that you can do about it. You just have to try to move on."

"There's nothing to move on to. I've got nothing in New York City. The only reason I came here was to be with Howard."

"Jennifer, you've got a bright future. You're at one of the top law schools in the country. You'll have plenty of other options."

"Howard wasn't just an option. He was all I had."

"You just have to calm down, Jennifer. This will all be better in a couple of days. Just try not to get too broken up about the whole thing."

"I know you're right, Luke. But I just can't imagine getting over this. I couldn't sleep last night."

"You have to try to focus on law school. Maybe I'll come up to the city to see you over Christmas break."

Jennifer sniffled. "That would be nice."

"In the meantime, just forget about Howard. That guy wasn't that great anyway. He was a little goofy."

Jennifer laughed a little. "I feel stupid calling you like this, but this whole thing has me very upset. I don't know where else to turn."

"It's okay, Jennifer. I'm here if you need me."

They said goodbye, and Lucius realized that he was tearing up himself. Jennifer would be better off without Howard, but hearing her like that made him sad.

Dolores spoke when he came back in the room. "What was that about?"

"Just a friend of mine. Her boyfriend broke up with her."

For a moment, Lucius swore that a look of jealousy went across Dolores' face. "Someone you're interested in?"

"Nope, we're just friends."

Over the next month, Lucius talked often with Jennifer. Her mood gradually improved and soon she was beginning to put the whole thing behind her. Their conversations occasionally drifted back to Robert, but for the most part they talked about the future. Lucius told her about the law firm he was going to work for, but he didn't mention the name or their connection to the mystery.

As their conversations started to space out more and more, Lucius realized that only sadness had been bringing them together ever since she left. They had only talked at the time of Robert's disappearance and at the time of her breakup.

Lucius called and accepted his offer at Leeder & Schrum. He was one of the first in his law school class to receive and accept an offer. He felt good about himself. He was doing well in law school, despite all of the interferences.

One day in the middle of November, Lucius received another phone call.

"This is Robert Collins, Sr., the father of your classmate."

"Yes, sir. What can I do for you?'

"I'm going to be in Charlottesville this weekend for a conference. I was wondering if you might be willing to sit down with me to talk about my son."

"Of course."

Lucius agreed to meet him at an expensive inn right outside of town. The meeting time arrived before Lucius really knew what he would tell the solicitor general. He drove out to the inn wondering if he had made a mistake.

When he arrived, Mr. Collins was already waiting for him. As soon as they ordered their drinks, he started talking.

"Mr. Dixon. I know that you were close with my son. His disappearance has really cut me deeply. I was hoping you could shed some light on it."

"I wish I could, Mr. Collins, but I don't think I can."

"The police are telling me that it may have had something to do with Dolores Martinez, the suspected murderess of Daniel Sandberg. Did you or Robert ever know her?"

"No sir. The only person other than myself that Robert spent a lot of time with was Lindsey Coleman."

"His name keeps coming up as well. But unfortunately we lost track of him a few months ago."

"He was the one who told me the story about your son going to New York after Jennifer Morgan."

"Did you ever hear anything from her?"

"I've talked to her a few times. She hasn't seen him in New York."

"Something odd was going on with my son. He was always such a bright student, and yet his grades dropped drastically in that last semester. You don't have any idea what was wrong?"

"No sir. He did like Jennifer a lot, and perhaps that interfered with his studying, but he was also spending a lot of time with Lindsey Coleman." Lucius worried about steering so much attention toward a person whose body he had helped throw into the swamp, but he wanted to steer it away from Dolores and Jennifer.

"Cole was always an odd fellow. He was very smart, but he never really fit in at the Justice Department. I only approved his hiring because of a strong recommendation from an old friend of mine."

"I didn't like Robert hanging around him. I think Cole was bad for him."

"And you don't have any idea where Cole is now either?"

Lucius had to lie again. "I don't. I haven't seen him since that day at the law school when he told me the story about Robert going to New York."

Robert Collins, Sr. choked up a little. "It's just that my son was very important to me."

"I know, sir. He was very important to me, as well."

"We had always been very close. I had always been very proud of him."

"He was...is a good person. I'm sure he'll be okay, Mr. Collins. I'll do whatever I can to help you find him."

Mr. Collins brushed a tear off his cheek. "My son is all that I have."

Chapter Twenty-One

Mr. Collins pulled out a handkerchief and dabbed his eyes. "I'm sorry. This whole thing has hit me very hard."

"I understand. I miss Robert a lot."

The two of them ordered their food and sat in silence for a few minutes.

Finally, Mr. Collins took a deep breath and spoke up. "So this girl Jennifer? She and Robert were close?"

"The three of us were all very close. I don't think I would have made it through my first year of law school without them."

Mr. Collins smiled. "I'm glad to hear that. Robert was a gifted child. He always excelled in school."

The rest of the meal was uneventful. When Lucius left the inn, rain was pouring down. He ran to his car and climbed quickly inside, but he was soaked to the skin anyway.

Lucius drove home as carefully as he could with his face next to the windshield, but he could hardly see anything. He arrived in the parking lot and used a grocery store bag to cover his head as he ran from the car to his apartment.

It was pitch black inside. Lucius tried to turn the lights on before realizing that the power was out.

He closed and locked the door behind him. He immediately stubbed his toe on his easy chair as he stumbled through the darkness. He put one hand on the wall and tried to edge forward an inch at a time.

It was at that moment that Lucius remembered that he no longer lived alone. He had a roommate. Where was Dolores?

He thought about calling for her before thinking better of it. What if someone else were in the apartment? He continued to inch forward toward his bedroom. He didn't have any candles or a flashlight. He only hoped that his eyes would adjust to the lack of light.

He moved carefully into the bedroom and toward his window. Maybe he could get some more light by opening the blinds.

As he was opening the blinds, he heard a rustling noise behind him and wheeled around. A shadow emerged from his closet and moved toward him.

It was Dolores. "Luke, it's you."

"Yeah, why were you in the closet? What's going on?"

"The power went off about an hour ago. I was a little afraid, but I was okay just sitting in the dark. Then, there was a loud knock on the door."

Dolores was breathing heavily and her heart was pounding. "I thought it might have been you, so I tiptoed over to the door and looked out the peep hole. It was a man. He was Latino and had a large mustache."

Lucius tried to think. "Was it Detective Torro? Have you ever met him?"

"No...I mean...no, I've never met him, but this was probably him. He identified himself as the police and starting yelling to open the door. I walked quickly into the bedroom and climbed into the closet. I didn't come out until you got here."

"How long did he stay at the door?"

"At least fifteen minutes. He was banging on the door so hard that I thought he might break it down. I was worried, Luke."

"I know you were, Dolores. We need to talk to Garland. This is serious."

"We'll get him on the phone tomorrow and see what he has to say. I may have to leave here, though, Luke."

"Maybe he was just looking for me. Detective Torro's had it out for me from the beginning. It's my own fault, though. I think he was just good at reading lies, and I was lying to him from the beginning."

"What do you mean?"

"I never told him about the spying that Robert, Jennifer, and I were doing. I didn't want to make us look like suspects."

"Well, there's no use worrying about that now. I'm going to try to go to bed. Wake me up if he comes back."

"I will, Dolores. Let me know if you need anything."

196

Almost as soon as Dolores left the room, the power clicked back on. Lucius nearly jumped out of his shoes as the entire apartment filled with light and noise.

He sat on the couch watching television for the next few hours. There was nothing on, but changing the channels helped to soothe his nerves. What was Torro doing? The last time they had talked, he had said that Dolores was the killer and to let him know if he heard anything. So why would he have come back unless he had some reason to believe that Dolores was here?

Lucius fell asleep on the couch and didn't wake up until the next morning.

When he opened his eyes, his phone was ringing. He answered it.

"Hello"

"Luke, this is Garland. Dolores told me to come over. Will you open the door?"

Lucius opened the door, and Garland entered the room coughing violently.

"I'm sorry about that, Luke. Now what can I do for you both? I told you we had to stop meeting like this."

Dolores entered the room. She seemed relieved to see Garland.

Lucius spoke, "We had something of an incident last night. Do you remember the detective that I told you about? The one who claimed Dolores was the killer?"

"Yes, I believe so."

"Well, he came here last night while I was away. He banged on the door and yelled for someone to open the door. The thing is, he had told me the last time we talked that Dolores was the killer and to let him know if I saw her. It seems weird that he would come back to talk to me unless he thought I knew something about Dolores."

"Perhaps he just wanted to ask you some more questions about the murder scene?"

"It's been nearly six months since that happened."

"You were right to call me. I've got a friend who can find out what's going on. For now, stay here. If he comes back, let him in, but make sure Dolores is well hidden. Don't give him permission to search if he asks."

"How soon can we expect to hear from you?"

"Hopefully, in the next few hours. I'll call you."

Garland left the apartment.

Lucius sat down and turned on the television. He rested his head on his pillow, and in a few minutes, he was asleep.

When he woke up, it was already early afternoon. He walked into his bedroom, where Dolores was on the computer.

"I didn't want to wake you, Luke," she said over her shoulder.

"Thanks. Any word from Garland?"

"Not yet. I was just looking for places that I could go. Since the police are after me, I'm not going to travel by plane."

"You may not have to leave." Lucius didn't want her to go. She was the only friend he had left.

"I know. I'm just getting prepared."

"I can take care..." Lucius was interrupted by the ringing of his phone.

He ran into the other room and answered it.

"Luke. Has Detective Torro returned to your apartment?"

"No, sir."

"Do not let him in if he does. Sergio Torro was kicked off the force in August."

"What?"

"He's no longer a police detective. He wasn't a detective when he told you that Dolores was the killer. I don't know what he's doing."

"Are you sure?"

"I'm very sure. You have to be especially careful, Luke. I don't know what he's doing, but he could be dangerous."

"What should Dolores do?"

"She has to leave."

"Are you sure? Isn't that dangerous?"

"It's more dangerous for her to stay with you. I don't know what Torro is up to, but if he finds Dolores with you, you're both in trouble. Let me talk to Dolores."

Lucius carried the phone into the bedroom and gave it to Dolores. He couldn't remain in the same room. He walked back into the living room. Tears were welling up in his eyes. He didn't realize how much he had come to rely on her company.

He sat on the couch for a few minutes before Dolores walked in.

"I'll miss you, Luke."

Lucius was choked up. "I'll miss you, too."

Dolores grabbed his hand with both of hers and pulled it near her face. "I'll be okay, and I'll see you soon."

"I know you will."

Nothing more was said. That evening Lucius drove Dolores to the train station and watched as she got on her train.

They were still worried that the police were looking for her, so they didn't think it was a good idea for her to try to get on an plane. Garland had given her several thousand dollars and a fake ID, so she could take care of herself. She was going to Ohio.

Lucius drove home, thinking about how he was going to adjust to living alone again.

The next day he woke up early and drove to a local gun store.

When he entered, the man behind the counter spoke up. "I'm Gary. I own this place. Just let me know if you see something you like."

After looking around for a few minutes, Lucius pointed to a gun.

"A derringer?" Gary was smiling.

"I suppose."

"That's a girl's gun."

"That's okay. I just need something small that I can use to protect myself."

Gary laughed. "Well, this certainly meets both of those criteria. Is this the one you want?"

"Well, is there another small gun that you think would work better?"

"Yeah, follow me. I've got a Kahr MK9 that might be exactly what you're looking for."

Lucius followed him across the store to another glass counter top.

Gary unlocked the counter top and pulled out a small, stumpy looking gun.

"It's perfect."

"All right, you'll have to fill out some paperwork. I have to do a background check."

Lucius filled out the paperwork and waited in the store while the background check was run. He had decided that it was time to buy a gun. Things seemed to be getting more and more dangerous. He didn't know what Torro was doing now, but he was probably working for the Ramsdens. Why else would he be looking for Dolores even after he was dismissed from the police department?

And Lucius had already had a gun pointed at him once. At least if it happened again, he would have a chance to fight back.

"Mr. Dixon. You're clear. You've bought yourself a gun."

Lucius took the gun out to his car and drove home. He felt a little safer.

Months went by without event.

Torro didn't come back. There was no sign of him. It seemed strange. According to Dolores, he had banged on the door for at least fifteen minutes. Why would he no longer have any interest in talking to him? Maybe he realized Dolores was gone. But how? Or maybe he realized that Lucius now knew that he was no longer on the police force. But how would he know that either?

December came and went without a trip to New York City. Jennifer had stopped calling almost completely. She seemed to be recovering from the split with Howard.

His third semester as a law student went as well as any of the others. He had more time to concentrate on his studies this time, and he felt better about his performance. He even participated in the moot court competition, a competition in which the students prepared an appellate court argument, and then performed the argument in front of judges. Lucius worked hard and advanced to the second round.

It was in the middle of January when Lucius received a phone call.

"Luke, this is Garland."

"How are you?"

"Unfortunately, I'm not well. That's why I'm calling you. I'm in the hospital."

"What's going on? Are you sick?"

"Yes, I'm very sick. In fact, I'm almost certainly dying."

Lucius didn't know what to say.

"It's okay, son. I'm dealing with it, but I need your help."

"Of course, anything. Just tell me what to do."

"You can't come to see me. We can't have my family seeing you here. I need you to go to your law school's parking lot…the one nearest to the library."

"Okay…why am I going there?"

"Lavindra will meet you there and tell you the rest. The two of you have work to do."

"Yes, sir. I hope things go well for you at the hospital."

Garland laughed. "Well, they won't go too well. That's why it's very important for you to get this done."

"I'll be pulling for you."

"Thanks, son. I'll talk to you soon."

Lucius started panicking again. He had lost Dolores, and now he was going to lose Garland. Everything seemed to be falling apart.

He tried to calm himself down as he drove to the law school. Lavindra was waiting for him when he arrived. The warm glow that had been on Lavindra's face on the day of their road trip was gone. His brow was furrowed, and he looked as if he had been crying.

Lavindra's smile seemed forced. "It's good to see you, Mr. Dixon."

"It's good to see you, as well."

"I'm sorry we have to meet under such trying circumstances."

"I'm sorry as well. I know you two are close."

"We have to go to Garland's house. There are certain things that he doesn't want his family to have."

"Like what?"

"Well, we'll talk about that on the way."

The two of them climbed into Lavindra's car and began driving.

"We have to get the other copies of the manuscript. We have to get his computer. We have to get all of the copies of the newspapers and the copies of the journals written by Ambrose and Cassius."

"What are we supposed to do with all of that?"

Lavindra chuckled. "You're supposed to keep it."

"What? Why can't you?"

"Garland wanted me to, but I can't. If Garland lives, then I will throw myself into this thing. I will do everything I can to ensure that Garland's family is exposed because that's what he wants. But if he dies, this is no longer my fight."

"What do you mean?"

"I'm only involved in this thing for one reason. I want to help Garland die at peace with his legacy. I am not a crusader for truth."

"So you don't care about this? You don't want to expose the evil that this family has done?"

"Of course I do. But I'm old. If Garland passes, I have other things that I need to do. You and Dolores will have to take charge."

They drove for a while in silence.

"You won't help us?"

"I'll help in whatever way I can, but I won't be running things."

"Okay, I'll take the stuff."

They drove for nearly half an hour before pulling into the driveway of Garland's house. They entered and walked up the stairs into a large office.

Lavindra knelt in the corner of the room and began turning the knob of a safe.

"I hope you don't think poorly of me, Mr. Dixon."

"I don't. I understand."

"I'm glad you do because I'm not entirely sure I understand it myself. I just can't see myself carrying on with all of this if Garland dies."

Lavindra opened the safe and produced a large stack of papers. They were separated by binder clips and had hundreds of tabs on them. He placed them on the desk, then pulled out another stack and placed it next to them.

"I'll leave these here while we unhook the computer."

Lucius flipped through the stack of papers while Lavindra worked. It was all here. He moved his fingers over the copied pages...over the copied handwriting of Ambrose Ramsden and his son Cassius. He flipped through the stacks of copied newspapers and through the heavily edited manuscript pages.

"I don't know where to begin. What do I do with all of this stuff?"

"Luke, you've done pretty well for yourself so far. I have no doubt that you'll know exactly what to do with all of this."

Lavindra continued pulling out wires from the computer and placing the different components into a nearby cardboard box.

"But this is different. I've always had someone to rely on. If Garland dies and you leave, then I'll be all alone."

Lavindra sighed. "If it makes you feel any better, I'll let you talk to Garland. Maybe he can tell you what to do."

"I'd like that."

Lavindra pulled out his cell phone and dialed a number.

"Garland? Luke wants to talk to you."

Lavindra handed the phone to Lucius.

"Hello?"

"Yes, Luke. What can I do for you?'

"Lavindra wants me to take all of this stuff, but I don't know what to do with it."

"You know exactly what to do Luke. Get the journals of Blackbeard and publish the real family history of the Ramsdens. Expose them for what they are."

Chapter Twenty-Two

Lucius didn't know how to reply. "But...but why me? I'm part of the reason why we lost the research in the first place? We wouldn't be in such a bad position, if I had done a better job."

"I have confidence in you precisely because you contributed to the loss of that research. You've learned from the mistakes you've made, and you will be much more careful this time."

"I just don't know if I'm ready for this."

"You're ready. Now, I have to go. If my nurse catches me on the phone again, I'll be in big trouble."

"Goodbye, Mr. Ramsden."

"Goodbye, Luke."

Lucius gave the cell phone back to Lavindra and accepted the task, "Okay, I'll do it."

"I'm glad to hear that, Mr. Dixon. You should go ahead and carry one of those boxes down to the car. I'll be behind you with the other one once I get this computer packed up."

Lucius picked up the box and walked down to the car. He was nervous but confident that this new material would be safe in his hands. He wouldn't be so careless this time.

After the two of them finished packing up the papers and the computer, they climbed into the car and drove toward Lucius' apartment.

"In the Documents folder on that computer, there is a hidden directory called 'Ramsden Family History.' All of the written material is on the computer, and all of the copied material has been scanned into the computer. It's all in that folder."

They arrived at Lucius' apartment, and Lavindra helped him to carry everything inside. Before leaving, Lavindra shook his hand and wished him luck. Lucius watched him drive away, his eyes a little watery once again.

He went inside and began working. He unhooked and moved his own computer, before setting up Garland's computer on his desk. He plugged in all of the peripherals and turned on the power.

Lucius found the hidden folder and began looking at the files. There were 242 scanned document files, and fifteen files created by a word processor.

Lucius then began changing the file names. He changed each of the 242 scanned document files into files named "Contracts Research" and their number. He then changed the name of the word processing documents to things like "Memorandum Rough Draft" and "Memorandum Final Draft."

When he had finished changing all of the file names, Lucius went through the process of signing up for a new e-mail account. He then began e-mailing all of the files to the new account. He wanted to have an electronic copy in case the physical copy was taken. An anonymous e-mail account seemed to be the safest place to store such an electronic copy. It wouldn't be tied to any particular computer.

Once he had finished e-mailing the files, he saved them on a flash drive. He then deleted all of the files from the hard drive of Garland's computer. Lucius next turned off Garland's computer and opened it up.

He pulled out the hard drive and took it into the kitchen. He took the hammer off his refrigerator, put the hard drive in a plastic bag, and smashed it. He then wrapped another plastic bag around the remains and put both bags in the bottom of his trash can. Lucius was going to do everything that he could to make sure that no one else got this information.

Lucius took the flash drive into the living room. He pulled a DVD out of the middle of his collection and put the flash drive inside. He slid the DVD back into its place. He had nearly two-hundred DVDs. Someone looking for information would have to go through a lot of trouble to find it.

Lucius left his house and locked the door behind him. He drove to the bulk supply store and picked up three boxes that were small enough to slide underneath his bed.

When he arrived back at home, he took a large marker and wrote on each of the boxes, "Summer Research for Professor Franklin." He then piled all of the paper material into the three boxes, before sliding the boxes all the way under his bed. His bed fit into one of the corners of his room, so the bed would have to be moved in order to see the boxes. Lucius then took the old boxes, along with the trash from his kitchen and the remains of Garland's computer, drove them to a neighboring apartment complex, and threw them into a trash bin.

When Lucius got home, he sat down on his couch with a smile on his face. Maybe he would be able to handle this after all. He wouldn't mention the location of the information to anyone, nor would he write it down. If someone did break into his home when he was in class, they would have to devote a good deal of time to find anything. Even if they did find the papers under the bed and the flash drive in the DVD case, he still had an extra copy in an anonymous e-mail account. He wouldn't lose the information this time.

Just as Lucius' confidence was reaching an all-time high, he looked across the room and caught sight of the gun he had bought. That image brought him back to reality. He remembered Sandberg's lifeless face. He remembered his friend Robert, and how optimistic he had been when they began law school. He remembered Lindsey Coleman being shot in front of him, and he remembered throwing his body into a swamp.

His mind flashed back to Sergio Torro, the former police detective who had been snooping around the night the electricity went out. This was going to be dangerous. Lucius was now in the middle of it. It would be difficult to remain an anonymous cog for much longer.

But there was nothing else to be done. Garland was in the hospital. Lucius couldn't cure him of whatever was killing him. Lavindra would help only if Garland survived. And Dolores didn't plan to return until after the summer. Lucius just had to wait.

So Lucius waited. Once again he focused his attention on law school. He spent several weeks working hard for the moot court competition. He and his partner overwhelmed their opponents both times. A few weeks later, he found out that they had been selected to be among the final sixteen participants. The competition had begun with more than two-hundred.

His favorite class of the semester was Trial Advocacy. The idea of the class was to replicate a trial court setting and to see how the students could perform in their roles as the attorneys. Lucius enjoyed it a great deal.

His other classes were also enjoyable. His ability to read cases had improved tremendously. He began reading horn books during the semester to better prepare himself for the final exam. He paid attention during class, and he could tell from the other student's responses to the teacher's questions that he was far ahead of most of them.

His grades from the previous semester were finally posted. He once again received three A's and a B. Despite all of the distractions, his law school career was actually going very well. He was proud of his performance.

Summer finally arrived. He finished his exams and sublet an apartment in Norfolk. It was time to go into the belly of the beast. He left Garland's research behind in Charlottesville, feeling that it would be safer there than with him in Norfolk.

As Lucius Dixon walked toward the office of Leeder & Schrum for the first time, he didn't know what to think. He could be walking into a death trap. After all, if Sergio Torro wasn't working for the police, then he was almost certainly working for the Ramsdens. And the fact that he had stopped coming to Lucius' apartment after Dolores left, led him to believe that Torro had known about her presence.

But Lucius didn't turn around. He walked boldly into the office building and took the elevator up to his office on the third floor of the building. He had come too far now. There was no turning back.

He was greeted by the receptionist and guided to the office that he would be sharing with another summer associate who would be arriving later in the summer.

As soon as he had settled into his chair, Marcus Henry limped into the office. Marcus was one of the young associates he had met during his interview. He had graduated from UVA law only a few years ago. Despite his young age, he had gray hair.

"I'm glad you decided to come to work here, Mr. Dixon."

"I'm glad to be here. The firm is very impressive."

"Well, you're an impressive young man. I was taking a look at your transcript. You're really doing well for yourself at UVA."

"Thank you. That's nice of you to say."

"You know, I won the moot court competition when I was there, so you'll be the second winner at Leeder & Schrum when you get here."

Lucius laughed. "I'm not entirely sure I'll win."

"I've got confidence in you. Anyway, let's get started with the orientation process."

"Sure."

"All right, the first thing you need to understand is that you should keep track of all of your time. Most law firms want to know every tenth of an hour. We're more specific than that. We want to know every minute, so keep track of it."

"Yes, sir."

"You don't have to call me sir. I'm not that much older than you. Anyway, next you need to understand the phone system. I've included in your materials a brochure that explains that system - how to transfer calls and how to do conference calls, etc. You should read it when I leave."

"Okay."

"All right, next I need to explain our filing system. We keep all of our research and make it available to all of our attorneys."

Lucius' attention was piqued. That meant that they probably still had a copy of the research that they had stolen...and he could get it.

"Okay, so type your name and password in the appropriate boxes. Your user name is your first initial and your last name. Your password is the last four digits of your social security number. You can change your password later."

Lucius did as he was instructed.

"Now you want to open the program called Document Storage. There should be an icon for it on your desktop. Now click on Find at the top of the screen. You can enter search terms or the author's name here to try to find the document you're looking for. You'll get better at it with practice. Now come with me. We have another filing system."

Lucius followed Marcus out of the office and into the elevator. They took the elevator all the way down to the basement of the building. Marcus used a key card to open the elevator doors, and they exited into a small, dark hallway.

"There is a key card in the packet that was sitting on your desk. You'll need it to access this floor."

"What's down here?"

"This is our primary filing system. Our managing partner has always believed strongly in keeping hard copies of everything, so we keep all of the copies down here."

Lucius was a little frightened. He didn't like being down here alone with Marcus. He was still afraid of what the firm knew. "Should I come down here? Or should I just access the electronic information."

Marcus led Lucius down the hallway, opening the different doors to large rooms filled with filing cabinets. "You should normally just use the electronic information. However, if it is something very important, you should come down here to check the physical copies."

Once the tour was completed, Marcus led Lucius back to his office.

When they arrived, he spoke again. "I'm also going to be giving you your first project. You worked for a professor last summer, so am I right to assume that this will be your first job at a law firm?"

"Yes, sir."

Marcus smiled. "I could have sworn that I told you not to call me sir. Anyway, your first assignment will be a document review. One of our clients is planning to acquire another company, and we have to review all of the information given to us by the target company."

"What will I be looking for?"

"I'll send you an e-mail listing all of the key terms and phrases that you should be looking for. If you find anything that seems relevant, you should mark the page with a tab and move along. You won't need to write anything for this project."

"Sounds good."

"Can I use your phone?"

"Sure."

Marcus turned on the speaker phone and called his assistant. "Could you provide a copy of all of the documents relating to the Ramsden-Coastal Mining Company matter to the new summer associate, Mr. Lucius Dixon?"

"Certainly, sir."

Marcus hung up the phone. "If you have any questions about the project or anything else, just drop by my office. I'll be glad to help you."

"Thanks. You've been very helpful."

Lucius sat back in his chair and let out a sigh. It seemed like a very normal beginning. Maybe they didn't know anything after all. He thought about the electronic and physical filing systems. There seemed to be a very good chance that the research done by Sandberg and Martinez was still in existence somewhere.

He logged into the computer filing system while he was waiting for the documents to be brought to him. He did a preliminary search with Daniel Sandberg as the author. Thousands of documents came up.

He tried to limit the search by including the word 'Ramsden', but that still left him with over three-hundred documents. He tried the word 'Blackbeard' but received zero results.

He then attempted to use Dolores Martinez's name. As he was typing her name into the search tool, he was startled by a knock at the door. He quickly minimized the program and looked up.

At the door was a heavyset man with a two-wheeled dolly. On it was a stack of four boxes. He wheeled the dolly into the office. "Where would you like these?"

"These are the documents that I'm supposed to review?"

"Yes, sir. Where would you like them?"

Lucius directed the man to drop the boxes next to his desk. When the man left, he opened up the first box and saw that it was filled to the brim with papers.

He picked up his phone and dialed Marcus.

"This is Marcus Henry. How can I help you?"

"This is Lucius Dixon. I was just looking at these documents, and there were more than I was expecting. How long should this review take me?"

"Approximately one month."

"Oh, okay. I just wanted to make sure that I wasn't supposed to get this done for you by tomorrow or anything."

"No, it's fine. The acquisition is nearly a year away. These are just preliminaries."

"Thank you."

"You're welcome."

Lucius hung up the phone. This was not exactly the sort of excitement he was hoping for. He would be reading company documents for the next month, looking for key words and phrases. He couldn't imagine anything much more boring.

Lucius picked up a stack of documents and plopped them on the desk beside him. He opened his e-mail and read the message from Marcus. He printed out a copy and placed it beside the documents.

Before beginning, he went back to his search for documents written by Dolores Martinez. There were fewer results this time, but there were still too many for him to read them all. He closed the program and began his assignment.

The next few days were very boring for Lucius. He had really enjoyed his job for Professor Franklin the previous summer. He was hoping that this job would be similar. He wanted to do research, not document review.

He kept working, though. There was nothing he could do about it. They were paying him a lot of money, and he was in a position to get back the research that had been lost. It was an ideal situation. He just had to deal with a little boredom.

One day he came across a line in one of the documents about some research that had previously been performed by Leeder & Schrum. He decided to use it as an excuse to visit the filing room in the basement. He pulled out his key card and headed for the elevator.

He got on the elevator by himself and headed down to the basement. The doors opened at the first floor. He recognized one of the assistants standing outside the door. She spoke. "Is this going up?"

"No, I'm going down."

"Oh, okay."

The elevator doors closed. He was hoping to make it down to the basement without being seen. So much for that.

He arrived at the basement floor and unlocked the doors with his key card. He waited for a minute at the door, trying to hear if anyone else was down here. When he was satisfied that he was alone, he let the elevator doors close and walked down the hallway.

He entered the door to the first room and went inside. He didn't know where to begin. He found a filing cabinet labeled 'Index' and opened it up. He found a section called 'Attorney Work Product' and a sub-section called 'Research Memoranda."

The sub-section was divided by topics. There were too many pages of memos written on property issues, and he struggled to think of how to narrow his search. There were no subject headings for 'Blackbeard' or for 'stolen property.'

The 'Research Memoranda' were also indexed by the client's name. He looked up 'Ramsden,' but there was far too much information. There were several different listings for different Ramsdens, as well as companies named after the Ramsdens. Each of the listings had at least a few dozen cases, and some of them had hundreds. Wilfred Ramsden's listing had thousands.

Lucius realized that he was not going to be able to find anything of substance on this visit. He would come back at a later date with a better idea of how to conduct his search.

He walked to the elevators and made his way back to the law office on the third floor.

He was thinking about other ways to look for the research when he turned the corner. He wasn't watching where he was going, and he ran right into Sergio Torro.

Chapter Twenty-Three

For a moment, they just stared at each other.

Torro spoke first. "Mr. Dixon? What are you doing here?"

"Detective Torro...it's been a while. I'm working as a summer associate for Leeder & Schrum."

Torro's eyes got a little bigger. "Why'd you pick this firm?"

"I liked the idea of a smaller firm that did a little bit of everything. Plus, they gave me an offer before I had even interviewed anywhere else."

"No other reason?"

"No, sir. What about yourself? What are you doing here?"

"That's, unfortunately, none of your business."

"Well, if you need anything, my office is right down the hall."

"Thanks, Mr. Dixon. I'm sure I'll see you soon."

Lucius walked past Sergio Torro and toward his office. He had wanted to ask about his dismissal from the police force, but he didn't want to draw any more attention to himself than he had already.

As he walked back toward his office, he considered the possibilities. What did Torro know? If he had known that Martinez had been in the apartment, wouldn't he have gone in? But if he didn't know, why did he stop coming by as soon as she left?

Torro had always been suspicious of him. Even if Torro had no idea that he and Martinez knew each other, this could be dangerous. Of all the law firms in the world, he had chosen to come to the former law firm of both the man whose body he had discovered and the dead man's suspected killer. This couldn't look good.

He walked into his office and sat down at the desk. He couldn't concentrate on work.

Lucius tried to come up with an explanation in which Torro's presence here at the law office was purely innocent. Perhaps he had simply continued investigating Sandberg's death after his dismissal. And perhaps that investigation had led him to Leeder & Schrum. After all, both Garland and Dolores thought that this firm may have had something to do with Sandberg's murder.

But more likely, he had been working for the Ramsdens while he was at the police department. He had been dismissed, probably because his loyalty was to the Ramsdens, not to the department. And now he was working directly for the Ramsdens, just like everyone else at the firm. If that were the case, Lucius was in trouble.

He briefly considered leaving and never coming back. But then they would know for sure that something was up. His best bet was to act as normal as possible and to deny everything if he were to be questioned. Surely they wouldn't kill him on a hunch.

The next two days were very tense for Lucius. He studied everyone that he met. He read far too much into every look that he got and every snippet of conversation that he overheard. Had Torro told anyone about Lucius' discovery of Sandberg's body or about his relationship with Dolores? Did anyone at the law firm even care? Maybe they knew nothing about Sandberg's murder.

Two days later, there was a message on his phone when he arrived at work. "This is Marcus Henry. Come to my office as soon as you get here."

Lucius got out of his chair and started walking down the long hallway toward Marcus' office. Perhaps he just wanted an update on the review of documents. Maybe he wanted to make a change to the project. This wasn't necessarily a bad thing. After all, it was doubtful that Marcus Henry would be the one to kill him.

"Come in, Mr. Dixon."

"Sorry. I was a little late getting in this morning."

"That's okay. Close the door behind you and have a seat."

Lucius did as he was told.

"I've got some questions for you...some concerns that we have."

Lucius swallowed hard. "Okay. Go ahead."

"Mr. Dixon, did you ever know a man by the name of Daniel Sandberg?"

The questions were starting again. Lucius debated how much truth he should tell this time. "Yes, sir. He was my Torts professor."

Marcus smiled. "What did I tell you about calling me 'sir'?"

"Oh...sorry."

"That's okay. Now, was that the extent of your relationship with Mr. Sandberg?"

"No...I mean, not really. I was also the person who found his body when he was murdered."

"That must have been traumatic."

"It was."

"But you didn't witness the murder?"

"No, sir...I mean, no."

"Did you know that Daniel Sandberg was an attorney here before he was a professor at UVA?"

Lucius fibbed. "Someone told me that when I said that I was coming here."

"That didn't bother you? That you were coming to the firm where the man whose body you found once worked?"

"I thought about it, but I'm not superstitious. It seemed like it was just a weird coincidence."

"The fact of the matter is, Luke, that some of the higher ups are a little worried. We just found out about this a couple of days ago, and it seems like more than a coincidence to some people."

"What do you mean?"

"Well, no one ever figured out why Daniel Sandberg was murdered, so there's always a possibility that he was murdered because of his affiliation with this firm. Perhaps there is an angry former client out there somewhere, or maybe someone is angry because we represented his opponent in a case and defeated him."

"But what does that have to do with me?"

"Maybe you are that someone."

"What are you saying? That you think I killed Professor Sandberg?"

Marcus feigned surprise. "No, of course not. But maybe the killer sent you here to find out information."

"That's crazy! I chose to come here myself."

"Calm down, Luke. We're just trying to investigate this thing. Like I said, this only came to our attention a couple of days ago."

"Honestly, I'm sorry about that. Maybe I should have said something, but it just seemed unimportant."

"I'm sure it is, Luke. You had no connection to Sandberg other than being in his class and finding his body?"

"That's right."

"And you have never been involved in any litigation that Leeder & Schrum was involved in?"

"Never."

"And you don't know anyone who has been involved in any litigation with Leeder & Schrum?"

"Right."

"Okay. Just a few more questions, Luke, and then we can put this behind us."

Lucius doubted that he would ever put this behind him. "Okay."

"There was another attorney who worked closely with Sandberg when they were here. She has disappeared since Sandberg's murder. Do you know or have you ever met Dolores Martinez?"

"No. I've been asked about her before, though."

"This is very important, Luke. Dolores Martinez is one of the primary suspects in the murder of Daniel Sandberg, and she has a lot of bitter feelings toward this firm. We need to make sure the police find her before she does something drastic."

"Why does she have bitter feelings toward the firm?"

"There were a lot of hard feelings over her dismissal from the firm. She's an excitable girl."

216

"Can I ask you a few questions?"

"Sure, Luke."

"I know where this information is coming from. I ran into one of the detectives who was investigating Sandberg's murder case in the hallway. He was always very suspicious of me, and he always asked about Dolores Martinez."

"You're right so far."

"I just wanted to know why he was here. Was he still investigating that case?"

"No, he was dismissed from the police force a few months ago. Someone at the firm met him while he was investigating the case, and we decided to give him a second chance as a security guard after he was fired. I suppose it's just a coincidence that two people involved in the murder investigation of Daniel Sandberg ended up at his old firm."

"I'm being honest with you, Marcus. I've got nothing to hide."

"It's okay, Luke. I trust you."

Lucius got out of his chair and left the room. By the time he arrived back at his office, he realized that he'd been sweating profusely.

Once again, he was unable to concentrate on his work. He hadn't gotten any work done since he ran into Torro two days ago. He was too nervous.

Now his mind was continually going back to the conversation with Marcus Henry. Had his lies been obvious? Was there a possibility that they could catch him in a lie?

He tried to figure out what it was that they knew. Then he remembered the flash drive in the book that he had failed to get from Sandberg's house. Sergio Torro knew that he had gone by Mrs. Sandberg's house trying to get a book, but did Torro know the significance of the book?

Lindsey Coleman had either beaten him to the book or taken it from Robert. And he had given the flash drive to the firm according to Dolores. But had he told the firm where he found it?

The worst case scenario was that the firm knew that Lucius was trying to get the very book that contained the flash drive. If they knew that, then they knew that he was much more involved in this whole thing than he had admitted.

The best case scenario was that the firm didn't know anything about Lucius' visit to Mrs. Sandberg's house, nor did they know where Lindsey Coleman had gotten the flash drive from. If that was all they knew, then he was okay. They might suspect that he was lying, but they didn't have any proof.

Lucius tried to put his focus on his work. He started reading the piece of paper that was on his desk, but he only succeeded in reading the first sentence over and over. There was too much to worry about. Someone might walk into the office at any minute with a gun pointed in his face. Even if they didn't have any proof that he knew anything, they might kill him just in case.

Now that Garland was in the hospital, he had no way to find out if they were on to him. He would just have to be careful. There was nothing else he could do.

For the next few weeks, Lucius did his best to be careful. He only walked in crowded areas, and he never left his new apartment after dark. He could only manage to work for about five minutes at a time before his mind drifted back to his concerns for his own safety.

He started carrying the gun with him in his car. He kept it on the seat beside him and put it under the seat when he got to work. He didn't know if he had the nerve to shoot anyone, but he felt better having the gun there. It gave him some comfort.

One Thursday night, Lucius was coming home from work, and he began glancing back at the lights that were behind him. Every time he made a turn, the car behind him made a turn. His mind flashed back to the night when he had picked up Dolores from the airport. She had glanced back a few times, before deciding that they weren't being followed. Unfortunately, she had been wrong.

Lucius decided to make an extra block or two...just to make sure. He made a loop through an old downtown area, but the car was still behind him. He picked up the gun off the passenger seat and placed it in his own lap. If anyone tried to kill him, he was going to fight back.

He finally pulled into his parking lot after an extra thirty minutes of driving. The car pulled in behind him.

He thought about driving out the other side of the parking lot, but he felt that it was time to face whoever this was. He couldn't drive around all night. He pulled into a parking space next to his building and picked up his gun.

Just as he was making sure that the safety was off and the gun was ready to fire, he noticed the lights going by him. They drove by and went out the other side of the parking lot. Lucius breathed a sigh of relief.

Lucius walked slowly into his new apartment, clutching the gun to his chest. His heart was beating so loud that he could hear it.

He walked down the stairs that led to his apartment and three others. He looked in every shadowy corner, expecting to have to kill an assailant, but there was no one to be found.

He put the gun in his left hand and dug out his keys. He unlocked his apartment and entered carefully. He turned on the lights and looked around. It seemed safe. He closed the door and locked it.

He walked into the main room and looked in the closet that contained the air conditioning unit. He checked the kitchen. He walked into his bedroom and looked in his closet. He even got down on the floor and looked under his bed.

This had become his routine. He remembered how much he had wanted to be involved in all of this. He hadn't realized at the time that he would be concerned at every moment for his own safety. It was almost too much to handle.

Lucius put the gun down on one of the two couches in his sublet apartment and walked into the kitchen. The sublease part worried him, too. That meant that someone else had a key to his apartment. Someone could unlock the door and come in at anytime.

He decided to cook himself a hamburger in the skillet. He wasn't particularly hungry, but he knew he needed to eat. He pulled the hamburger meat out of the refrigerator and rolled a hunk of it into a ball. He patted it out with one hand while he turned on the oven with the other hand.

He would be glad when he got back to Charlottesville. He felt safer there. Charlottesville was more in his comfort zone, even though he really didn't have anything there anymore. Robert was gone. Jennifer was gone. Dolores was gone. And Garland would probably be gone soon. Anyway, he couldn't talk to him as long as he was in the hospital.

Lucius dropped the hamburger meat onto the skillet. It sizzled, and grease popped up slightly burning his hand. He turned the temperature on the stovetop down. Why had he come here? Why was he involved in all of this? If he were smart, he would have realized, like Lavindra, that this wasn't his fight.

Lucius finished cooking his hamburger and ate it quickly. He was hungrier than he had thought.

He turned on the television and flipped through the channels for a few hours before falling asleep on the couch. He slept soundly.

The next morning Lucius woke up early and got ready for work. He was going to have to try to concentrate. He needed the money from this job to pay off some of his student loans. He didn't need to get himself fired. He tried to tell himself that he was overreacting. No one at the firm wanted to kill him.

As he drove into work, he was feeling better. No one had said anything to him since Marcus called him in a few weeks ago. Maybe Marcus had believed everything that he had said, and the firm had decided that Lucius was no threat.

His optimism was shattered when he got to work. Once again, there was a message on his office phone, and once again it was from Marcus Henry. "Luke, I need to see you. This is Marcus."

Lucius got up and slowly walked down the hall. Maybe it was about the work this time. After all, the due date was fast approaching.

His legs got heavy as he reached the door. "Come in, Luke."

Lucius walked inside the door. There had been no order to close the door this time. That must be a good sign.

"I've got a little job for you, Luke."

"Okay."

"You haven't had much experience with our filing system, have you?"

"No, I haven't."

"All right, well, I've got some filing for you. I know this seems like secretarial work, but you need to figure out our system, and there's no better way than by filing something yourself."

"Sure."

"You need to file this carefully. This is discoverable information. Do you know what that means?"

"That if the other side requests it, we have to give it to them."

"That's right. So be very careful with it. I want to file it in the appropriate filing cabinet in room B-4. Can you do that?"

"I think so."

Marcus picked up a box off his desk and handed it to Lucius. "All right, here you go. Give me a call if you have any problems."

Lucius carried the box out into the hallway and into the elevator. Once he got in the elevator, he glanced down to see what it was he was looking at. The top piece of paper in the box was an e-mail from Dolores to Daniel Sandberg.

Lucius quickly flipped through the information as the elevator went down. These were hard copies of the research that had been taken from Sandberg's safe. They had to be. This was what he had come here for. He considered leaving immediately with the information, but that would draw too much suspicion. He could just get the research later. After all, now he would know exactly where it was. He could make copies late one night and return it without anyone being the wiser.

Then Lucius became suspicious. What are the odds that they would give him this particular information to file? And why would it be discoverable by anyone? It didn't make sense. This had to be some sort of a setup.

The elevator doors opened. He hesitated, and then slowly stepped into the hallway. He walked past a few doors and turned a corner. There was a man standing in a suit in front of room B-4.

"Mr. Henry told me you'd be coming. Go on inside."

Lucius braced himself. This was going to be it. He hadn't brought his gun. He couldn't protect himself. And Garland wasn't going to come to his rescue this time.

Lucius looked around the room as he entered. There were no filing cabinets in the room. There was only a single large paper shredder. Lucius looked back at the man in the suit who was now standing in the doorway. The man nodded at Lucius. "Go ahead, son."

Chapter Twenty-Four

The box fell out of Lucius' hands and landed on the ground with a thud. The man at the door chuckled.

Lucius didn't know what to do. The man didn't have a visible weapon, but he was clearly trying to intimidate Lucius. He could try to pick up the box and run, but what good would that do him? Even if he made it out of the office, where would he go? What would he do?

The man looked impatient. Lucius picked up the first piece of paper out of the box. He knew that it was unethical and probably illegal for him to shred a discoverable document, but he didn't know what else to do. He also knew that without the research, there would be no way to bring the case that would force the release of Blackbeard's journals.

Lucius fed the first piece of paper into the shredder. The man in the doorway smiled and closed the door. Lucius' eyes darted around the room, looking for a place to hide the research.

The room was completely empty. There were no vents. There were no windows. Lucius picked up another piece of paper and fed it into the machine. There was another copy, after all. There was the electronic copy that had been on the flash drive in the book at Sandberg's house. Perhaps the firm had kept that copy as well.

He tried to look at the information as he fed it into the machine, but it was too exhaustive. There was no way he could remember enough of it. For the next forty-five minutes, Lucius fed the research into the shredder one page at a time.

When he finished, he took a deep breath before opening the door. Again he braced himself for a gunshot. He walked out into the hallway. There was no one around. He walked slowly back to the elevator doors and stepped inside.

He briefly debated going to the ground floor and leaving the firm without looking back, but that seemed like a waste now.

If they wanted to kill him, they would have done so already. If this was some sort of test of his loyalty, he had passed it by shredding the research. Either way, the best thing to do would be to go back to work.

He pushed the button for the third floor and waited as the elevator doors slowly closed. He had done what he had to do.

When he arrived back at his office, no one was waiting for him. He sat down at his desk. There were no voice mail messages. There were no e-mails. Everything seemed normal.

He just sat there staring at his computer screen for what seemed like hours. He couldn't possibly concentrate on his work now. He wanted someone to come into his office. He wanted someone to explain to him what was going on.

Finally six o'clock arrived, and Lucius left his office. He again expected someone to meet him at the elevator, but there was no one to be found. The receptionist waved goodnight to him as he passed.

He took the elevator down to the parking garage and walked through the dark and to his car. He drove home in silence.

There were no lights behind him as he pulled into his parking lot. He got out of his car clutching his gun.

He got to the door and unlocked the dead bolt, but the door didn't open. The lock on the door itself was locked. Lucius stepped back. He never locked the door. Because the door could be locked from the inside and the dead bolt had to be locked from the outside with a key, he always locked the dead bolt only to avoid locking himself out of his apartment.

Lucius held his gun firmly in his right hand as he unlocked the door. He opened it slowly and stepped inside.

He took a few steps into the apartment. He turned on the light in the main room. There was no sign that anyone had been in there. He checked his bedroom and the kitchen. There was no one in his apartment now, and there was no sign that anyone had gone through any of his things.

But Lucius was absolutely sure that he had only locked the dead bolt. Someone had been in there. Could his landlord have come by? Or the person who was subleasing the apartment to him?

Lucius didn't think so. The firm had sent someone to his apartment. They had broken in while he was shredding the documents. He was sure of it. Thankfully, there was nothing in the apartment for them to find. He had left all of Garland's research in Charlottesville.

Charlottesville.

If they had tracked him to this apartment, then they could easily find out about his other apartment.

Lucius had nothing to do for the weekend, so he quickly packed a bag, climbed into his car, and drove toward Charlottesville. Maybe they had no intention of searching that apartment. Maybe they hadn't even been the ones who were in his apartment earlier that day. But just to be safe, Lucius wanted to check.

About halfway there, he got a call on his cell phone. He answered it without looking at who was calling.

"Luke?"

"Yeah, it's me. Who's this?"

"It's Jennifer. I'm sorry I haven't talked to you in a while."

"That's okay, Jennifer. How's the summer going?"

"Well, it was going pretty well until today."

"What happened?"

Jennifer hesitated. "Robert's dad came to see me."

"What? What did he want?"

"He wanted to talk to me about his son. It was weird. He just came walking into my office in the middle of the day."

"Well? Go on, Jennifer. What did he say?"

"He wanted to know if I knew where Robert was. I told him that I didn't, and he said that he had heard otherwise."

"I didn't tell him that you knew where he was, but I did tell him what Cole told me...you know, that Robert went to New York to find you."

"Well, he wouldn't let up. He said that I had done something to his son, and that he wanted to know where he was."

"Did you tell him anything?"

"No. I wanted to tell him everything because he was so forceful, but I didn't want to get us in trouble. I just told him that Robert was going through a lot."

"Well, that's true. He was struggling."

"Luke, I don't know what to do. This is all becoming a little too much for me to handle."

"There's nothing left to do. Just go back to work on Monday. Mr. Collins probably won't bother you again."

"I hope you're right."

"Listen, Jennifer. I need you to keep silent about the whole thing for a little longer. They'll find Sandberg's murderer at some point, and then it won't matter anymore."

"Okay, Luke. I'll talk to you later."

"Bye, Jennifer."

Lucius drove on through the night. He missed his friends. He remembered that first year and how much fun they had together. They had suspected that something strange was going on, but more than anything investigating the mystery had been a lot of fun. Ever since Sandberg's murder, it had all become so serious.

He finally pulled into the apartment complex a little after ten o'clock. It was dark, and there were only a few cars in the parking lot. Most people were out of town for the summer.

He got out of his car with his bag on one arm and his gun in the other hand. He walked to the door and entered his apartment. After some investigation, he determined that there was no one inside.

Lucius pulled out the DVD case that contained the flash drive and checked inside. It was still there. He walked into the bedroom and looked under the bed. The boxes were still in place, as well.

He walked back into the living room and collapsed onto the couch. He never moved back into his bedroom after Dolores left. He preferred to sleep on the couch with the television on. He needed the noise. The weight of silence was too much for him.

The next morning Lucius woke up and loaded the boxes into his car. He left the flash drive. It seemed to be safely hidden. He drove to a storage center and walked inside. The employee behind the counter looked up.

"What can I do for you?"

"I need to rent a storage unit to store a few boxes."

"Yeah, I can do that. What size do you need?"

"I don't know. How deep are the units?"

"It depends on what you're looking for. How big are your boxes?"

"Hold on a second." Lucius walked out to the car and brought the boxes inside.

"That's it?"

"Yeah, that's all of them."

"All right, we can rent you a small unit. That'll give you plenty of room."

Lucius started thinking. If he had to give them his driver's license, this place wouldn't be any safer for the boxes than his apartment. "What do I need to rent the box? I don't have any sort of identification with me."

"We normally don't rent without ID, but I'll let you get it if you can pay me cash for the full year."

"Yeah, I can do that."

Lucius paid the employee and took his key.

"Your unit is at the very back of the complex. You should drive back there to it. Number K-43."

"Thanks."

Lucius put the boxes back in the car and drove to the unit. He unlocked it and slid the boxes inside. He hesitated for a moment. Under his bed, the boxes just looked like innocent research. In the unit by themselves, they looked more important.

Lucius closed the unit and locked it. He had paid cash for the unit. No one that cared about these documents would have any idea where to look for them now. He got in his car and drove home.

He relaxed for the rest of the day by watching television. He got a good night's sleep and drove back to Norfolk on Sunday.

His nerves had settled a little. The firm had been suspicious of him, but for whatever reason, they had decided not to kill him. Instead they had chosen to make him shred some important documents. Maybe they wanted to let him know that the documents were no longer available, or maybe they just wanted to test his loyalty. Whatever their reason, his actions should have made them trust him a little more.

Nothing unusual happened for the rest of the summer. The other summer associate showed up about halfway through the summer and was always in the office with him, so Lucius didn't have a chance to try to look on the network for the electronic copy of Sandberg's research. It was probably better anyway. He didn't want to draw any more attention to himself, and the firm might have some way of tracking his searches.

He finished his project on the day it was due. His next project was more of the same. He wasn't sure if they had chosen to give him the most boring projects possible in order to test his fortitude, or if the only things they trusted him with just happened to be boring.

He had a couple of conversations with Marcus, but none of them addressed the shredded documents. No one else mentioned it, so Lucius didn't mention it either.

With only a week left in the summer, Marcus came into their office.

"Hey guys, how are you?"

The other summer associate, Derek Donner from Yale Law School spoke first. "We're doing well."

"I want to invite you guys on a yacht cruise. After your last day on next Friday, we're going to take one of the partner's boats out. It will be sort of a going-away party for you guys. What about you, Dixon? Are you in?"

A boat trip seemed harmless enough. "Yeah, it sounds like fun."

"Donner?"

"I'm not going to be able to go. I've got to catch a flight back to Connecticut that Friday after work."

"Oh, well, I'm sorry to hear that. I'll see you next Friday, Mr. Dixon."

Marcus Henry walked out of the office. This wasn't good. Lucius had agreed because he thought Derek would be going. It seemed safe with Derek there. Now he wasn't so sure. Maybe they had just been waiting for the right opportunity to knock him off. Maybe they knew Derek had a flight that Friday afternoon.

"Derek, had you mentioned that flight to anyone?"

"What?"

"Your flight out next Friday. Had you mentioned that to anyone at the firm?"

"Yeah, I thought that was kind of weird. I told them a couple of weeks ago that I would have to leave a little early on that Friday to catch my flight. I've got a wedding to be at that weekend."

"I wonder why they didn't schedule the cruise around that."

"I don't know. They probably forgot. I hope this doesn't affect my offer."

Derek talked about his offer constantly. Leeder & Schrum wasn't one of the firms who offered all of their summer associates a position with the firm after they graduated, so Derek was paranoid that everything he did would prevent him from getting an offer.

"I'm sure it will be fine, Derek."

"Yeah, that's easy for you to say. You're going on the cruise."

"I promise not to impress anyone too much."

Derek didn't laugh. "This is serious, Luke. This firm is very prestigious. I mean...it doesn't show up in the rankings, but those in the know are aware of how good this place is. I want to work here next year."

"You did a good job with all of your projects. That's all that matters."

"I don't know if I did well on those projects. All I know is that I completed them."

"Well, worrying won't accomplish anything. Anyway, I've got to get back to work."

Lucius lowered his head and looked at the papers in front of him, but he wasn't able to concentrate. He now had a boat trip to worry about.

The last week went by quickly. Lucius said goodbye to Derek when he left early that Friday. He told Derek that he would e-mail him, but he didn't plan to follow through with that promise.

He rode with Marcus to the dock, and they climbed aboard the yacht. After a few nervous minutes, two partners arrived: Franklin Norski and Gregory Stevenson. They were both nearly seventy years old.

Mr. Norski was the friendlier of the two. "How are you doing Mr. Dixon? I'm glad you could make it."

The four of them made small talk for a few minutes. After a while, two more carloads of attorneys arrived, and they launched the boat and sailed out into the Atlantic Ocean.

Lucius did pretty well, despite his nerves. He managed to carry on several conversations with the different partners.

After about an hour, Marcus called him below deck. Lucius walked slowly behind him into a small bar.

"Luke, I wanted to tell you that we all thought you did a very good job this summer."

"Thank you."

"I'm particularly proud of you. I fight for UVA kids all the time. I really wanted you to do well."

Lucius didn't say anything.

"Well, what I'm getting at is that we want to give you an offer. We want you to come back to the firm next year."

Lucius was surprised. "Wow, that's quite an honor. I'll need some time to think about it, though."

"Of course you will. Did you enjoy your time with the firm?"

Lucius lied. "I did. The work was very challenging."

"We wanted to give you more research projects, but it just didn't work out that way this summer. If you come back next year, you'll definitely get more research."

"Well, thanks very much. I appreciate this."

Marcus walked behind the bar and crouched. Lucius was terrified that he was going to come up with a gun. Lucius had left his own gun in his car at the parking garage.

Marcus rose up with a bottle of bourbon. "Want a drink?"

"Sure. Just pour it over some ice."

230

Marcus picked up a couple of glasses and filled them with ice. He poured the bourbon slowly over the ice.

The two of them sipped their drinks for the next few minutes. Not many words were exchanged. Lucius didn't know if it was a good sign or a bad sign that he had been given an offer. Did it mean that they now trusted him? Or did it mean that they wanted to keep him close, so they could keep an eye on him?

When they finished their drinks, they went back up to the deck. Lucius started talking to one of the partners but was interrupted when his phone started buzzing. Lucius didn't recognize the number, so he excused himself to take the call.

"Luke, this is Dolores."

"Where are you?"

"I can't get into that over the phone. I've got some bad news."

"What is it?"

"Garland's dead."

Chapter Twenty-Five

The news wasn't completely unexpected. "Are you going to be okay?"

There was a pause. "Yeah, I'll be all right. It's just...I didn't have a father growing up, Luke, and both Daniel and Garland filled that role for me. Now I've got no one."

One of the attorneys was staring at Lucius. He was careful not to say anything that would give away who he was talking to. "Just try to be strong. Are you going to stay where you are?"

"Yeah, at least for a while."

"Can you call me back later tonight? I'm at a firm event right now."

"Okay, I'll call you in a couple of hours."

Lucius ended the call and walked back over to a group of attorneys.

The partner Franklin Norski had a grin on his face. "Girlfriend checking in on you?"

"No, sir, just a friend."

The next few hours passed peacefully. At nearly midnight, the boat docked, and the attorneys departed.

Marcus Henry called Lucius over to his car. "Do you need a ride, Luke?"

"Actually, that would be nice. Could you give me a ride back to the office?"

"Sure, get in."

Lucius climbed into the car, and Marcus cranked it up.

"So do you have a girlfriend, Luke?"

"No, not at the moment."

Marcus paused for a few seconds. "Well, I'm sure we'll remedy that soon."

Lucius laughed uncomfortably.

They drove the rest of the way in silence. Marcus dropped Lucius off at his car but grabbed his arm before he could exit the car.

"Luke. I just want you to know that you did a really good job this summer. We are all very proud of you."

Lucius could smell the alcohol on his breath. "Thank you. I really enjoyed the summer."

"I hope you'll keep in touch. Let me know if you're in town."

"I will."

Marcus' grip loosened, and Lucius climbed out of the car, shutting the door behind him. He looked back at Marcus as his car accelerated off.

Lucius climbed in his own car and drove home. As soon as he arrived at home, his phone began ringing.

"Hello?"

"Luke, it's Dolores. Are you done with your firm event?"

"Yeah, I just walked in the door."

"So I guess you're wondering what we should do next? About the whole Ramsden situation?"

"We don't have to think about that right now, Dolores. I'm sure this isn't an easy time for you."

"I'll be fine, Luke. I have to stay here for a few more months. Then I'll come back to Charlottesville, and we'll move forward. We can't stop just because Garland is dead."

"Are you sure you want to do that? Maybe we should quit while you and I are still alive."

"We're not going to quit. This is important, Luke. It wasn't just about Garland."

"Where's Lavindra? The last time I talked to him, he seemed to imply that he was no longer going to be involved after Garland died."

"He left for Sri Lanka the day after it happened. He's accepted a two-year teaching assignment at the University of Colombo in Sri Lanka. He's going to teach Medieval poetry."

"Well, maybe he's got the right idea, Dolores."

"Luke, if you don't want to help me anymore, I understand. I can carry on by myself."

"No. If you're going to stick this thing out, then I'm going to help you."

"Thanks, Luke. That means a lot to me."

Lucius braced himself. "Unfortunately, I've got some bad news. Leeder & Schrum made me shred the research that you and Sandberg did."

"What?"

"They gave me a box filled with the research. They told me to file it, but they sent me to a room with a paper shredder and an intimidating man standing in front of it, telling me to go ahead. I shredded it."

Dolores was silent.

Lucius tried to reassure her. "There's still an electronic copy. They probably have it on their system."

"Yeah, we'll figure it out, Luke. Just be careful."

"They also offered me a job for next year. Should I take it?"

"No, Luke, you shouldn't. We'll figure out another way to get into their system to get the research, or you and I can start the research over from the beginning. There's no reason to put you at risk again."

Lucius wasn't going to argue this time. He had been on edge the entire summer. "Okay, Dolores."

"I have to go now, Luke, but I'll try to call you soon."

"Okay. Be safe, Dolores."

"I miss you, Luke."

"I miss you, too."

"Bye."

"Goodbye, Dolores."

Lucius had been pacing around the room while he talked. After hanging up the phone, he turned on the television and sat down. He fell asleep in his chair.

The next day Lucius packed up all of his things and moved back into his Charlottesville apartment. He felt much safer there.

He called Marcus Henry the next afternoon.

"Marcus?"

"Yeah?"

"This is Lucius Dixon. I just wanted to let you know this soon, so you could go ahead and start interviewing others for the position. I'm not going to take the job with Leeder & Schrum."

"I'm really sorry to hear that Luke. Do you have a reason for us?"

"It's just not the type of work I see myself doing. It's nothing against anyone at the firm. Everyone was great."

"Everyone at the firm will be very disappointed to hear the news. Nonetheless, I hope you do well this next year, and I hope you find a job that better suits your needs."

"Thanks, Marcus."

Lucius went into his bedroom and began signing up for on-grounds interviews. He wanted to interview for as many different positions as possible. He signed up for firm jobs, as well as clerkships and government jobs. Because he had been so distracted by the Ramsden affair, he hadn't really had a chance to consider his future. Now that he was considering it, he realized how bright it was.

He had excellent grades and would graduate from a prestigious law school. He even had a good shot at winning the moot court competition. His credentials were very strong.

The interviews went well for Lucius. He felt that he learned a lot about the different law firms that he talked to, but he was more attracted to government work. It seemed like a good way to begin his career. For the most part, young government lawyers were thrown into the fire and gained more experience than young lawyers at law firms.

His classes began and Lucius again focused his attention on law school. He had one more year of school, and he wanted to finish strong. While most of the third-year law students slacked off, Lucius focused harder.

He began receiving offers from law firms in October. He had until December to make a decision. He talked to Dolores nearly once a week. They talked about what they would do to get the research back, but they also talked a lot about Lucius' future. Dolores was very supportive and wanted him to do something that would make him happy.

He advanced through the next two rounds of moot court. His speaking skills had improved tremendously, and he had become much better at thinking on his feet. His briefs were never as good as his opponent's, but he always made up for it by outperforming them during oral arguments.

The judges would do their best to stump him with a hard question, but he always had the perfect answer or deflection. His confidence in his own ability also began to grow. He was beginning to think that he would win the whole competition.

Instead of accepting a job at a law firm, Lucius decided to clerk for a year. He got a job offer as a clerk for the Virginia Supreme Court, and he took the offer. It would be a great jumping off point for his legal career.

Lucius took all of his exams and felt that he did well. He decided to stay in Charlottesville for the winter break. He wanted to relax for a while.

Professor Franklin called him in for a meeting on the day after his final exam.

"Hey, Luke, I'm glad you could make it."

"It's not a problem, sir. I'm staying in town for the break."

"I just wanted to thank you for all of your help. That research project of ours is going to be published in the Harvard Law Review."

"Wow...congratulations, sir."

"I couldn't have done it without you."

"Thanks."

"I mean it, Luke. You've done very well for yourself. After all that you went through last year, I'm very proud of you."

"Thank you, sir. You've been a big help."

"What are you going to be doing after you graduate?"

"I'll be clerking for the Virginia Supreme Court for the first year. I'm still undecided as to what I'll do after that. I decided not to defer any of my offers. I want to keep my options open."

"That's very impressive. I think you'll do well for yourself."

The two of them chatted for what seemed like hours. Finally Lucius excused himself and headed home.

The next semester arrived. Lucius was ready to be done with law school, but he knew he had to focus for one more semester.

About halfway through the semester, he received the final moot court problem. He began staying late at the library preparing his brief. His briefs had always been less than impressive, and he knew that if he could match his opponent's brief, he could win the competition.

He set his other studies aside. He was confident that he could catch up in the reading when the competition was over. It was more important to win. If he won the moot court competition, he could write his own ticket. He could go anywhere that he wanted to go.

One night he was in the library near closing time. He was deep in concentration, when he was disturbed by a loud banging noise behind him.

He turned quickly to see what the noise was, but there was no one around. In fact, he hadn't seen anyone in the library for a while.

He put his pen down and got out of his chair. He walked slowly around to the other side of the book shelf. There was no one there either.

Lucius was confused and a little frightened. He was sure that he had heard a noise, and he was sure that someone had caused it. Had someone been watching him? Or had someone just rushed by quickly, accidentally bumping into a shelf.

Lucius walked back to the front of the library.

Gretchen Lewis, the librarian, smiled at him.

"Ms. Lewis, have you seen anyone else in the library?"

"No, Luke, I'm pretty sure you're the last one. I'm locking up in five minutes."

"I could have sworn I heard something a minute ago."

"Well, I wouldn't be surprised. These old book shelves creak sometimes."

"It was louder than that. It was a thud."

Ms. Lewis smiled again. "Maybe a loose book fell off a shelf or something. I wouldn't worry about it, Luke."

But Lucius was worried. For weeks now he had managed to keep his imagination in check. He hadn't worried very much about the Ramsdens or Leeder & Schrum or any of that. He had focused on school.

But now it was all coming back to him. His life could still be in danger. He had turned down that offer. What if they took that the wrong way? What if they took that as confirmation that Lucius knew something?

Lucius walked back to the desk he was using and collected his things. He wished he had his gun.

He walked out into the darkness and toward his car. He jumped at every noise.

Finally he reached his car and drove toward his apartment. He tried to tell himself that he was being ridiculous.

Lucius arrived at home but was unable to sleep that night. For the next week, he was tense. Every face seemed suspicious.

He lost the moot court final. It wasn't even close.

He had tried to work hard on his brief. He had spent countless hours staring at it, trying to think of how to improve it, but he was unable to concentrate. What did it matter anyway? His law school experience wouldn't be defined by any of this. It would be defined by his mystery, and ultimately his failure to reveal the truth about the Ramsden family.

He hadn't been very good at the oral argument either. All of the talent that he had developed over the last two years had left him when he walked up to the podium. He stuttered and stammered when he was asked questions. His answers weren't terrible, but they were poorly delivered and unorganized.

Lucius left the law school with his head hung low. He had come so far in the competition only for it to all fall apart at the end because he lost concentration. He was ashamed of himself.

A few weeks later, he got the news that he had been waiting for, when his phone rang one night after midnight.

He had been asleep with the television on, but he managed to get to the phone before it stopped ringing.

"Hello?"

"Hey, Luke. It's Dolores."

"Dolores, it's been a while." He hadn't spoken to her in a few weeks.

"I'm sorry about that. I had to change cities and cell phones. I felt like I was being followed."

"By who?"

"I'm not sure, but it's okay. I'm safe now, and I've got some good news."

"What's that?"

"I'm coming back to Charlottesville."

"That's fantastic. You can stay here again."

"Yeah, I'll take you up on that offer. I've also got an idea as to how we can get that electronic copy of the research."

"What's that?"

"I know where one of the Leeder & Schrum tech support guys lives. We can get the firm's remote software from him, and then we can log on from any computer and find the file."

"How would we get the software from him? He's not going to just hand that over. He could get fired."

"We'll bribe him or something. Those people don't make much money. He'll be happy to hand it over for a couple of hundred dollars. We'll give him fake names, in case he tries to turn us in."

Lucius didn't like the plan, but he couldn't tell her that. He was too excited to see her. "Sounds good, Dolores. When are you coming in?"

"I'll be there tomorrow morning."

"So soon?"

"Yeah, I've missed you. I can't wait any longer to see you again. You're pretty much the only friend I've got left."

"I've missed you, too, Dolores. I'm looking forward to seeing you again."

"How did the moot court competition go?"

Lucius didn't want her to worry. "I did well, but not well enough. I lost, but it's okay. I'm proud of my performance."

"That's all that matters. Second place out of two-hundred kids is pretty good anyway."

"Yeah, thanks."

"Well, I've got to go. I need to get some sleep."

Lucius lay back down on the couch, but he was too nervous to sleep. When his clock said 6:00 A.M., he got off the couch and went into the bedroom. He lay down in his bed for the first time since Dolores had left.

He wasn't sure when she was coming, but he wanted to be ready. He decided to skip his classes for the day. He got out of bed, cleaned the apartment, and took a shower. He kept his phone with him at all times.

Before Lucius knew it, it was afternoon, and then it was evening.

Where was she? Had she decided not to come after all? Or was she just running late? Maybe she realized that it was too dangerous, or maybe she spotted the person who was following her again.

Lucius stayed up until about midnight. He was afraid to try to call the cell phone that she had given him. She switched phones pretty often, and he didn't want to give whoever was following her an inadvertent clue.

Lucius didn't sleep well that night either. He tossed and turned, thinking about Dolores and what had happened to her.

The next morning, he showered and left the house. He couldn't sit around waiting any longer. He had to go to class.

He was sitting in his Constitutional History class taking notes, when he noticed some of the students whispering in front of him. He glanced at one of their computer screens.

It was on a news page. The headline read, "Suspect Arrested in Murder of UVA Professor."

Lucius strained his eyes to read the first line of text: "Dolores Martinez, a former co-worker of Daniel Sandberg, has been arrested in connection with his murder."

Chapter Twenty-Six

Lucius sat in his chair stone-faced.

Now he was really alone. Dolores had left him before, but he always knew that she could come back at any time. Now he didn't know what to do.

He wanted to rush down to the police station. He wanted to tell them everything that he knew. But he knew that Dolores wouldn't want that. The police would probably only arrest him and charge him with conspiracy to commit murder. If the Ramsdens were powerful enough to have an innocent woman charged with murder, then they wouldn't have any trouble going after him as well.

And surely they didn't have enough evidence to convict her. Detective Torro had said something about her fingerprints being all over Sandberg's office. But even if that were true, they'd need more than that. The murder weapon was at the bottom of a swamp, and Dolores didn't have a motive for killing Sandberg. There were also secretaries and other professors who would have seen the murderer. They would surely testify that they didn't see Dolores up there that day.

Lucius briefly considered the possibility that Dolores had murdered Sandberg, but he quickly discarded that thought. She had to be telling him the truth.

The professor dismissed the class, and Lucius gathered his things. If she needed his help, she could get in touch with him. She was probably safer in the hands of the police than she had been while traveling anonymously in rural Ohio.

The next few months went by very slowly for Lucius. He wanted badly to finish the job that Sandberg and Dolores had started. He wanted to expose the Ramsdens for the evil family that they were. They had killed Professor Sandberg and Robert, and they had caused Dolores to be accused of a murder that she didn't commit.

But he didn't know what to do. He wouldn't know where to begin researching the legal issues that Sandberg and Dolores had researched, and he didn't know how to go about getting the electronic copy of that research from Leeder & Schrum. He was stuck.

So Lucius focused on his schoolwork as much as he could. He followed Dolores' case in the news. He worried about her every night as he tried to sleep. She was tough, but she wasn't prison tough.

Her trial was set for the following August. Lucius didn't know how he would do it, but he planned to have her free before the trial began.

In the meantime, Lucius finished law school. He didn't study as hard for his finals as he had in the past, but he still felt confident that he had done well. About a week after school, he finished a research paper for his Separation of Powers course, and he graduated from law school in May.

It was a somber occasion. It was supposed to have been one of the high points of his life. He was graduating from one of the best law schools in the country. He had done well there and was prepared to begin his legal career as a clerk. But Lucius didn't have a smile on his face as he walked across the lawn in the early afternoon. It was all he could do to keep from crying.

But he continued to move forward. He had signed up to take the Multi-State Professional Responsibility Exam and the Virginia Bar Exam. He purchased some study manuals and settled in at his apartment in Charlottesville. He began studying for nearly eight hours a day. At least he had control over this.

His routine was broken one day in late May by a phone call.

"Mr. Dixon?"

"Yes?"

"This is Arnold Shiflet. I'm calling on behalf of the Virginia Character and Fitness Committee."

"Yes, sir. What can I do for you?"

"We need you to come in. We have to talk to you about your bar application."

"Okay. Can you give me a better idea of what this is about?"

242

"I'm sorry. I can't do that. Are you free this Friday?"

"Yes, sir."

"All right, we need you to come down to Richmond."

"Where exactly?"

"The Virginia State Bar. We're located at the corner of 8th and Main. I'll see you at ten o'clock Friday morning."

Lucius said goodbye, but Arnold Shiflet had already hung up the phone. "Great," he whispered aloud. "Something else to worry about."

Lucius got up early Friday morning and drove to Richmond. He didn't know what to expect when he walked in the door.

The secretary took him into a room with three men sitting behind a folding table. They introduced themselves and shook his hand. The one in the middle was the man he had talked to on the phone.

"Mr. Dixon, please take a seat."

Lucius sat down in the lone chair in front of the table. He was sweating.

"A very disturbing video tape came into our possession, and we wanted to see if you could explain it."

"Okay. I'll do my best."

One of the other men got up and wheeled a television out to their left. He pushed in a video tape and turned up the volume. "We've even got sound," he said with a half-smile.

The tape began inside Marcus Henry's office. Lucius recognized it and immediately realized what this was.

There was a timer at the bottom of the screen, which revealed that the tape began at 9:30 in the morning. Lucius entered Marcus Henry's office, and Marcus told him to file the information. He also told him that the information was discoverable.

The tape then cut to different angles following him down the hallway toward the elevator, as he carried the box of research. Where were all these cameras? Lucius hadn't seen a single camera the entire time he had been there.

The tape continued. It showed Lucius taking the elevator down to the basement level and looking through the material as the elevator descended. It showed him exiting the elevator and walking down the hallway. The man who had stood in front of the door was not on the tape. It cut immediately from the hallway to a view inside the room.

The tape showed Lucius standing inside the room for a few seconds. It showed him looking toward the door. If he didn't know better, it would have seemed like he was looking to make sure no one else was around.

Then the shredding began. The tape continued as Lucius shredded the entire box full of documents. One of the men stood up and fast-forwarded the tape through all of the shredding.

When the tape ended, the man who had moved the television ejected the tape and turned off the television.

Arnold Shiflet spoke up. "So, Mr. Dixon? Do you have an explanation for what we just watched?"

Lucius didn't know what to say. "I don't know, sir."

"What do you mean you don't know? We just watched you shredding discoverable documents. Unless you have a pretty good explanation, we're going to have a real problem."

"I was confused. I didn't understand what I was supposed to do."

"Didn't the attorney tell you to file the documents? Didn't he tell you that the information was discoverable?"

"Yes, sir. Apparently, he did. But I misunderstood him. I thought I was supposed to shred the documents."

"Well, I'm sorry, Mr. Dixon, but that explanation is not good enough. This is one of the most egregious acts that I've ever seen performed by a potential lawyer. There is no way that the state of Virginia can license you to practice law."

"But, sir..."

"I'm not finished, Mr. Dixon. Not only is there no way that the state of Virginia will ever license you to practice law, there is no way that any state in this nation will ever allow you to practice law. I hope you'll learn a lesson from this."

"It was just a mistake, sir."

"I'm sorry, Mr. Dixon, but no one is going to believe that."

Lucius just sat there in disbelief. His life was coming apart at the seams.

"That's all there is to say, Mr. Dixon. You can go now."

244

Lucius got up and stumbled out of the room. Three years of his life down the drain. How would he pay back his student loans? What would he tell his parents?

His vision got blurry, and he collapsed in the hallway.

When he woke up, he was surrounded by secretaries.

"Are you okay?"

"I think so. I just blacked out."

Lucius sat up and put his back against a wall. He tried to stand up, but his legs felt like jelly. One of the secretaries brought him some water. After a few minutes, Lucius got up and walked out to his car.

He didn't even turn on the radio as he drove home. He rode in silence. His life was in shambles.

His phone rang when he was halfway home.

"Luke, this is Detective Snow."

"Hey, what can I do for you?"

"Actually, I wanted to apologize to you."

"For what?"

"For the way Detective Torro and I behaved. He was so certain that you had something to do with all of this. I thought he was crazy, but I went along with it anyway. And for that, I owe you an apology."

"That's okay, Ms. Snow." Lucius thought about telling her everything. Maybe she could help to get Dolores out of jail. Maybe she could help them in bringing the truth out.

"If there's ever anything you need, just let me know. I'm willing to help."

But he couldn't tell her. He couldn't tell anyone now. He had to handle this on his own. "Thank you, Ms. Snow. I will."

"I should have known that Sergio wasn't behaving properly. When he was dismissed from the force, it didn't come as a surprise to me. I don't know why I didn't tell someone about his behavior. I guess I was just intimidated by him."

Lucius didn't say anything.

"Well, anyway, I just wanted to let you know that I was sorry about the way I behaved."

Lucius said goodbye to Detective Snow and continued driving. Maybe he would call her back when he was feeling better. Maybe they could work together to release Dolores. And then the three of them could go after the Ramsdens.

But then again, her call had come at a very suspicious time. It was right after his meeting with the ethics board. Perhaps they were checking on him or testing his responses. Maybe Detective Snow also worked for them.

When he arrived at home, he had an e-mail on his computer from Professor Franklin. He had forgotten about Professor Franklin…one of the few friends he had left.

Luke,

Please come see me tomorrow at the law school.

Jonas Franklin.

Lucius went out to the living room and sat down to watch television. Professor Franklin might be his final hope. Maybe he could help him to fix all of this.

The next morning, he walked into Professor Franklin's office. It was filled with boxes.

"What are all the boxes for?"

"They're moving me up to the third floor of the library...to a dusty old corner. They've got to make room for the new hot-shot professors. I think this office is going to one from Yale."

"That's absurd. You're the best professor at this school."

Franklin smiled, but only briefly. "Luke, I wish we could just sit here and chat, but we have something more important to talk about."

"What's that?"

"We heard here at the law school about what happened yesterday with the Virginia Bar. I'm very disappointed in you."

"It was a big mistake, sir."

"I heard that the whole thing was recorded."

"That's true, but what I did was a mistake. I didn't understand…"

"I know you too well to believe that, Luke. You're an intelligent young man."

Lucius didn't know how to defend himself, even to his friend.

"I brought you into my office after the incident that happened here two years ago. I saw the potential in you. You could have been a great attorney, but you threw it all away."

"I didn't know what I was doing."

"You wasted so much potential, Luke. Most people never have the opportunities that you had. Why did you do it?"

"I was trying to tell you that. It was a mistake. I thought that was what I was supposed to do."

Professor Franklin's eyes began to water. "That's just too hard for me to believe."

"It's the truth. Why would I shred documents like that? What would my motive be?"

"You have to go now, Luke. I hope you'll learn from this. I hope you'll find your way. I just keep thinking of the wasted opportunity."

Lucius got up and left the office. There was nothing else to say. He could try to tell the truth about Leeder & Schrum, but no one would believe it.

His only chance now was to force the truth out. If he could release Blackbeard's journals to the public, then all of this would be fixed. The people would learn the truth about the Ramsdens. Dolores would be set free, and his reputation would be restored.

It was pouring down rain when he left the law school. He ran to his car. He drove home and sat down in his chair. His eyes settled first on his gun sitting on the coffee table. His eyes then moved to Garland Ramsden's manuscript. He got out of the chair and walked over to it.

A clap of thunder resounded through the room, as he picked it up and began flipping through the pages. His studies had forced him to put it aside with one chapter to go. Now he had nothing better to do. He might as well finish it.

Chapter Twenty: The Pirate King

In some ways, Wilfred Ramsden was the culmination of everything toward which his family had worked.

He was powerful. He graduated from Wharton and became one of the youngest CEO's in American history. He handled the family's corporate assets better than any Ramsden before him. He would nearly double their wealth by the time he was fifty.

He was unafraid of immorality. As much as he had tortured his brother as a child, he tortured his employees as an adult. He invested in industries as they rose, and they would collapse when he pulled his investments.

He was also eccentric. He was more obsessed with the Blackbeard story than any of his ancestors. He read every book that there was to read about Blackbeard. He shared anecdotes about the famous pirate at board meetings.

As of the time of this writing, he still attends the Blackbeard Festival in Hampton, Virginia. He goes incognito dressed in full Blackbeard regalia. He even walks around at the festival with a silver cup that he claims is the cup that was made from Blackbeard's skull so many years ago.

He was elected to the United States Senate in overwhelming fashion and served two full terms. He fought against any sort of restraints on corporate freedom. He was most famous for sponsoring legislation that made it significantly easier for his former corporations to buy political influence.

He was briefly talked about as a potential presidential candidate, but he always waved off such talk. He knew that he had too many family secrets. He knew that they might come out if he made such a run.

He named his son Ambrose, but he was always disappointed in him. He feared handing over the corporate reigns to him.

Lucius' reading was interrupted by a soft knocking at the door.

At first he wasn't sure if the sound was created by the rain or if there was someone at the door.

He put the book down on the coffee table and sat staring at the front door.

There was another knock.

Surely they wouldn't have come to kill him now. They had already ensured that he could never practice law.

Lucius didn't want to get up. He just wanted to go back to his reading.

There was another knock.

Lucius picked his gun up off the coffee table. He walked slowly over to the door and looked out the peephole.

There was a dark figure standing outside his door, but he couldn't tell who it was. Whoever it was, they were covered in water and looking down.

Lucius unlocked the door with his left hand while he held the gun firmly in his right hand. He slowly opened the door and looked out.

The man at the door had long hair, and his face was covered in stubble. He was also soaking wet.

But there was no doubt about it. It was his old classmate Robert Collins.

Chapter Twenty-Seven

Robert brushed his hair back out of his face and smiled. "I wasn't expecting the rain."

Lucius was startled. "Robert...what...come in..."

"Thanks, do you have some clothes I can change into."

"Yeah, go in the bathroom. I'll go get some from my room and toss them into you."

Robert did as he was told, and Lucius handed him some jeans and a button-up shirt. "What the hell, Robert? Where have you been?"

Robert answered through the door. "Arizona, New Mexico, Idaho..."

"What were you doing?"

"I just did odd jobs for people and traveled. I had some savings, so I used that also."

"No, I mean...why did you disappear? Everyone was worried about you. Your dad thinks you're dead."

Robert emerged fully dressed from the bathroom. "I know. He's the reason I had to leave."

"What do you mean?"

"He was putting too much pressure on me. I failed a class last semester, and there was no way he was going to forgive me."

"Robert, he's your dad."

"You don't know my dad. He expects great things from me."

"But Robert...I thought you were dead, too. I thought Cole had killed you."

Robert laughed. "Why would Cole have killed me?"

Lucius hesitated. He didn't know how much to tell Robert. "Well, you gave him the address to Sandberg's house. The address you took from me."

"I thought it might have been a clue for the murder investigation, and Cole wanted to continue that investigation after I left."

"Cole wasn't a good guy."

"Wasn't?"

"He's dead."

"What?"

"There's a lot that I have to catch you up on. Are you interested in helping me?"

"More than ever."

"I shouldn't tell you any of this. But right now, I'm all alone, and I need some help."

"You can count on me this time, Luke."

Lucius looked at Robert and smiled. He looked ridiculous with long hair and half a beard. "All right, Robert. Here goes. Dolores Martinez is innocent. She didn't have anything to do with Sandberg's murder, but she's now been charged with it."

"How do you know that she's innocent?"

"Because she told me, and I believe her."

"Okay, Luke. If you trust her, I trust her."

"So I went to get her from the airport one night, and Cole followed us back to my apartment. When we got out of the car, he confronted us with a gun."

"Lindsey Coleman?"

"Yeah, he walked right up to us. Apparently, he was the one who killed Sandberg. He apologized to me for what he was about to do. He was about to kill us, Robert. At the last second, an SUV came flying into the parking lot, and the driver shot Cole several times."

"Who was the driver?"

"I'm getting to that. The driver was a guy named Lavindra Padmini. He is the closest friend of Garland Ramsden."

Robert's eyes got big. "Wilfred Ramsden's brother?"

"Yeah, how'd you know that?"

"Wilfred Ramsden is very close with my dad. When I was growing up, I was best friends with his son Ambrose."

Lucius didn't know what to think. Should he stop the story right now? Was his friend Robert somehow involved with the Ramsdens? He couldn't bring himself to believe that, and after all, why would Robert be revealing his hand if he were involved with the Ramsdens?

"You have to believe everything I tell you from here on out. It's going to sound a little crazy."

"Crazier than Lindsey Coleman pointing a gun at you and then being shot by the companion of a United States Senator's brother?"

"Yeah...much crazier."

"All right, let's hear it."

"Okay, so we took Cole's body and threw it into a marsh outside of town. Then Garland Ramsden gave me this book. It's a history of the Ramsden family."

"Okay?"

"Apparently, there were these two brothers who came to America in the early eighteenth century. They were on the boat that took Blackbeard's ship, and one of them helped to kill Blackbeard."

"Blackbeard...? The pirate?"

"What other Blackbeards do you know? Yeah, Blackbeard, the pirate."

"I'm sorry, Luke. I'm just trying to follow your story."

"So the night after they took Blackbeard's ship, these two brothers sneaked back out to the ship and stumbled upon these journals kept by Blackbeard. One of the brothers was Ambrose, who later killed his brother and kept the journals for himself."

"Luke, I hate to interrupt again, but what makes you think any of this is true?"

"They've shown me newspapers, and I trust Dolores. It's true, Robert. I can assure you that it's true."

"Okay...I'm just trying to process all of this."

"All right, so Ambrose then used the journals to collect Blackbeard's treasure. Then he passed the journals down to his son, who passed the journals down to his son and so forth. They kept the secret of the journals from everyone else and used them to create a vast wealth."

"And they've kept the secret ever since?"

"Yeah."

"Garland Ramsden has the secret now...or Wilfred...or both?"

"Just Wilfred. Garland found out about it when he stumbled upon some documents in Wilfred's house. He wants to expose his family's secrets."

"So what does that have to do with Dolores and Sandberg and what they were doing in the library?"

"They were doing research to try to force the release of Blackbeard's journals. Because they were stolen originally, they thought they could get them released to the public through legal channels."

"And Sandberg was killed because the Ramsdens found out?"

"Exactly. And the book at Sandberg's house contained a copy of the research. Cole stole it and gave it to the Ramsdens. He was then supposed to eliminate Dolores, but we were saved by Garland. It's a crazy story, but it makes sense."

"So where is the research now?"

"That's another long story. One copy of it has been shredded, and the other copy is probably still in the hands of an evil law firm that works for the Ramsdens called Leeder & Schrum."

"The firm that Sandberg and Martinez worked for?"

"Yeah...that's how they found out about the whole thing, and they left to help Garland release the journals."

"So can we get the research?"

"I don't know how. I worked for Leeder & Schrum this summer. They made me shred the paper copy of the research, and I never could find the electronic copy."

"You shredded documents?"

"Yeah, and it cost me, too. They taped me doing it and used it to make sure that I couldn't pass the bar. So I've got a law degree, but I'll never be able to pass the bar."

"Luke, this is the craziest story I've ever heard."

"But it's all true."

Robert looked thoughtful for a moment. "I'm guessing we don't have any idea where the journals themselves are."

"We do know where they are. There was a letter that gave the account number and the bank's location. The journals are in a bank somewhere in Virginia. I've got a copy of the letter somewhere."

"So why don't we just go get the journals. We'll steal them and release them without worrying about all this legal stuff. It'll be like the Pentagon Papers."

"There's a problem with that plan. There are two keys that have to be used simultaneously to open the safety deposit box that contains the journals."

"And who has the keys?"

"Wilfred Ramsden probably still has one of them. We don't think he's passed it on to his son. He is supposed to wear it around his neck. But we don't know where the other one is. He was supposed to give it to someone he could trust."

Robert's eyes got even bigger. "Luke..."

"What?"

"I know who has the other key."

"How could you possibly know who has the other key?"

"I told you...Wilfred Ramsden was very close with my dad."

"Are you saying that your dad...?"

"I don't know for sure...but ever since I was a kid, he's worn a key on a piece of red string around his neck. I've asked him about it before, and he's always told me that it was a very important key that he had to keep for a friend."

This was unexpected. Lucius' mind started churning. "If we could get that key, then all we would need is Wilfred's key. If I can find the copy of the letter that was given to Wilfred, it has the location of the bank and the bank account."

Lucius darted into his bedroom and grabbed his keys. "Come on, Robert. We've got to go get some boxes."

"Luke, how do you expect to get the keys?"

"We'll figure that out later. But for the first time since this whole thing began, I see the solution. I see how we can get the journals."

Lucius picked up his gun off the coffee table.

"You have a gun?"

"Did you miss the part of the story where your old friend Cole had a gun pointed in my face?"

Robert laughed. "You've lost your mind, Luke."

"Are you going to help me?"

"Of course I'm going to help you."

They climbed into Lucius' car and drove directly to the storage center. Lucius loaded the boxes into the back of the car, and they drove back to his apartment.

Once they were inside with the boxes, Lucius explained. "All right, Robert...you take those two boxes over there. What we're looking for is a letter from Wilfred Ramsden's father to Wilfred. It tells about the keys, and it tells where the bank account is."

"All right, I'll see what I can do."

For the next hour, very few words were exchanged. They both had a singular focus. Lucius didn't know how they'd get the keys either, but he would think of that when they got to that part.

After an hour, Lucius found the letter. The bank account was A-4-1436, and the bank was in Cape Charles, Virginia.

"All right, Robert. Now you have to tell me how we can get the key from your dad."

"I don't know, Luke. I haven't seen my dad in two years. I'm pretty sure he's going to be just a little angry with me."

"Yeah, but you're his son."

"Yeah, all the more reason for him to be angry with me."

"Dolores is in jail for a crime she didn't commit. One of our professors is dead, and who knows how many others have been killed by this family through the years. We have the power to end all of that, Robert."

"Okay, just let me think."

Lucius sat on the couch staring at Robert for a minute. They had started this together, and they were going to finish it together.

Robert spoke up after a few minutes. "We need to get another key from a hardware store. We're going to confront my dad and tell him to switch the keys. That way he won't have to tell Wilfred Ramsden that the key is gone."

"That's a great idea. Then when we steal the key from Wilfred Ramsden, he'll still think everything's okay because your dad still has his key. It's perfect."

Lucius slept well that night for the first time in a long time. He dreamed about Dolores.

The next morning they woke up and drove to Washington, D.C. They used Robert's key to go into his father's apartment, and they waited for him to come home.

After a few hours of waiting, Robert Collins, Sr. walked in the door. He dropped his coat when he saw his visitors.

"Robert...son...you're alive."

"Yeah, dad. I'm alive."

"Where have you been?"

"I had to get away from all the pressure."

"Why didn't you tell me that you were okay? I've been worried sick about you."

"I know. I'm sorry."

"I've got some calls to make. I have to let everyone know you're okay, and I have to try to make sure that this doesn't cause you any legal problems."

"I have to ask a favor, dad."

"What is it?"

"The key that you wear around your neck."

"What about it?"

Robert pulled the replacement key out of his pocket. "I need you to switch this key for that one, and I need you to never mention to anyone that this switch happened."

"What are you talking about, Robert? I haven't seen you for two years, and you walk in with your friend asking for a key that I've held in trust for over half my life."

"Yes, dad. I have to have the key."

"No, you don't."

"You're my father. Please trust me."

Robert Collins, Sr. stood staring into his son's eyes. Both pairs of eyes filled with tears. "I don't know what to think anymore, Robert. I'll do what you're asking me to do, but I need you to help me to understand."

Robert Collins, Sr. took the key off the string and put the new key on. His son took the key from him, handed it to

Lucius, and gave his father a hug. "This will all make sense soon, dad. Thanks."

Lucius and Robert climbed back into Lucius' car and drove back toward Charlottesville.

"I'm sorry you had to do that, Robert."

"It's okay. That's the first time in my entire life that I've faced my dad. I've always run from him in the past."

They drove in silence for a while, until Lucius slammed on the brakes after thinking of an idea.

"I've got it, Robert."

"Got what?"

"How we can get the other key."

"Okay, tell me."

"I was reading the last chapter of that book about the Ramsdens when you came in the other day. It said that Wilfred Ramsden attended the Blackbeard Festival in costume every year. He'll have the key, and I'll take it from him."

"How?"

Lucius looked at the gun in the back. "By force."

"Luke, are you sure that's a good idea?"

"I've come too far now, Robert."

"How will you figure out which one is Wilfred Ramsden? I mean there will probably be a lot of people there in costume."

"He carries around a silver cup that he claims was made from the skull of Blackbeard. I'll find him."

When they arrived at home, Lucius looked up the Blackbeard Festival. Luckily, it was taking place on June 2. It was only a couple of days away.

Lucius drove to the Charlottesville costume shop and rented a pirate costume, including a plastic pirate mask. He left a cash deposit and didn't give them his name.

When the day arrived, Lucius and Robert drove to Hampton. They pulled into a hotel parking lot outside of town, and Lucius began putting on his costume.

"I need you to stay here at the hotel, Robert."

"What?"

"Please...just trust me...I have to do this alone."

"Okay, Luke. I trust you."

Robert got out of the car and walked into the hotel lobby. Lucius drove into Hampton and found festival parking.

He walked around the festival for a while. There were thousands of people wandering around. A couple of hundred of them were in costume. There were even authentic-looking pirate ships out in the harbor. After a few hours of wandering, he stumbled upon a man dressed like Blackbeard and carrying a silver cup.

He stalked the man for the next few hours. The man talked like a pirate to everyone he passed. He told everyone that he was the real Blackbeard and that he wanted his treasure back. He was a big hit with the kids. Lucius couldn't see his neck to determine if he had a key hanging on a string around it, but he was sure that it had to be him.

Finally as it started to get dark, the man left the crowded streets and walked away from the festival. Lucius pulled his mask down over his face and followed him until they began passing a dark alley.

Lucius approached him quickly and shoved the gun in the man's back. "Get in the alley, old man."

Chapter Twenty-Eight

The man did as he was told. Lucius walked immediately behind him and held the gun hard against his back. He didn't know what he had gotten himself into. Was this really the best way to proceed?

When they had walked about fifteen feet down the alleyway, Lucius stopped walking.

He tried to speak firmly. "All right, stop and turn around."

As he was turning around, the man reached for his back pocket.

"W...what are you doing? Stop that."

"I was just getting my wallet for you. There's no reason for anyone to get hurt. Just stay calm."

"I don't want your wallet. I want what's hanging around your neck."

"What are you talking about?"

"You've got a key hanging around your neck. I want that. I want you to give me the key right now."

The man looked uncomfortable. "I don't know what you're talking about. Please just take my wallet and leave me alone."

Lucius began to wonder if he had the right man...or maybe it was Wilfred, but he had already passed the key down to his son. Lucius might have made a big mistake. "Let me see your neck."

The man looked sheepish. "Okay, okay, I'll give you the key, but it won't do you any good."

"Just give it to me."

Wilfred Ramsden began fiddling with the back of his neck. "I don't know what you've heard about this key, but you won't be able to do anything with it. It doesn't open anything of importance. Who are you anyway?"

"Stop talking and give me the key."

Wilfred reached out to hand the key to Lucius.

"Put it on the ground."

He did as he was told.

"Now take two steps back and get down on your stomach."

"This isn't necessary, young man. Just take the key and go."

"Just do what I'm telling you to do, and you'll be fine. Lie on your stomach and don't move for five minutes."

Wilfred took two steps back and lay down on his stomach. Lucius scooped up the key and backed slowly out of the alley. He shoved the gun into his pants pocket. He hadn't thought through this part of the plan. He thought that perhaps he should try to change out of his costume in a nearby alley and walk calmly back to his car.

Instead Lucius pulled the plastic mask off his face and ran for his car as soon as he was out of the alley. He got there in less than five minutes. He climbed into the driver's seat and stripped off the rest of the costume. He put it under the seat in the back of the car and drove out of the parking lot. He ducked his head as he passed the security guard who was standing in front of the lot.

He kept looking in the rearview mirror for police lights, but they never appeared. Would Wilfred Ramsden even call the police? Wouldn't he be too paranoid that someone would find out what the key opened if he reported it stolen? He arrived back at the hotel where he had left Robert. He walked inside and looked around the lobby and its immediate surroundings, but Robert was nowhere in sight.

He approached the hotel desk. The wormy concierge looked up at him from beneath his glasses. "May I help you?"

"My friend was supposed to wait for me here. Have you seen him?"

"What's your name?"

"Luke."

The man reached under the desk. "He left this for you."

The man handed Lucius an envelope. It contained the key that they had gotten from Robert's father and a note. Lucius

ripped the envelope open in front of the concierge. For a
moment, he wondered if his plan was falling apart.

> Luke,
>
> I've got to go back to D.C. to try to patch up the
> relationship with my father. I'm sorry to leave
> you like this, but I'm sure you'll be better off
> without me anyway.
>
> Good Luck,
> Robert

Lucius didn't have time to be shocked. He closed the
envelope and walked quickly back out to his car. He unscrewed
the license plate and took it off. In case someone saw him
arriving at or leaving the bank, he didn't want them to be able to
track him later. He climbed into his car and headed for Cape
Charles, Virginia. He had printed out directions from the
Internet. It was supposed to take one hour and one minute.

He drove at the speed limit. There was no need to draw
any more attention to himself. He had to pay a toll, and he drove
through a long tunnel before emerging right outside of Cape
Charles.

After an hour and fifteen minutes, he pulled into the
parking lot of a small grocery store next to the bank. He put
Wilfred Ramsden's key in the envelope with the other one and
walked inside.

There was only one bank teller inside, and there were no
customers. He walked up to the bank teller.

"I'm here to see a safety deposit box."

"Which one, sir?"

"A-4-1436."

The clerk looked startled. "Are you the owner of that
box?"

"Well, not exactly. You see the owner wishes to remain
anonymous, so he sent me in to collect its contents."

"I only ask because I had a phone call about that very account. I was told not to allow anyone to have access to that safety deposit box."

"Well, I need to have access to that box. I was sent here because the owner is worried that someone else is after what's inside. I'd appreciate it if you'd direct me to it immediately. I don't have time for this."

"I'm sorry, sir. I'm afraid I won't be able to help you. I could be fired if I let the wrong person take something from one of our safety deposit boxes."

Lucius was panicking. He didn't know what to say. "Listen, this is an anonymous account. You have to rely on the owner retaining possession of the keys which open the box. You can't legally keep me from accessing it. I have the keys, and I want to collect the contents of my safety deposit box. I have my cell phone in the car. I can call the police if you want me to."

"That won't be necessary, sir. Follow me."

The clerk led Lucius into a room at the back of the bank behind an opened steel grate. He unlocked a small section of safety deposit boxes and pulled out A-4-1436. He put it on the table in front of Lucius and walked out of the room.

Lucius pulled out the two keys and stuck them into the two keyholes on the safety deposit box. He took a deep breath as he turned the keys. The box unlocked and opened with a creak.

Lucius ran his hands across the plastic that was wrapped around the ancient journals. Unfortunately, he didn't have time to admire them now. He picked them up and practically ran out of the bank.

"Sir..."

Lucius didn't look back. He climbed into his car and drove off. Once he was out of town, he pulled into a gas station and put the license plate back on his car.

The attendant confronted him. "What'd you do? Rob a bank?"

Lucius forced out a fake laugh. "Nah, I just got the plate, and I forgot to put it on. Thankfully, I didn't get pulled over."

The gas station attendant laughed and walked back inside. "If that's what you want me to believe..."

Lucius got in his car and drove slowly back to Charlottesville. He stopped once more to throw the costume into a trash bin outside a hotel.

When he arrived at his apartment complex, he sat in his car for a minute, allowing his mind to rest. Then he took the journals into his apartment.

He didn't breathe normally again until he had locked the door and put the gun on the coffee table. Now he could see what he had.

He examined the journals carefully. They appeared to be exactly what he had been told they were. The journals of Blackbeard the pirate. Lucius smiled. After all of this time, he had them in his hands. The pages of the journals were yellowed. The ink was faded in many places, and nearly every page was torn.

But these journals had survived for three-hundred years. He was the first person other than the Ramsdens to see these journals since Blackbeard wrote them. It was all a little too much for Lucius to take in.

But what would he do now? He had committed armed robbery in the process of obtaining the journals. Even if there were a chance that the police weren't in the pocket of the Ramsdens, he couldn't go to them. They would just arrest him when he told them the story of how he obtained the journals.

Garland was dead. Robert had other things on his mind. Dolores was in prison. Lucius didn't know where to turn. He wanted to release the journals. He wanted to finish the plan that Garland had set into motion years before. He wanted to grant a dying man's request. He wanted to do the right thing.

But maybe that would be impossible. Maybe he should just keep the journals. The Ramsdens didn't have them any longer, so maybe their power, and with it their evil, would slowly wane. Lucius could use the journals to retrieve the remaining treasure. He could use the money for good instead of evil. He could try to cancel out all of the evil that the Ramsdens had brought into the world.

But how would he know which treasures were left unfound after all these years? The Ramsdens had probably found nearly all of the treasure. And if there were unfound treasures, how would he be able to find treasures which had eluded such a wealthy family for nearly three-hundred years? He didn't have any treasure-hunting ability.

And he wouldn't be safe as long as he had the journals. The Ramsdens had been suspicious of him in the past. They had been so suspicious that they made sure that he'd never be able to practice law. If they took a picture of Lucius to the bank clerk, he'd surely be able to identify him. And then they'd come looking for him and the journals that he had stolen.

Lucius knew what he had to do. He had to release the journals to the public. He had to make sure everyone found out about what the Ramsdens had done. He had to honor Garland, and he had to try to free Dolores from prison. And he had to do all of that before the Ramsdens found him. He knew what he had to do. He just didn't know how to do it.

He looked around the room and noticed the manuscript that had been written by Garland. That gave him an idea.

Lucius went into his room and retrieved the typewriter that his grandfather had given him when he was a boy. He had brought it to Charlottesville as a decorative item, but now he planned to put it to practical use.

He pulled some paper out of his printer and fed the first sheet into the typewriter.

Chapter 21: How It Ends

Lucius started telling the story. He left out his own name and the names of Robert and Jennifer. And for obvious reasons, he left out the murder of Lindsey Coleman. But he told the rest of the story in its entirety.

He wrote about stalking Dolores in the library. He wrote about Sandberg's murder and revealed Lindsey Coleman as the murderer. He wrote about his meeting with Garland Ramsden, and he wrote about Garland's death. He wrote about the family's connection to Leeder & Schrum, and he wrote about Dolores' wrongful arrest.

When he had finished, he had nearly forty pages. It was a long chapter.

Lucius looked out the window. The sun was coming up. It was morning.

Now that he had finished his masterpiece, he didn't know what to do with it. Who would believe it?

He sat in his apartment staring at the journals and the manuscript. He looked at the papers scattered about the room and the half-empty boxes. He had left everything as it was since the night he and Robert found the letter from Wilfred Ramsden's father. He hadn't had time to clean.

Lucius laughed. Just a few hours ago he had been pointing a gun at a former United States Senator to get the key to a bank vault which contained the long-lost journals of the world's most famous pirate. This was much more than he had ever expected from his law school experience.

But how would it end?

He thought about going to Detective Snow. She had been very nice to him, and she had even called recently to apologize for Torro's behavior. But she wasn't the right person. Even though she was a police detective, she might not have the power to release the journals. She would probably try to go to her superiors, and they would probably ship the journals right back to the Ramsdens.

He thought about trying to get in touch with Lavindra in Sri Lanka, but that didn't seem like a good idea. Lavindra wanted to put all of this behind him. He wanted to move on.

He thought about Robert Collins, Sr. He certainly had the power to release the journals, but he was a close friend of Wilfred Ramsden. He might be hesitant to involve his friend in such a scandal. And anyway, the Collins family had enough to worry about right now. He didn't need to bother them.

Finally his mind settled on Jonas Franklin. He had the respect of his peers and the necessary connections to get the journals released. And he had shown a great deal of integrity in his dealings with Lucius. After a lot of thought, Lucius decided that he was the ideal candidate. Jonas Franklin could be trusted to do the right thing.

He put another piece of paper in the typewriter.

Professor Franklin:

Everything that you will read in these boxes is true. Please ensure that the manuscript and the journals are released to the public. As you read the manuscript, you will see why it is so important. I am relying completely on you. Don't mention this to anyone until the information has been released. Dangerous people want to make sure that this information never gets out.

Your friend

Lucius thought about signing his name to the letter but thought better of it. Professor Franklin didn't have too high of an opinion of him right now.

Lucius packed up two boxes full of research and in one small box he put the journals of Blackbeard and the manuscript that he had completed earlier that morning. He carried all three boxes out to his car.

He drove to the law school, his windshield wet with the morning dew.

He got out of the car and carried the boxes into the law school. He went to Professor Franklin's room, but there was no one there.

Then he remembered. Professor Franklin had said that he was being moved to the third floor of the library.

Lucius carried the boxes into the library and up the stairs. He thought about Gretchen Lewis as he walked by the empty desk where she normally sat. As he walked up the stairs, he felt like he was walking back into the past.

He remembered that first night. He had been sitting at a desk on the third floor of the library. He was trying to study for his first exam. She had startled him and dropped that card. That one chance meeting had set the table for all that would follow. His life had changed so dramatically. If he had left the library just a few minutes earlier, none of it would have happened.

After a few minutes of searching, Lucius found Professor Franklin's new room. He could tell by the light coming from under the door that the professor was inside.

Lucius walked slowly over to the door. He put the boxes down softly and placed the letter on top.

He knocked on the door loudly and darted behind a nearby bookshelf. He heard Professor Franklin calling for him to come in. He knelt down, so that he wouldn't be visible.

After another minute, Professor Franklin opened the door and looked out. He looked down at the boxes, and the letter that was sitting on top of them.

He picked up the letter and read it. He took a few steps outside his door and looked around. Lucius considered running but held his ground.

Professor Franklin picked up the boxes one by one and carried them back into his office. After one more glance to make sure no one else was around, he closed the door.

Lucius walked slowly down the steps and outside the law school. Everything was now in Jonas Franklin's hands. He sat down on the wet grass in front of the law school. He looked up at the sun as it peered out from behind the clouds.

Professor Sandberg was dead. Dolores was in prison. His friend Robert had his hands full in trying to save the relationship with his father. And Lucius, even if the Ramsdens didn't come after him, could never practice law.

In spite of everything, Lucius Dixon smiled.